SPACE DETECTIVE

A SCIENCE FICTION PRIVATE EYE NOVEL

Duane Spurlock

Illustrated by Mike Fyles

InterroBang Tales
Louisville, Kentucky

InterroBang Tales
Louisville, Kentucky
www.duanespurlock.com

Publisher's Note: This is a work of fiction. Names, characters, places, and incidents are a product of the author's imagination. Locales and public names are sometimes used for atmospheric purposes. Any resemblance to actual people, living or dead, or to businesses, companies, events, institutions, or locales is completely coincidental.

Cover and interior illustrations by Mike Fyles
InterroBang Tales colophon by J.T. Lindroos

Space Detective – A Science Fiction Private Eye Novel/Duane Spurlock - 1st ed.
ISBN 979-8-9877970-1-3

Dedications

In memory of
Thomas Bouchoux
A great college roommate and a great pal
RIP

and
Yesterdays Bar and Grille
If it's not world famous yet, it should be
—Duane

To all the book, magazine, newspaper and comic book illustrators, who created such a rich seam of information and entertainment for a post-war childhood.
—Mike

I'll descend upon your Earth from the sky.
—*The Seven Seas of Rhye*, Freddie Mercury

CONTENTS

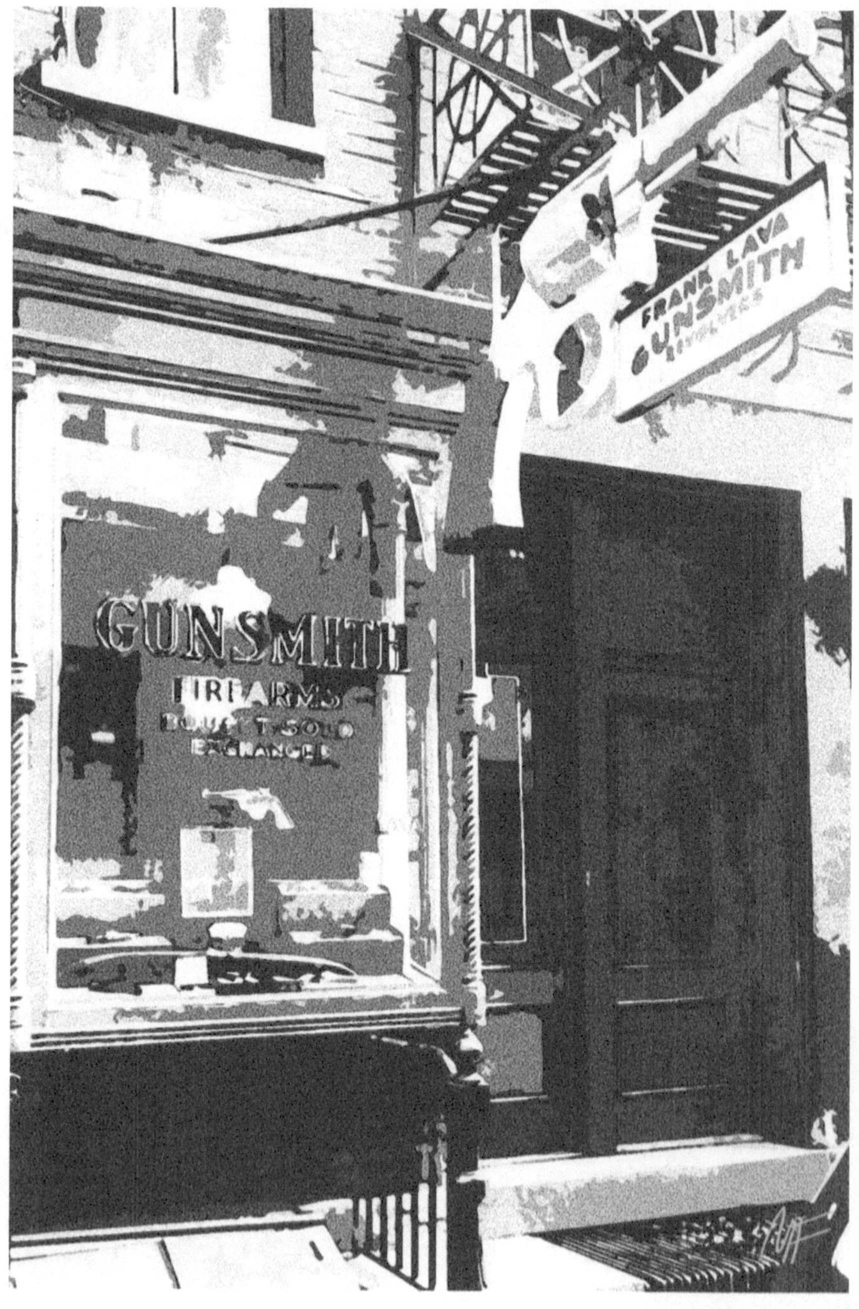
FRANK LAVA
GUNSMITH
GUNSMITH
FIREARMS

PART ONE

Uncas

CHAPTER ONE

Despite the Model 6's well-documented flaws, the Space Detective preferred the Model 6 Rigelian Hand Zapper to the Model 8. He found it a better-balanced blaster that fit his hand just so. The Model 8 felt barrel-heavy to him. And the way the 8 molded itself to his hand was very unsatisfying—and a little disturbing. (More than once I heard him say, "I just don't know what they were thinking when they started using those Nevian Octo-ambient grips on the Model 8. When I let go of the gun, it wouldn't let go of me. Had to pry it off my fingers.")

So the Space Detective radiated absolute confidence as he leveled his Model 6 at Ronnie Roquette, whose recent activities might better be described as invasion assistance rather than mere smuggling. But although Ronnie was staring down the cannon-sized blow hole of a lethal hand blaster, his face began to glow with confidence. Uh oh.

I alerted the Detective:

<<Your helmet must have a breach—short-wave Confidence radiation is infecting Ronnie. Better shoot fast.>>

The Space Detective pulled the Zapper's trigger, and the Model 6 demonstrated one of its flaws: Instead of firing with a warm and satisfying POM, the charge drum flew to the right with a PLING, leaving the Detective gripping a gun frame with a barrel attached. As usual, he was not at a loss for words—at least, one word: "Poot!"

As the drum escaped the frame, its locking pin had shot forward and struck Ronnie in the face. "Hey! That coulda put out my eye!"

Radiated by confidence leaking from the faulty helmet, the smuggler charged, arms extended.

Whatever Ronnie was feeling, it wasn't really radioactive

confidence—that was just the Earth human metabolic response to the frequency escaping the helmet.

The Detective's left forearm batted aside Ronnie's right arm. He brought up the handgun and wobbled the smuggler by rapping Ronnie's collar bone with its barrel. The pistol, even without the drum, weighed enough to stun the outlaw. The Detective lunged forward, smacked Ronnie in the face with the front of his helmet and dropped him to the floor. Even unconscious and battered, Ronnie's features suggested an attitude of easy accomplishment.

"Gotta get this helmet patched," the Detective said.

<<The Studie is coming around the corner.>>

I maintained a telepathic link from the office with the Detective. Not "telepathic" in any organic sense, because it worked thanks to some technological modifications, but telepathy is the easy way to refer to it.

It would be a misnomer to say I manned the office, as my genetic forebears are Plutonian—I sat in a container lined with dry ice and kept operations flowing while the Detective handled the leg work. After all, he had legs.

The Detective dropped Ronnie's sidearm into a coat pocket, picked up an egg carton-sized container from the floor with one hand and with the other slung Ronnie's inert form over a shoulder. Grit cracked under his Florsheims as he crossed the vast concrete floor to the open door. As he stepped out from one of hundreds of warehouses lining this part of the Great Mohegan River, a car skidded to a stop before him: a modified 1950 Studebaker Commander Starlight Coupe, Milky Way black. The passenger door opened, and he plopped Ronnie into the seat, closed the door. He got into the driver's seat—because I had directed the auto's robot to the door, no one was actually already in the seat—and set the carton between him and Ronnie's slumped form before putting the Studie in gear and driving off.

CHAPTER TWO

At the office—a second-floor walk-up over a tobacconist's shop that ran numbers from the back room—the Detective opened the top drawer for one of three filing cabinets and touched the Containment tab of a file folder. He moved Ronnie, still on his shoulder, closer to the drawer, and the smuggler was sucked into the Containment folder like something in a Tex Avery cartoon. The Detective closed that drawer, opened another and manipulated the Evidence tab, and the egg carton likewise slurped into the cabinet like a wet noodle.

From a third drawer, the Detective opened a Workroom folder and stepped in.

As every schoolboy knows, as New Angoulême had spread horizontally across the landscape since the arrivals of Giovanni da Verrazzano and Henry Hudson, the search for more space had eventually led to the creation of the skyscraper to exploit vertical space. The technologies the Detective relied on let him use the space between spaces—much as a tesseract is a four-dimensional cube, the Detective employed science that allowed him to use rooms within rooms that weren't even visible from outside. Some of the spaces within the file cabinets' folders were larger than the office within which they sat.

Sitting sealed in a dry ice container all day gave me time to think about these things. Luckily, I didn't get headaches.

In the Workroom, the Detective found the fault in the helmet that had allowed Ronnie Roquette to be contaminated during their little skirmish. He returned to the office proper after retrieving and donning a fresh helmet from Storage.

Just in time. The office door opened and revealed Chief Inspector Jonathan Brewster Uncas. His figure briefly fuzzed around the edges as he stepped over the threshold, and Uncas shook for a moment as if from a chill. The fuzz and chill resulted from the transport process that moved any visitors from the second-floor walk-up to the actual location of the Detective's office—using the same tesseract-like science, the office was Neither Here nor There, but "Nere," as the Detective described it. Just by pressing a switch, the New Angoulême office could appear to be empty, and the office in Hong Kong or Paris would appear to be occupied.

Whoever crossed the threshold remained unaware that he had been transported from one reality to another. It was one of those little secrets we kept that made our work tricky.

"Always cold here," Uncas muttered.

His name was pulled from Mohegan history, but he actually belonged to the Pequot tribe; still, both were Algonquian, and Uncas wore on the lapel of his topcoat the traditional black feather pin of the Algonquian nation. The police department ranks were filled with Mohawks and Irish, and the newspapers occasionally ran a story about dissent in the precincts caused by Uncas—or one of the other officers from a competing tribe—rubbing someone in uniform the wrong way.

He didn't doff the non-standard-issue black beret. "Where have you been tonight?" he asked.

The Detective moved casually, sat in the captain's chair behind his desk. His helmet was opaque, therefore it would do him no good to smile, so he tried to put a smile in the sound of his voice. "Why should I have been anywhere but here?"

Uncas remained all business. "The hood of your car was still warm."

Note to self: expect a reprimand and a request for a better heat sink for the Studie's engine.

Experience proved that putting Uncas at ease helped keep relations less difficult. The Detective gestured to a visitor's chair with a gloved hand: "Go ahead, have a seat. I bet you need a break from chasing down all those JDs."

Crimes committed by teenagers had been fodder for bold headlines in the newspapers recently. Juvenile crime was nothing new, but its nature had gotten more violent lately—beatings, shootings, rapes, small-scale riots—and the spike in this sort of activity had both shocked and frightened a large part of the population.

The chief inspector ignored the effort to make things warm and friendly. He remained standing. He kept that stiff, professional posture that alternately drew praise for his unyielding focus to the particulars of his job—or scorn for his lack of reasonable human empathy when dealing with citizens or members of the competing news outlets. He might well have served as a model for *Dragnet*'s uber cop, Detective Joe Vrijdag.

"Where were you three weeks ago, May 28 through June 6?" Uncas asked.

"Working a case," the Detective said.

"Where?"

"Out of town."

"Four weeks before that?" Uncas asked.

"Another case."

"Where?"

"Out of town."

"For whom?" the inspector pressed.

"That's a confidential matter between me and my client," the Detective responded. "I'm sure you can understand that, Inspector."

Uncas said nothing, but stared without blinking at the Detective. It was the sort of look that would prompt those irritated news writers to include the words "stoic Indian" in their blocks of copy.

Finally he spoke: "You disappear for days at a time, supposedly on a case. Business must be good," and he almost smiled, "but no clients ever appear at your door. You could meet them at other locations, of course, but there is no evidence of that, either."

The Detective didn't respond. He seemed content to let his uninvited guest air his thoughts to see where they would carry him.

Uncas raised a hand, touched one finger to his chin. "You show up at interesting places—crime scenes where you seem to have no business, you just happen to be in the neighborhood, or you are exercising your professional interest.

"And I have not even mentioned this gaudy outfit. Do you ever take off that ghastly mask?"

The Detective shook his head, silent.

"I pegged it for an interesting business gimmick when you first came to my notice," Uncas continued, and he put both hands in the pockets of his coat. "Masked wrestlers were gaining fans in the rings, so it made sense you might draw attention to likely clients with a mask of your own. And Space Detective probably has a nice ring for those souls who get a tingle from those low-budget UFO movies. Your paperwork is all clean and on file, but how you got approval without using an actual, legal name, I have yet to determine."

"Space Detective is my legal name," the boss answered.

Uncas gave him another one of those time-stopped stares.

Now he placed his hands on the back of the visitor's chair and leaned forward. The light from the desk lamp blazed on the enameled lapel pin. "Your existence puzzles and bothers me. I do not like puzzles in my city. Puzzles mean problems in my world." He turned to leave, then stopped at the door. "For the past three years, you have struck me as a problem I just have not unpuzzled yet." Then he exited, fuzzing around the edges as he left, and shut the door behind him.

"Hm." The Detective remained silent in his chair awhile. Then: "I'd expect someone who considers absolute zero a balmy day to know something about cooling car engines."

Ah, the expected zinger.

<<I'll get on it.>>

"What do you suppose all that was about?"

<<What do you mean?>>

"That uncharacteristic, un-Uncas-like unburdening?"

I thought about it.

<<Does he think we're criminals?>>

"He might think I'm a criminal. He doesn't know about you."

True. I considered. I started to be distracted by thoughts of the Studie's heat sink.

<<What do you think?>>

The Detective tapped his fingers on the desktop in some sort of rhythm he'd heard on the radio. He answered, "I think I need a gunsmith."

CHAPTER THREE

The Space Detective looked up at a gun nearly the size of an automobile. It hung over the sidewalk, its barrel pointed across the street, suspended above the display window of a storefront. The sign over the door read

Frank Lava
Gunsmith

This establishment resided on a short street—Central Market Place—that was home to a number of gun shops, newspaper crime reporters and photographers, tattoo parlors, and drinking emporiums. This block served these businesses and residents well, as it was located close to the building that was the target of Frank Lava's wooden gun: Police Headquarters.

<<What do you suppose the cops across the street think, having a gun pointed at them all day every day?>>

No answer.

<<Think Uncas will look out and see you here?>>

"What if he does?" He reached for the door handle. "He's probably too busy to look out the window."

Inside Frank Lava's shop, the Detective stood across a Formica-covered counter from the man named on the sign. He was a short, dark man with black hair that fought the bonds of its morning pomade, and he had a pencil-thin mustache. He was broad-chested, and had long arms that appeared longer because the sleeves of his shirt were pushed up and held from falling by green garters.

"Mr. Space Detective, I've heard of you! What brings you here? Need an atomic pogo stick for moon travel?" He winked and laughed and slapped the counter with one wide, long-fingered hand.

The Detective produced a hearty chuckle. "No, no moon trips today. It's a new moon tonight, not much up there right now to land on. I might miss and who knows where I'd end up?"

"Ho ho! That's good! That's a good one!" Lava smacked the counter again.

The telepathic link meant I was party to all this hilarity, which was hindering my heat-sink thinking.

"What caliber is that big boy hanging outside?" the Detective asked.

"Oh, you like that? Brings in lots of customers, some of them didn't even think about wanting a gun until they saw that beauty. My cousin, Salvadore, does woodworking over on the next block, he made that with his own hands." Lava clapped, then rubbed his hands together like he was making hamburger patties. "That's really nice, Salvadore does good work. A working model. Well, all the parts move like they're supposed to in a real pistol. It's a .38 Police Special."

"Ah." The Detective nodded. "No, I mean in real life, in the actual gun's scale, what size cartridge would it fire?"

Lava cocked his head, like a puppy confused by a command from its master. "It don't fire."

"No, of course not." Another hearty chuckle. "But if it did fire, let's say I need to shoot a pellet to the moon with a message inside, what size shell would I need?"

"Oh! Oh ho! That's good! I see!" More counter smacking. If I'd had a head, it would have been aching. "Let's see. Well, I don't know, really. I'd have to measure. Or maybe Sal would remember."

"Just curious." The Detective put a smile into his voice. Somehow. I didn't understand how he did that. But it was effective, because people reacted the right way, even though they couldn't actually see him smile through the helmet.

He placed a package on the counter. "I've got a gun I'd like you to look at. It needs some repair, and I asked around, heard you were about the best to be found."

"About?" Now Lava smacked his chest. "I am the best, and satisfaction is guaranteed. Let's take a look."

He cut the twine around the packet, unwrapped the paper, and opened up the oiled fabric within to reveal the parts of the Model 6 Rigelian Hand Zapper.

"What is this?" No one had to see Frank Lava's face to hear the surprise expressed in his voice.

"It's a—well, it doesn't have a name," the Detective explained. "It's a collector's item, really, so I would very much appreciate your, um, discretion."

"Uh huh."

"It was liberated from a facility in Berlin during the war—"

"A foreign model, eh?"

"Oh, very foreign. It's a prototype, very hush-hush project, never actually went into production."

Lava picked up one piece, then another, turning each in a very delicate manner using just his fingertips—giving evidence of his artist's heart for the machinist's skill. These weren't just polished pieces of metal, they were a finely crafted engine, a designer's dream given functional shape and form.

"What are these grips?" he asked. He touched one side with just a fingertip, as if he wasn't sure it wouldn't bite.

"Some new Berlin material," the Detective answered. "More hush-hush stuff. I don't think it's in production anywhere yet."

"This must take a very unusual load," Lava said, eyeing the charge drum.

"Indeed." The Detective remained very still, not wanting to distract the expert from his examination. Finally he said, "The principles aren't so different from those of a normal revolver. Do you think you can fix it?"

Lava suddenly looked up at the helmet's eye holes. "Think? There's no thinking. I can repair this. If it's a gun, I can fix it. No thinking. Guaranteed."

"Excellent."

CHAPTER FOUR

The Space Detective was in the Evidence folder examining the carton he'd confiscated from Ronnie Roquette. It sat inside a sealed containment box. The Detective watched through its tempered glass walls as he manipulated mechanical claws to lift the lid on the carton.

Inside, the carton was divided into sections.

Inside each divider was a vial.

The claws lifted out one after another so the Detective could study each, then returned the vial to its divider before grasping the next.

While this was going on, the Detective was speaking: "The papers say Uncas never drinks, never swears."

<<In public, at least.>>

"He's driven, wound up tight to be—what? A role model? In control?" He eyed more closely the contents of one vial. He shook it a bit with the claw. "Let's think about this."

<<I thought we already were.>>

"Snarky today. Hot engine giving you trouble?"

<<No, no. Just trying to figure out where to put a couple more vanes to draw off heat. Please continue this riveting psychoanalysis.>>

He shook the vial again. "He's a figure of authority in New Angoulême. He sees the world as a system of alliances—networks of power or politics, kinship, clans or tribes. Uncas' job is to keep order where those lines intersect."

<<Makes sense.>>

"So when something doesn't belong to or fit into one of those known alliances, exists in its own domain—"

<<Like us.>>

"—Uncas sees a potential conflict, a bit of chaos that might disrupt the order he's paid to maintain."

<<So that's why he visited and spouted off yesterday?>>

"Could be." The Detective replaced the last of the vials in the carton.

<<What was he trying to do? Give us an ultimatum? 'Get out of

Dodge by noon, pardner?' Or warning us?>>

"Maybe he was asking for help."

<<From us? Didn't sound like a question.>>

"That wouldn't be his way." The claw closed the carton. The Detective left the Evidence folder, stepped out of the filing cabinet into the office proper. He closed the drawer behind him. "He's giving us an opportunity to explain ourselves. To reassure him that we're not a disruption."

<<You could tell him the truth.>>

"I've thought that once or twice. But what would I say?"

<<Um, we're part of an interstellar peacekeeping mission called The Reseau, sent undercover to various planets to prevent unauthorized incursions by outlaw extraterrestrial regimes?>>

"Do you suppose telling him that we're two aliens sent by other aliens to keep out still more aliens will make him feel relieved?" The Detective barked a laugh. "Sounds like the invasion already happened, and we're part of it."

<<Well, he's the one wants to know.>>

"We don't fit into his map of power structures and subway lines. We're terra incognito—'Here be monsters.' Well, after checking out Ronnie's cargo, I'm thinking he may be right. But we may be the least of his worries if that carton really holds what I think it does."

He drew open another cabinet drawer.

<<What do you mean?>>

"What does every city dweller hate?"

<<The super? Traffic jams? Chewing gum on the sidewalk?>>

"Cockroaches."

And he whipped into the Containment folder that held Ronnie Roquette.

CHAPTER FIVE

Ronnie was in a cocoon. It maintained all his metabolic functions at optimal levels while keeping him in a sort of sleep. But his psychological functions were kept healthy by the automated programs plugged into the cocoon. A sort of lucid dreaming.

The cocoon was arrayed in a harness that moved slowly within a clear-sided sphere. The movement prevented fluids from building up in extremities and also prevented pressure ulcers or blood clots from forming.

A video screen with a strip of buttons along the bottom edge was plugged into the sphere. It sat on a plain table, and the Detective sat in a straight chair before the screen and pressed a button. This inserted the Detective into Ronnie's consciousness just as Ronnie's face appeared on the video. In the mind of our prisoner, he and the Detective were sitting across from one another in a typical Earth-style interrogation room that could be found in any of New Angoulême's precincts.

Ronnie smiled. In appearance, he was still a young man, not yet thirty years old. He displayed youthful bravado and disdained authority.

<<He's a knucklehead.>>

He showed his teeth like an ape at the zoo. "Time for some fun and games?"

The Detective ignored the question. "Ronnie, whatever your experiences with the local law, you are in a completely different position now. No defense lawyer will be showing up. No bail will be set or paid."

"So why are you talking to me? According to you, I'm *persona non gratis.*"

"*Grata.*"

"What?"

"Nothing."

Ronald Roque was a local boy who earned his way picking up odd jobs from New Angoulême hoods. He was happiest behind a wheel, so his chores usually involved driving stolen goods—for example, a connection made sure a load of dresses was in a certain address in the fashion district at a certain time, Ronnie would appear, step into the cab of the truck, and drive away.

"Gelinda will get me outta this," Ronnie said. "I'm persona somebody to her."

We knew who Gelinda was. We're not alone: the Detective and I are part of a network, and we had access to its records on suspected pirates and worse from a multitude of systems. Gelinda was a recruiter from Grasnius 6—a moon of the gas giant GrassoGolandoGoro, which really was now Grasnius 5, since the Grasnians accidentally blew up Grasnius 3 when a badly aimed warhead missed a diplomatic convoy that had been mistaken for an invading fleet from Grasnius 8. Fortunately, Grasius 3 was uninhabited.

Gelinda didn't work for any of the GrassoGolandoGoro moons' governments. She had stowed away at a young age on a cargo shuttle from the system. Now she provided her services to a guild of Hyrnavian pirates. They wanted access to the considerable mineral wealth found on Earth. That was one theory, anyway. Gelinda's remarkable sexual allure for nearly any species of creature made her a valuable tool to the pirates.

True, her eyes were dark and could melt anyone's resolve. She had two long, sweetly curved legs. (See, I don't have legs and even I found her fascinating.) Thick, long, shiny black hair. Gelinda also had three tentacles and blue skin pocked like the surface of Earth's moon, but that didn't matter to anyone smitten by her pheromone attack and persuaded by her Universal Dissembler—a small electronic unit she wore like an amulet that could convince anyone that she exceeded whatever their personal image of pulchritude might have been.

And so, Ronnie was smitten and seduced. He left home to fly blast buggies for Gelinda. He changed his name to Roquette and roamed the hidden spaceways.

He remained a knucklehead.

The Detective scoffed. "Gelinda doesn't know where you are. And she's probably already found another guy by now to do her bidding."

Ronnie scoffed in his turn. "Boy, what you don't know."

"I know that Gelinda is smart. She knows you for what you really are. It's easier to find a new gull than to attract attention trying to rescue you. By getting caught, you've made yourself a liability, Ronnie. Think about that. Your mob pals, back before you hightailed around with

Gelinda and her bosses—if they considered someone a liability, what happened to that person? A long ride off a short pier? Burial in a garbage scow?"

Ronnie scowled.

The Detective continued: "I also know that if anyone on this planet gets hold of you, the authorities will consider you a traitor—aiding and abetting an invading force. You won't last long then." The Detective paused. "I'm your best bet for a long and happy life, Ronnie. Think about that."

The Detective punched the button, and Ronnie's face faded with a blue flash that quickly shrank to the size of a white BB pellet in the center of the screen. Then the dot disappeared.

<<Boss, you better take a look at this.>>

CHAPTER SIX

By the time the Detective stepped back into the office from the file cabinet, I'd already set up and turned on the retractable video screen from what would normally be his desk's typewriter storage well—a section of the desktop flipped and locked into place.

During Ronnie's interrogation, I'd been watching a surveillance screen for a covert camera placed at the warehouse where we'd tracked down the smuggler. These cameras didn't use telephone lines, but functioned with frequencies outside the ranges used by Earth communications devices: the waves were relayed by a network of drone craft placed in geosynchronous orbit around the planet. The concept had been published by the scientific community here, but had yet to be put into development.

The Detective sat.

<<It's the warehouse. A Louie is trying to get in.>>

A Louie is a Local Entity—a native to the planet—who works for extraterrestrial parties. The Louie may realize his bosses are aliens, or he may have no notion that they are other than humans working on the shady side of the law. The Louie may not even understand that he's doing something illegal—not everyone had such loose allegiance to his home planet as Ronnie Roquette.

"Might be a juvenile delinquent looking for trouble."

<<Too old.>>

"Then he looks like a Louie."

<<Ronnie didn't tell you anything?>>

"Nope."

<<Did you expect him to?>>

"Nope."

<<You could use the cocoon controls—make him tell you.>>

"I could."

<<But?>>

He sat straighter in the captain's chair. "I want him to want to tell me. The information will be cleaner that way. He'll tell me more if he cooperates."

He pointed at the video screen.

A skinny, bald guy—about five-five in height—was trying the doors to the building with no success. Apparently he had no keys, so he clearly expected the doors to be open or he had plans to meet someone.

I shifted the focus and resolution. An enclosed delivery truck sat in the parking area.

<<He came in that truck.>>

It was a murky green. The name of a business on the truck sides had been painted over.

"Do we know him?"

<<Not in the files.>>

"Can you capture the license plate?"

<<Running it now. . . Billy 'Goat' McGraw. His address is on a card in the drawer.>>

He retrieved it from the micro-component printer located there.

"Ronnie's not going to make this date."

Billy Goat must have realized the same thing. He climbed into the truck and drove out of range of the camera.

The Detective stood to go.

<<New heat sink is all ready.>>

"Really?" He stopped before the open door. "How do you do that? Fix the car, get those cameras in place? You never leave the jar."

<<The magazines here say it's good to have some mystery in a relationship.>>

He didn't move. It was a momentary thing, but noticeable. Then he left.

CHAPTER SEVEN

The Detective had no worries about catching up with Billy Goat McGraw. He knew McGraw would eventually return home. So he first made a visit to the warehouse where we'd spotted Billy Goat.

A key couldn't enter the lock on the door. The Detective had inserted a self-molding plastic circuit into the slot. He just touched the circuit's partner component—about the size of a matchbox—to its exposed end, and the circuit responded by clicking open the lock.

Inside, he closed the door and switched on a flashlight. He whipped the beam back and forth, but nothing had changed since he had left with Ronnie over his shoulder.

He strode across the floor—vast and empty—until he reached the far corner of the structure, whose large doors opened up to the river. The doors were shut. Pencil lines of light ran along their edges. Standing before the doors was Ronnie's blast buggy.

It rested on stubby struts that extended from notches in the body, which was shaped vaguely like an egg that had been flattened a bit.

A single gull-wing hatch was raised on the left side of the buggy. The Detective clambered in.

Two thickly upholstered seats were arranged before the control panel. There was no observation port of any kind. All visual contact would have been made through displays generated by the onboard systems.

The surface of the material wrapping the cushioning of the seats was cracked and dull. And that marked the end of any amenities. The rest of the interior was given over to cargo space.

<<Empty?>>

"Looks that way." He opened bins, lifted the hatches on bays sunk into the body of the craft.

<<And?>>

"And either the carton I have in the Evidence file is all Ronnie brought with him, or he brought more and the rest are already out there. Somewhere."

<<And?>>

"And that's bad."

The Detective had returned to the gull-wing hatch to swing down to the warehouse floor when a red light flared into life on the control panel. He paused and gazed at the light: it blinked rapidly before shining steadily for several moments. Then it went dark again.

The Detective remained half in, half out the hatch. He looked at the panel.

<<What was that?>>

"I don't know."

And then we both forgot about it. He dropped to the floor, the soles of his Florsheims making a satisfyingly solid rap on the concrete.

CHAPTER EIGHT

Billy Goat didn't show up at the address immediately. Understandable: the time was still within daytime business hours. The Detective waited.

It was dark, nearly eleven o'clock when the apartment door opened and let in light from the hall, silhouetting Billy in the door. He pushed a button, the lights came on, Billy shut the door. He stopped in the act of hanging his jacket on a hook on the wall.

He turned. His arms were still cocked upward, his hands holding the green jacket. Billy looked at the Detective sitting in a blue chair.

He recognized the Detective. Once you've seen a picture in the paper, read the name, you know him when you see him.

"Whadda you want?"

The Detective gestured to the tatty sofa. "Have a seat. You look like you've had a big day. I bet you're tired."

Billy sat. He wrapped his hands in the jacket. It lay in his lap.

"So?"

The Detective leaned forward. "What are you doing for Ronnie Roquette?"

Billy's eyebrows climbed his forehead.

"Who?"

"Ronnie Roque."

Billy's face changed. Not much, but just enough.

"Don't know him."

"You paid him a visit today. At a warehouse. Mohegan River."

"I didn't see Ronnie today."

"You're right. He wasn't there. But you were." The Detective touched up the crease of his trousers where it crossed his knee, one leg over the other.

Billy stayed quiet.

The Detective continued: "Let's say you had already met Ronnie earlier. Maybe a few days ago. Picked up a load of . . . something from him. Carried it . . . somewhere." The Detective tapped the top of the lamp table between his chair and the sofa. First softly, with his fingertips. "Is that the way it was, Billy?"

Silence.

He rapped once, harder, with his knuckles. "Was it?"

Billy looked unsure, then nodded.

"What was it? What did you pick up?"

Billy's head moved back and forth, like he wasn't sure of the answer. His mouth stayed closed, but his jaws moved, like something wanted out.

"Big boxes? Or small?"

Billy's eyebrows started to rise again.

The Detective prodded: "Small, like egg cartons? Billy, did you deliver eggs for Ronnie?"

Billy nodded.

<<This talkative fellow is making my ears tired.>>

"You don't have ears."

When Billy heard this, those eyebrows hopped up high on his forehead. Then Billy was off the sofa and charging the door.

But he didn't make it, tackled from behind by the Detective. Billy's nose smacked the floor and blood popped from his nostrils. He rolled over on his back, curled up like a bug. He held his nose with both hands and groaned.

"Sorry, Billy." The Detective patted the man's shoulder. From a coat pocket he plucked a capsule about the size of his thumb. He pressed this against Billy's neck, to which it adhered. Billy relaxed into sleep immediately. The Detective stripped off his necktie so he could use the material to pack Billy's nose.

"Bring the Studie—"

<<To the back door in the alley. Got it. I'll also get the Medic unit ready in Containment.>>

"You're reading my mind."

<<That's my job.>>

CHAPTER NINE

Billy was in a cocoon of his own, but the Detective had manipulated the controls so that in the minds of Billy and Ronnie, they were sitting together at a table in a bar, sharing a pitcher of beer between two glasses. The program didn't provide a lot of detail, just sketchy outlines that allowed the two prisoners' minds to fill in particulars from their memories. So Billy might imagine he was sitting in a Bowery tavern, while Ronnie might smell marinara simmering in a back kitchen in Little Italy.

"I don't care what you say," Billy protested. He pointed a finger at Ronnie. His nose wasn't broken and he didn't have black eyes in this shared mental confab. "I delivered those cartons like you asked, and now I'm in trouble with the Space Detective. That guy spooks me."

"He's just a guy. He's not a cop." Ronnie made a dismissive gesture. "If he spooked you, that's just what he wants. You're doing just what he wants you to do. Go ahead, be spooked. He's happy now."

Billy stewed. Ronnie swirled the beer in his glass, turned it up for a long, slow drink.

Billy looked up at Ronnie. "What's in those cartons?"

Ronnie filled his glass from the pitcher. "No need for you to know."

"Do you know?"

"They got good service here. I didn't even see anybody refill this pitcher."

Billy grabbed Ronnie's glass. "Do you?"

"Look, Billy, I'm telling you, it's better you don't know."

Billy pushed the glass at Ronnie. "Who are you working for? Who am I working for?"

"Billy—"

"Look, the cops are one thing. But this Space guy, he works different. Look, I done jobs for Raoul the Shark, Joey Fingers—those guys are scary guys. I got no problems working for scary guys. But this Space guy—if I'm spooked, it's 'cause he's spooky for real. Something bad is up if this guy is messing around with you and your cartons."

"Billy—"

"Who am I working for, Ronnie?"

"You're working for me."

Billy barked. It was a laugh, but it sounded like a bark.

Then Billy disappeared. His chair was empty, his beer glass left behind.

Ronnie shook his head. He took a drink.

Then he disappeared, too.

CHAPTER TEN

Ronnie's face was back on the video screen before the Detective.

"Ronnie, I'm not the only one curious about your employers."

Ronnie sneered. "I'm still waiting for the fun and games, Mister."

"And you're still waiting for Gelinda?"

Ronnie ignored the question.

"Aren't you curious about your employers, Ronnie?" The Detective adjusted the knot of his new tie. "Why do you suppose they want to come to Earth?"

"The pastrami."

"Maybe. But let's say they want the minerals, the fuels."

"So?"

"So. They can get all that—except the pastrami, certainly not the rye—from the asteroid belt. With much less trouble, as well." Ronnie stared. "You know about the asteroid belt, Ronnie?"

"I've seen it."

"So. What does Earth have that the asteroid belt is lacking? Besides pastrami."

Ronnie still stared.

"So." The Detective continued. "No guesses?"

Ronnie just stared.

"All right, I'll tell you." The Detective tapped Ronnie's nose on the screen. "Slaves."

"Slaves."

"To work. Here, or maybe other planets. Or maybe just to sell. There's a market for cheap labor throughout the galaxy. I'm sure the pirates Gelinda works for—who you work for—have plans for everyone here once they're in control."

No word from Ronnie. His eyes jittered beneath his lowered lids.

"Are your employers religious zealots, Ronnie? They might just kill anyone who doesn't convert."

Ronnie frowned. "I'm not a convert. They didn't kill me."

"You're an employee. A paid slave. Your conversion isn't required.

Yet. They just need your connections, your skills."

"They're not religious."

"At least not in any way you've seen or would recognize. Right?"

Again, silence.

"How's that feel, Ronnie? Helping strangers—aliens—come in and make slaves of everyone you know? Family. Friends. People across the country, in other parts of the world you've never met? Old men, old ladies. Children. Reading comic books one day, dead or picking away in an ore mine on some GrassoGolandoGoro moon the next." The Detective knitted together his gloved fingers. "How's that sound?"

Then he clicked off the screen.

Ronnie was returned to his cocoon with whatever thoughts the Detective had stirred up.

"You think he's safe in there, don't you?" the Detective asked.

<<He's swaddled in his warm and secure cocoon away from you. Sounds safe.>>

"But he's in there with himself. For him, right now, that's not very secure at all."

CHAPTER ELEVEN

The Model 6 Rigelian Hand Zapper lay shining on a clean cotton cloth. The flexible-arm desk lamp on Frank Lava's counter was twisted so that little flares of light danced about the barrel, frame, and charge drum, and swept along the curve of the trigger guard.

"Looks like new?" Lava's eyes were opened wide, his eyebrows up high, his head tilted forward, the craftsman sure of his skills—but his posture submissive, seeking a compliment.

"Very nice," the Detective said.

"Go ahead, pick it up."

The Detective did so. First with both hands, then he transferred it to his right. He weighed it, raised his arm up, stretched it out before him, and aimed at a plastic wall clock advertising FireWater Cream Soda. It hung over a curtained door at the back of the shop.

He brought the Zapper down, cradled the barrel in his left hand. "It's different," he said.

"There's a little more weight, right?" Lava nodded in response to his own question. "It's the locking pin. Too fragile. I machined a new one, custom fit. The length is a little different, too. Gotta balance the changes."

Talking about weight reminded the Detective of how he didn't like the barrel-heavy Model 8. Sensitive now to the changes made to the Zapper, he lifted it and aimed again.

He dropped it into his shoulder holster.

Drew it out, aimed.

All the while, Lava stood waiting behind the counter, the expression on his face unchanging.

All those wrinkles pushed up to his hairline by those eyebrows—

<<That's gotta hurt.>>

"Hm." The Detective's grunt was more to shush me than to express any feelings he had about the gunsmith's work.

He tucked the Zapper back into its holster.

Lava's smile appeared to grow wider, if possible. "So?"

"Exquisitely done, Mr. Lava."

Lava smacked the counter. "Ha! No Mister here for a happy customer, Mr. Space Detective. You just call me Frank." He slapped the counter again as he said his name.

"Thank you, Frank." The Detective shook hands with the gunsmith, whose hearty response caused the Detective to grip the counter edge with his other hand.

<<While you settle your account with Not-Mister Lava, you'll want to know I've picked up another visitor at the warehouse.>>

"Hm?"

<<Strike that: two visitors.>>

They were two cops—each wearing a dark navy beret and a blue line tattooed across the bridge of the nose that Mohawks wore to show their allegiance to the clan—its badges and its role in keeping New Angoulême safe and secure.

They arrived in a single patrol car, but separated after stepping out from its doors. One moved along the exterior warehouse walls in one direction, the second went the other way. They tried the doors, attempted to peer through the grimy windows.

<<Think Chief Inspector Uncas sent 'em?>>

"No," was the answer the Detective gave me when he was back in the Studebaker after completing his transaction with Lava—that is, Frank. "That's not Uncas' style."

<<So—just a routine check? Couple of guys on patrol in the neighborhood, picking a warehouse at random?>>

"How's that sound to you?"

<<Unlikely?>>

"Absolutely. If Uncas is checking us out, he'll take care of all the footwork himself. He won't delegate." He honked at an old Huguenot crossing the street against the light. "Can you take over the car, get me to the warehouse the quickest route?"

<<Will do.>>

CHAPTER TWELVE

"Do you have the car number?"

I had parked the Studie a hundred yards away, out of sight from the warehouse serving as Ronnie's garage. The Detective had trotted up to spy on the two cops.

<<Nope. Out of reach of the camera's eye.>>

"Okay." He kept low behind a cluster of fifty-five gallon barrels stacked outside a neighboring warehouse. He read off the car number from its fender, then gave me the plate number for good measure.

"How about the badge numbers?"

<<I have one. Once the second guy comes around, I'll have his. Here we go.>>

The Detective duck-walked to another vantage point behind cover. He watched the two Mohawks try to open the door—first with a key that wouldn't fit, then with a crowbar between the metal door and its frame. The influence of the plastic circuit in the lock—quite sophisticated technology from Corbel 12—encompassed the entire door, not just the lock, and it foiled the cops' efforts with the pry bar.

<<Aren't you going to confront them?>>

"I don't want to show our hand in this yet. If we let them know we're involved in something they're curious about, we'll have to hear questions we don't want to answer."

The two men gave up at the door, walked to the water's edge. They pointed and gestured. They couldn't reach the large bay doors that opened onto the river.

<<Think they'll come back in a boat?>>

"There's a good chance. But the Corbels will thwart any typical efforts to force entry."

The Detective observed until the two Mohawks gave up and drove away. He returned to the Studie.

"How about those IDs?"

<<The patrol car is authentic. The number and plates match a vehicle in the NAPD fleet.>>

"Okay."

<<The badge numbers are good, too. Isaac Kaghneghtago has been on the force five years, William Tagawininto for eight.>>

"Pull together the rest of their info. Time for another chat with Ronnie. I'm getting a bad feeling."

<<Hey.>>

"What?"

Back in Ronnie's blast buggy a red light began to blink rapidly on the pilot's control panel. Then it burned steadily for several moments before it went dark again.

<<Is that something to worry about?>>

The Detective was silent a few moments. "Nah."

<<Okay.>>

So we forgot about it.

CHAPTER THIRTEEN

Ronnie scowled.

Nothing new there. I didn't expect any better info from him, but the Detective had a different notion. So we went with his plan. After all, he's the boss.

Ronnie's face was on the screen again. The Detective didn't use the cocoon's controls to insert himself into any comfortable settings with Ronnie as he had earlier done with the smuggler and Billy Goat. He wanted to keep a psychological upper hand in his dealings with this prisoner, who had been playing a critical role in what appeared to be preparations for a major invasion.

The Detective steepled his fingers. "It's been a few days so far, Ronnie. No Gelinda. No escape attempts. You're still confined here. I don't anticipate any changes."

Ronnie's scowl intensified—his features seemed to draw together even more tightly.

The Detective continued: "Maybe your bosses weren't giving you the straight dope, Ronnie. Maybe they built you up because that's what they needed you to hear so you would go along. Gelinda was all smiles, I bet. All close and snuggly. Ronnie would do for Gelinda whatever Gelinda wanted, because she said the right things Ronnie wanted to hear."

No change in Ronnie's face.

"But who's been straight with you, Ronnie? Who told you that once you were out of contact, they had cut you loose? They don't really trust you, Ronnie. If so, they would have told you how things really stood. They wouldn't have used Gelinda to use you. She would have told you the truth. Now, even if I let you go—let's say I let you go, Ronnie. You hop back in your buggy, run back to Gelinda. You think they'll trust you any more then?" He let that work around in Ronnie's head a minute. "Nah. They'll just figure you ratted out on them. If you would betray your own people—your hometown, your world, your family—why wouldn't you do the same to somebody who's just paying you for a job?"

Ronnie looked down.

"Who's been straight with you?" the Detective repeated. "What would your mother say, Ronnie?"

Ronnie finally reacted, but he kept his head down. "Leave Momma out of it."

"I bet your mother would say, 'Trust the person who trusts you.'"

Ronnie turned away.

"I'm trusting you, Ronnie. I'm trusting you to listen to me, trusting you to make the right choice. I'm trusting you to tell me the truth."

Ronnie looked down.

The Detective let Ronnie breathe a few moments, then started again: "I looked in that carton I picked up at the warehouse, Ronnie."

Ronnie looked up. Something new was in his face.

The Detective reassured him, "Don't worry, I didn't let anything out. But I looked. Do you know what's in that carton?"

Ronnie nodded, just slightly, as if afraid to tip something off balance.

"Cockroaches," the Detective said. "Each one packed in there carefully for a safe little trip in a blast buggy: Zigging and zagging into the system, hugging asteroids, riding the sensor shadows of moons, able to drift from outside the system all the way into Earth orbit without tripping any AllEye sensors on the watch for any unauthorized craft. But they're not your typical tough-as-nails, chip-on-the-shoulder New Angoulême cockroaches, are they, Ronnie?"

Ronnie shook his head. It was a slow movement, as though he was pulling against some force trying to hold him in place.

"Those are special cockroaches, aren't they, Ronnie? Something the Hyrnavian pirates tinkered with before you brought them planetside."

Ronnie nodded. His neck had loosened up from whatever had gripped it so resolutely.

"Tell me." He did it again: The Detective put a Smile into his voice.

Ronnie heard it. He swallowed. It was almost comical, an exaggerated gulp more appropriate to an old silent motion picture or a short with Moe, Larry, and Curly.

But Ronnie wasn't smiling. Sweat shined on his upper lip.

"They're not like regular cockroaches," he said. "They're like—asleep—in those cartons. Then they get a signal—like an alarm clock, you know—wakes 'em up. Then they scurry off."

"And?"

"And do what bugs do—make more bugs. But they're fast. And they don't need a poppa bug and a momma bug. Every one of those bugs is both momma and poppa. After so long—not long—each one grows so big, then splits up into ten or a dozen more. That dozen grows, splits into another dozen. In a week or so, there will be enough."

"Enough? For what?"

Ronnie looked down again. "They attack. Whoever is around. And by that time, they'll be all over. Not just here in the city, they'll be all over the coast. It'll be chaos."

<<Bugs? Chaos? Has he been in the cocoon too long?>>

The Detective ignored me, focused on Ronnie: "Attack how?"

"Attack, man, they attack." Ronnie grew more agitated. "They'll take people down, like a pack of wolves. They'll attack cars, trains, you name it. All the time they'll be splitting up like throwing a deck of cards, with every card building up a new deck. Pretty soon they'll outnumber everyone."

<<Sounds like glory days for the exterminators.>>

"Why won't the DDT-fog trucks work, Ronnie?" The Detective's voice remained calm; he didn't exert pressure. Just asked questions. The pressure came from within Ronnie.

"They're not like regular bugs. They're something else—bugs and, and, I don't know, robots."

"Part cockroach, part robot?"

"Yeah, yeah."

"So the bugs attack, the usual chemical weapons don't work, people panic. Right?"

"That's it."

"The police, the military—how do you fight a growing army of cockroaches? There are no supply trains to bomb, no boatloads of reinforcements to capture. No planes or tanks or artillery to attack. How do you fight?"

Ronnie shook his head. "I don't know."

The Detective let Ronnie catch his breath before asking another question: "Is this going on anywhere else, Ronnie?"

Another head shake. "I don't think so. Not yet. Start in the biggest, most famous city in the world. People get demoralized, worried it might happen in their home next. Get people frightened before anything happens, that means they're even more afraid when something does happen. That's what Gelinda told me."

The Detective nodded. "And then?"

"While everyone is running around chasing bugs, nobody is paying attention to other threats. The pirates drop down out of the sky, squash the armies, and take over."

<<What about the bugs?>>

It was almost like Ronnie heard me, because he said, "The pirates, they have a way to turn off the bugs. Like a switch, they push the button, the bugs turn off. So the cockroaches are no problem to the pirates. But if they need to twist anybody's arm to get what they want, the pirates just threaten to turn the bugs back on."

"Okay. Sounds bad. Thank you, Ronnie. That's good. You can rest soon. I have another question."

"Yeah, okay."

"This alarm clock for the bugs—have they received the signal yet?"

"No, I don't think so. How long I been here?"

"Four days."

"Pretty soon, though, I think. Gelinda didn't tell me for sure."

"Ronnie, I have one carton. How many more are there?"

"Twenty-four."

The Detective breathed out a long, slow sigh. "Are all twenty-four of those cartons delivered?"

"Yeah, that's what Billy Goat took care of."

"Do you know where he took them?"

"Yeah, Grand Central, Herald Square, Eriksson Circle, Walloon Street, all the heavy-traffic places where people come in and go out to other locations outside the city."

"You know all the places?"

Ronnie nodded.

"Okay. I need those places, Ronnie. A list. All of them. Then you can rest."

Relief started to appear on Ronnie's face. "Okay. Yeah, okay."

When the Detective returned to the office from the filing cabinet, he dropped a piece of paper onto the desk.

"We need to call in some help," he said.

CHAPTER FOURTEEN

Chief Inspector Jonathan Brewster Uncas stood before the Detective's desk, attempting to hide the shiver that came over him after he'd entered the office.

The Detective stood on his side of the desk, and although he had offered the visitor's chair to Uncas, the inspector shook it off.

"C'mon, have a seat. You're on friendly territory."

Uncas looked at the chair. The black beret remained on his head, and he didn't remove his coat.

"Please."

The inspector sighed, then sat.

"Thank you." The Detective sat. "And thank you for coming."

Uncas got to the point: "What do you want?" His words sounded more like a statement than a question, but at least he was responding.

"A couple of things," the Detective said. "First, I want you to understand that I am not a threat. To you, to your authority, to the city."

"You do not operate with proper authority." Uncas' gaze was steely, unyielding. There was nothing warm in his voice.

"I'm licensed, by the same statutory authorities that oversee your department—you enforce the laws of the land. I provide an avenue toward the same goals you represent—justice, safety, security—for people who seek another route."

"Where is the oversight? Who prevents you from straying outside the realm of the law?"

The Detective put a Smile into his voice. "Right now, I'd say you're doing that. You've certainly been keeping an eye on me and my movements."

Uncas grunted, noncommittal.

"Look," the Detective said, "are we so different? You work as part of a big public bureaucracy. But I read the papers—you're always running into some sort of friction because you roam outside the pack, running your investigations in your own way. I'm outside the bureaucracy, running on my own. I hit my share of friction, too—and I'll admit a good bit of it comes from you."

Uncas didn't grunt. His expression didn't change a bit.

<<Stoic.>>

The Detective cleared his throat. "Okay. Second, I'm asking for your help."

Uncas still didn't move, except one eyebrow changed position—only slightly.

"I've learned there is a threat to the city. That means something to both of us. And if the threat goes unchecked, it will spread—quickly—outside the city. Not just to the state, but up and down the coast and beyond."

"What kind of threat?" The inspector's eyes had narrowed, as if their tighter focus might exert a force upon the Detective.

The Detective sat back in his chair. His voice now had a personable, intimate quality: "I've said I'm not a threat, Inspector. What we do—your work, my work—seeks the same thing: maintaining order in the face of chaos, the tiger that stalks beyond the walls of the authority we represent."

Uncas appeared immovable, but he must have shifted a bit, for the light from the desk lamp blew a spark from the enameled feather pin on the inspector's lapel.

The Detective continued: "I'm not at liberty to say explicitly what the threat is. But I can tell you that with your help, by your orders, it can be contained."

The inspector leaned forward and put his hands on the edge of the desktop. "You say you are no threat. You say you and I are the same and different. You say something threatens my city, but it must remain nameless. You are asking me to hold smoke in my open hand and to prevent it from escaping."

The Detective shrugged. "I know. And I'm sorry. I'm sure you've had to make similar appeals to your superiors."

Silence from Uncas.

The Detective said, "I understand that you are a very private man in a very public position, Inspector. I understand that every move you make depends on respect and integrity. You must instill trust, and you must provide trust to be successful in your job."

Uncas' eyes narrowed again.

When the Detective received no response, he said, "I recognize these qualities in you, Inspector. I only ask you to trust the man who trusts you."

The inspector frowned and stood. "You presume much."

"I stand on what my investigations and observations tell me."

<<I got a bad feeling we're gonna be all alone with our bug sprayer on this one, boss.>>

The Detective didn't even clear his throat in an effort to shush me. He simply waited for the inspector's response.

Then it came: "I will need proof."

CHAPTER FIFTEEN

It was after midnight. The Studie was on its way to the home of Isaac Kaghneghtago, the first of the two Mohawks we'd seen poking around the warehouse. A little surreptitious digging let me know he'd be off shift now and—supposedly—in bed asleep.

<<I can't believe you got away with telling Uncas the threat came from a foreign power.>>

"It's true."

<<Lucky for you the Recent Unpleasantness with Berlin has made everyone twitchy about foreign designs on . . . well, everything.>>

The Detective had prepared one of the cybernetic cockroaches from the Evidence folder before the inspector had arrived. He brought it out from a desk drawer when Uncas asked for proof. The bug lay inactive in an empty aquarium tank. A wire screen in a frame sat on the top, weighted down with a brick.

Uncas' expression was that of a man who realized someone was pulling his leg.

"You should read the paper more often," he said. "This invasion started long before we were born, and is ongoing."

The Detective shrugged. "Who do bugs obey?"

<<Whom. Whom do bugs obey.>>

"Bugs obey nothing but their own bug nature." Uncas nearly sneered. Disdain seemed to provoke expression in his face and voice.

"Watch this." The Detective removed a compact shortwave transceiver from a shelf. It warmed up, he dialed over to the frequency he wanted, then pushed a button on the microphone.

The cockroach hopped onto its legs. It scurried around the four corners of its glass box with furious speed.

It leaped and clung to the underside of the screen. The bug shook against its prison, and even the brick jittered atop the improvised lid.

Uncas stepped back from the desk, eyes wide.

"What is this?" he asked.

"Just the beginning of the threat. Instead of heavy artillery, an army of these little monsters will soften the target—us, the city—for the follow-up force."

The cockroach began to hammer its body against the brick. Red dust and little bits of fired clay dropped into the tank.

Uncas muttered something undecipherable.

<<The newspapers would love to witness the inspector at this moment.>>

"Shh!"

Uncas looked at the Detective, who thumped the top of the brick with his gloved hand. The bug dropped to the bottom of the tank, then immediately jumped back to the bottom of the brick with an audible smack.

A crack popped into the surface of the brick, halfway across its length.

The screen began to rattle, and through a sudden gap between the frame and the tank lip, the bug escaped into the room.

"Get it!" the Detective yelled.

Uncas started stomping in a decidedly un-inspectorish manner.

The cockroach launched itself toward the inspector, latched onto his trouser leg.

"Yeeow!" Uncas began swatting at his leg, thrashed about, stumbled, sat and landed hard on the floor. "Yaarh!"

The Detective grabbed the radio, leaped across the desk to land before the office door, then kicked Uncas' leg. The steel toe of the Detective's wingtip met the bug with a *Tang*! The cockroach went spinning, bounced off the wall, and hit the floor. The Detective slammed the radio set onto it before it scrambled away.

Blue fire flared from under the radio with an alley-cat screech.

The Detective raised the broken radio.

The remains of the bug clung to the radio and continued to dance a jig while sparks popped from its carapace.

The Detective beat the radio and bug into scrap with the halved brick.

Finally, he said, "I know where to find a vat of acid to drop this," and he dusted his trouser knees.

Uncas looked at the empty glass tank, at the smashed radio, and then at the Detective. A hole gaped in the black fabric of his trousers, and a bloody three-inch chunk of his leg hung by a scrap of skin.

"Okay," he said.

CHAPTER SIXTEEN

We'd left Uncas at the St. Olaf emergency room, where a physician looking at the inspector's wound said gangrene had already begun to set in.

Jonathan Brewster Uncas, Chief Inspector for the New Angoulême Police Department, narrowed his eyes at the Space Detective. "You are sure of this?"

The Detective nodded. "I always get my man."

<<Except that one time. The one who got away.>>

The Detective made a growl, so low that Uncas couldn't hear it.

The inspector's mouth made a thin, tight line. Then he made a nearly imperceptible nod. The two had reached an agreement.

Now the Studebaker's Milky Way black paint was almost invisible in the dark interval between the pools of light radiated by two lamp posts. It was parked before the apartment building Isaac Kaghneghtago called home.

The Detective stood inside the door of the third-floor apartment described in Kaghneghtago's employment records. The only light came between the bottom of a pulled-down blind and the sill of the window facing the street.

The air was thick. The steam radiator alongside one wall was piping hot.

"Were those Mohawks wearing jackets at the warehouse?"

<<Yeah.>>

"It was around eighty degrees today, right?"

<<Yup.>>

The apartment was a wreck. Nothing had been picked up, thrown away, or cleaned in weeks, based on the look of the place. Kaghneghtago lived alone, but this disarray took bachelor slovenliness to a whole new level of yuck.

The Detective walked through the kitchen, his helmet's lenses adjusting to amplify any available light so he could see plain as day. The mess continued in the hallway, where the cop's uniform and gun belt had been dropped in a puddle, and the bath, where the tub was filled with water that looked greenish and smelled like a foul pond.

A stripe of bright light marked the bottom of the closed door to the bedroom.

"You know what I think?"

<<Yeah, I know.>>

The Detective hadn't pulled his Zapper after picking the door locks. He didn't reach for it now, but pulled a pint jar from a coat pocket.

Then he pushed open the door.

On the bed lay the Mohawk.

Only he wasn't a Mohawk.

He was a large green mass shaped like a lumpy, fat starfish the size of a man, covered with moss. It was basking in the light of an array of lamps—the sort used by commercial gardening farms for stimulating plant growth.

<<Shapeshifter!>>

Shapeshifters from Demeter X were plant beings that could assume the forms and behaviors of other creatures. Not particularly smart, but they followed orders well.

This one rolled off the bed with a crackly roar—like a truckload of dry spaghetti being broken all at once—and lunged toward the intruder. It smashed into the Detective's gut, and they crashed against the wall. The Detective dropped the jar. It thumped into a pile of clothes, so it didn't break.

The two squirmed on the floor, then the Detective shoved the creature off with his legs. They scrambled to their feet. Talons—five inches long—grew from the shapeshifter's extremities like spines on a nightmare cactus. Thick as bear claws. Ridges formed in lines along its legs and back, then extended to form rows of sharp-tipped spikes of wood. The shapeshifter now had assumed its battle form. It looked quite formidable.

It swiped with one taloned paw, then the other, and caught the lining of the Detective's jacket as he leaped away. *Rriiiip!* The monster tossed aside the torn fabric while the Detective backpedaled. He stumbled and fell against the bed. The shapeshifter charged. Two clawed arms swatted downward. The Detective rolled off the foot of the mattress, and the creature's talons shredded the bed linens.

The Detective stumbled against the wall, grabbed the window

curtains to steady his balance. The shapeshifter attacked, full tilt toward the Detective. He ducked, the monster slammed into the wall, and the Detective yanked the curtains from the rod and tossed the heavy fabric over his attacker's head. The creature flailed, smacked the Detective so that he crashed against the window. The glass shattered and fell out into the dark. The Detective was off balance, but didn't go through the open frame. He clutched the sill, pulled back into the room and regained his footing. He lurched over to the pile of clothes swaddling his dropped jar. He grabbed the container, wrenched off the lid, and spun around.

The monster was free of the curtains. It rushed the Detective. He flung the contents of the jar onto the charging shapeshifter. It screeched and hit the floor. It withered and curled up into a tight ball that turned a dull brown and gave off a stench like moldy potatoes in an abandoned root cellar.

The Detective caught his breath and screwed the lid onto the jar. "Commercial defoliant."

<<Eewww.>>

"Get a picture. I'll take a look around. Then we'll go check on his partner."

<<He's a single guy, too. Think he's another shapeshifter?>>

"Yep."

<<What are you gonna tell Uncas?>>

"To be careful who he picks to locate those bug cartons."

CHAPTER SEVENTEEN

The second shapeshifter-in-the-shape-of-a-Mohawk lived with William Tagawininto's—the real cop's—widowed mother in a tidy little house on a narrow street. Tidy on the outside. The inside was as big a wreck as the first shapeshifter's apartment.

We found the shapeshifter in the basement under an array of naked bulbs similar to the one we encountered at the first apartment.

Both cops were there—dead—along with Tagawininto's mother. Their bodies were thrown into a pile under the coal chute. The smell of rot was horrible.

The Detective confronted the shapeshifter with an open jar of defoliant in one hand and a photo of the remains of the first shapeshifter in the other hand. He had printed it with a micro printer installed in the Studie on the way over.

"You can go one of two ways," he said. "Like your buddy in the picture, or quietly and still breathing—or whatever."

The shapeshifter put up its hands. The Detective directed it to crawl into an empty cocoon he had brought from the Studie. His prisoner complied, the Detective sealed the bag, punched the buttons on its control unit, then drug it up the stairs.

He called Chief Inspector Uncas at his office.

"How did you know I would be here?" Uncas asked.

"I don't know your home phone, and I figure you must live at work more than at home anyway."

"Why are you calling?"

"How's your leg?"

"It will be fine. Why are you calling?"

"Okay. I asked you to wait on starting that little project for a reason."

"I am waiting."

The Detective paused. "Is it safe to talk on this phone?"

Now Uncas paused. "Yes."

"All right. Two of your patrolmen are dead."

"What!"

"Isaac Kaghneghtago and William Tagawininto. They've been dead for—a few weeks, I'd say."

The inspector's voice was controlled and quiet, but the anger was obvious in the tone. "I do not like more games. I saw William Tagawininto three days ago."

"It was an imposter. They both had imposters. I know it sounds crazy, but think about the bugs." The Detective sighed. "And I've found both their bodies, and Tagawininto's mom, all here at her house. It's bad."

"Who are these imposters?"

"I don't know. Perhaps gone by now." That wasn't exactly true. The tumbleweed carcass of the first was in a bag in the Studie's trunk. The second, still-living shapeshifter would soon be getting a ride to the office and its spacious filing cabinet.

The Detective continued: "There may be other imposters. I'm guessing the likely candidates would be single cops who wouldn't have to fool an entire family about being fake."

"Fine." Uncas said *fine*, but the sound in his voice meant anything but *fine*. "I will hand-pick a squad. They will be ready to hit the streets in one hour. Is this list you gave me complete?"

"To the best of my knowledge, yes."

"Make sure your knowledge is better than best." *Click!*

<<That went well.>>

"Back to the office. Uncas will have a crew on this site and Kaghneghtago's apartment soon. And we have more to do."

<<What's next?>>

"We still need to call in some help."

<<We already have the Chief Inspector on board.>>

"We need more."

<<Who?>>

"Call Jupiter."

<<Oh, no.>>

PART TWO

Knifetongue

CHAPTER ONE

The Detective sat at his desk. The tumbleweed shapeshifter was in the Evidence folder. The cocooned and docile shapeshifter was in Containment with Billy Goat McGraw and Ronnie Roquette. Uncas had a photo of the bug carton, thanks to the Detective, and was now gathering his squad to locate and confiscate the remaining cartons.

The Detective tossed aside a paperback book. The title was *L'homme au sang bleu*. The author was Leo Malet. It had been face up on the desk in plain sight during the chief inspector's visit.

<<What was the point of that?>>

"What?"

<<The French crime novel.>>

"Ah." He picked it up, riffed the pages with his thumb. "Psychology."

<<Have you been going to night school? Picking up a sheepskin without my notice?>>

"Leo Malet writes about a private eye. A loner. Always an outsider in relation to the people around him. But always getting the job done, just the same."

<<So?>>

"So Uncas sees it while I'm talking to him about our relationship, how we're both loners, working against the tide of popular opinion or bureaucracy to do the job we're supposed to do. It's a little symbol reinforcing the message that we're on the same side, that we're really alike, no matter how things look from the outside."

<<You think he even noticed it?>>

"Uncas is a sharp cookie. He sees everything around him. He didn't get to his position by luck or inside influence."

<<Okay. You think he knows this French guy and his detective?>>

"Like I said, Uncas is sharp. He knows more than he lets on. And if he doesn't know Malet, he'll make an effort to find out about him after seeing the book on my desk."

<<Are you sure you're playing Uncas like you think you're playing him?>>

"I'm not playing him. It's all a form of negotiation to show him we're his allies."

<<Hmph.>>

"Okay, we'll see."

<<Now what?>>

"We wait for Uncas to let us know he's rounded up the bugs. Then we start the next step."

<<What's that?>>

"Pulling off an alien invasion by Hyrnavian pirates."

CHAPTER TWO

The bug cartons had been collected.

But Chief Inspector Uncas wouldn't turn them over to the Detective.

The Detective protested. "The people who control these cockroaches—all they have to do is turn a switch to activate them, and then you'll have those crazy bugs running all over the place anyway. It doesn't matter that you've got them in custody."

Uncas' gaze was sharp. His weight rested on an old hickory cane he carried, for he favored his injured leg, but he stood straight and displayed the rigorous might of his office. "I represent the duly authorized law enforcement organization in this city, paid to serve the public good. Who are you?"

"A concerned citizen?"

One of the inspector's eyebrows twitched. Just a bit.

"I am looking into these impersonators in the department. This is a terrible development."

"Perhaps I can help—"

Uncas cut him off: "This is my department. It is an internal matter. Outsiders are not a proper element to introduce to this investigation."

Then he turned and strode out of the office, fuzzing around the edges before he closed the door.

<<That went well.>>

No response.

<<What about the bugs?>>

"We have a few options."

<<Such as?>>

"We can bomb the holding facility, totally wipe out the cockroaches."

<<Is there a *but* in that sentence?>>

"We'd also destroy several—many—innocent lives."

<<Other options?>>

"Time to call in the Louies."

The bad guys use Louies.

So do we.

I like to think the quality of our Louies is better than that of the others, but I may be biased.

Anyway, we can't do everything alone. They make some tasks easier to do.

CHAPTER THREE

Uncas was on the phone. He wasn't happy.

"Federal agents confiscated the bug boxes."

The Detective nodded, even though his caller couldn't see him. "That makes sense. Foreign power. Invasion. Foreign weapons to support the invasion. Federal agents. That makes sense."

"What do you know about this?"

"Me? You're the duly empowered authority. Who am I? According to you, in the scheme of these kinds of matters, I'm nobody. They're Federal agents. Doing their jobs. Just like you and me."

There was silence from the other end. But just for half a minute. Then a *Click* ended the call.

I had a feeling *Click* wasn't all the noise being made at the other end.

CHAPTER FOUR

If J. Edgar Hoover ever found out that one of his Special Agents for the New Angoulême district simultaneously performed tasks for a network of extraterrestrial agents similar to his own earthbound, nationwide agency, he would probably have the agent burned at the stake. Hoover might even want to light the match.

The day after Uncas' call to share his disgruntled exasperation, the Detective went out to take possession of the confiscated bugs. I'd kept up a stringent surveillance of the block around the office—the Detective felt sure the chief inspector would have someone watching his comings and goings.

<<You think he'd trust it to someone else?>>

"He has a lot of irons in the fire now. He can't handle them all alone. He's already got his hands full checking out his men in the department for foreign agents impersonating police officers."

<<I bet right now he really appreciates how you two are allies working on the same side of the fence for the same ultimate goal. I bet he burned every copy of Leo Malet he could get his hands on.>>

"Isn't this a good time for you to keep silent and build some of that mystery into our relationship? Or did you stop reading the magazines?"

<<Yep, you and Uncas—best friends until the end of time. Aren't you stopping off to share a pitcher from the Hell Gate Brewery later?>>

"I think you're supposed to tell me if you've spotted anyone staking out the office."

<<The block's clear.>>

"Thank you."

He drove the Studebaker back to the warehouse district on the Mohegan River. He didn't return to the one housing Ronnie's blast buggy. Instead, the Detective kept a warehouse of his own—purchased through, and taxes paid by a company that served as a financial blind if anyone researched its ownership. Another handy service provided by our Federal agent friend.

The same Federal agent who met the Detective inside the warehouse.

"Detective."

"Van Eckk."

The two shook hands.

Agent Van Eckk had a military buzz cut, so his blond hair looked white against his head, and laugh lines around his mouth and eyes that softened the hard edges of his face—no fat on this man. Still, standing before the Detective in a black suit, he looked like a man who had no time for anything but serious business.

He gestured to the half-ton delivery truck parked behind him under the dome of light from a bowl-shrouded bulb suspended from the ceiling. All windows in the warehouse had been painted over when the Detective took possession.

Van Eckk smiled. "I trust the agency's stereotypically steamrolling over the local authority's jurisdiction has proven to be a successful ploy?"

"So far. But I'm not sure if Uncas is madder at me or the agency."

"He might be mad at the agency, but he knows he would have more luck striking back at you, if that's the way he works."

"Not normally," the Detective said. "But I'm pushing him into very uncomfortable territory. He may respond . . . unpredictably."

<<Maybe he still trusts you. No one is shadowing you.>>

"Yet."

"Pardon?" the agent asked.

"Thank you for your help," the Detective said.

"I'm available as needed," Van Eckk said. He walked toward a door to leave.

"Do you need a ride?"

Van Eckk laughed. "I'm a Federal agent. I have a badge that lets me ride in any car that rolls by."

The door slammed behind him.

The Detective contemplated the delivery truck, and walked two circles around it before raising the segmented door at its rear.

A metal trunk painted dark green rested in the cargo area. A padlock through a hasp secured the lid. The Detective knew that if the cockroaches were activated, the lock and the trunk's metal sides wouldn't last long against the furious bugs' attack.

I turned on more ceiling lights at his request. The far corners of the warehouse were illuminated, revealing various shapes—the arched backs of Quonset huts, large cubes the size of small apartments.

He drove the truck to one of the huts, backed it so the rear door faced the door of the hut. He dragged the trunk from the truck, left it on the floor between the truck and the hut.

From inside the latter he brought a two-wheeled dolly, which he used to move the trunk inside the Quonset hut.

Around the trunk he set up a collapsible frame of metal rods that formed a cube without walls. At each corner and midway along each rod was what looked like the reflector in a flashlight, but none contained a bulb. Instead, standing in the center of each shallow bowl was a little golden spike, like the nib of a fountain pen.

The Detective stepped back a few paces, then removed from his coat pocket a black box, about the size of a package of kitchen matches. He pressed a stud on the box.

The edges of the trunk seemed to fuzz, then the container was gone.

A little dust cloud rose from the floor, raised by the air displaced when the trunk disappeared.

The trunk still existed. But it was in another space.

Just as our office could be said to reside in a place the Detective called Nere, the trunk filled with bug cartons now rested in a storage site—what I liked to think of as a vast, endless closet—the Detective called NoWhere. A place where the trunk and its contents would be inert, held in stasis, like a steak in a deep freeze. Without the cold or freezer burn.

After dismantling and stowing away the transport frame, the Detective locked up the warehouse and returned to the office.

<<Now what?>>

"Time to shift the invasion into the next gear."

CHAPTER FIVE

ERICKSSON CIRCLE BESET BY BUGS

Commuter Cockroaches

STOCK EXCHANGE ATTACKED

Rabid Roaches At Large, Threat Growing

KILLER COCKROACHES INVADE

Exterminators Stymied

The morning and evening editions were black with dire ink. The dailies hawked hysteria. And the radio newsreaders were near breathless in their efforts to outdo the tenor of fear apparent in the newsprint headlines.

Yellow journalism had taken a back seat to white-knuckle fright.

Having Louies in the news reporting game was a great plus for our side. We rarely called on their expertise—the news, after all, was supposed to be factual, and fudging facts could be found out by some newshound with a sharp nose.

But the Detective had made a play with Van Eckk and a few high-placed media moguls. The result was a cacophony of headlines of the like that hadn't been seen since the war.

And the widespread panic in the newspapers probably had the populace puzzled.

Because no reports about attacking cockroaches had been made.

No one in New Angoulême had been attacked by a single invading bug.

Well, no more than usual any other day in any metropolitan area.

Newsstand customers bought papers that day and scratched their heads—certainly they had been in some of the areas reporting infestations, yet they hadn't noticed any unusual events that day.

But it was news—in the papers, on the radio—certainly the stories must be true. Right?

The Detective sighed and folded the last issue from a stack of papers and dropped it with the rest on the floor by the desk.

<<I can always note the satisfaction in your sigh for successful strategies.>>

"How are you at writing jingles for radio ads?"

<<The content surely wouldn't be more misleading than the stunt you pulled today.>>

"All for a good cause."

<<Will you recommend surgically removing toes to reduce the pain of pinching shoes? Or how about just amputating the whole leg?>>

"You've turned up the Snarky setting an extra notch today. Did you wake up on the wrong side of the jar this morning? Dry ice too warm?"

<<I simply have a lot of reservations about this . . . campaign, I guess.>>

"Understandable. Believe it or not, I do, too."

<<Didn't stop you from forging ahead.>>

"We're dealing with big stakes."

<<So you say.>>

"You heard Ronnie," the Detective said. "You saw what the shapeshifters from Demeter were willing to do—murder innocents—to push forward the pirate's plans."

<<How happy about all this do you think Uncas is going to be?>>

That's when the phone rang.

"I bet we're going to find out right now."

<<Actually, I'm surprised we haven't found out before now.>>

The Detective was right: Uncas was the caller.

"You need to come Downtown," he said. "Now."

"I'll be right there."

Uncas added, "Now, as in You are already late."

"I'll see you in your office."

Before the Detective could hang up, Uncas made his point clearer: "Not my office. The Commissioner's office."

Click.

The Detective paused two extra moments before hanging up.

CHAPTER SIX

In a town filled with impressive architecture, the Commissioner's office held its own.

He wasn't present when the Detective arrived, but the room certainly represented the Commissioner's presence.

The floor-to-ceiling walnut paneling gleamed with the rich brown glow some men found in the promise offered by a bottle of 12-year-old Kentucky bourbon.

Crystal chandeliers lit the exposed beams of the vaulted ceiling.

The desk looked big enough to seat an Automat's lunch rush crowd.

The vast black mouth of the stone fireplace behind the desk suggested medieval origins.

Above the mantel were arranged a double-bladed battle ax, a war spear, and a leather-covered shield decorated with silver wrought into knots and mazes. The ax and spear were linked where they crossed with a shiny pair of handcuffs.

It was a room for grand gestures, for photo opportunities, for intimidation.

The door behind the Detective slammed open.

The Commissioner entered, followed by Uncas. The chief inspector still used the cane.

A departmental flunky stayed outside the office and closed the door.

New Angoulême Police Department Commissioner Oswald Knifetongue bristled: His fiery red hair, though tamed by comb and pomade, seemed at any moment only a breath away from standing out from his skull; the waxed points of his mustache suggested the deadly ends of lightning bolts; and electricity seemed to fill the room simply because he had entered it.

Knifetongue was Big: Big of voice, of passion, of stature. The glare of his eyes and the breadth of his chest and shoulders were said to have made hardened criminals dirty their trousers.

He claimed direct descent from the Vinland Vikings—the Christian settlers driven from their Scandinavian homelands by persecution from the blood-feuding pagans to the land discovered by Leif Eriksson.

In his black uniform with its gold braid and medals, he looked more thunder god than Lutheran. The barely restrained rage evident in his face made me wonder if his ancestors might have been pagan stowaways at heart.

Knifetongue took his place behind the desk. He didn't sit. Chief Inspector Uncas stood beside the Detective. But not too close.

The Detective held his hat by the brim. He didn't extend a hand for a shake.

<<Might pull back nub.>>

The Commissioner opened proceedings. He skipped the introductory pleasantries:

"What is going on in My City, and who is causing it?"

<<Do you hear echoes thundering up there in the ceiling beams?>>

Neither the Detective nor Uncas appeared eager to be the first to respond. But the Detective finally asked, "Could you be more specific, Commissioner?"

It hardly seemed possible, but Knifetongue's scowl appeared to darken.

"Before the sun was up, before I'd had my first sip of coffee, the newspapers told me a monster movie is playing out on the streets of My City. Outside my office this morning is a crowd of reporters from the afternoon papers wanting to know what My Police Force is doing about this bug emergency threatening My City. No one on My Staff knows what they're talking about, what the papers are telling people, what the radio is ranting about. There's no evidence of anything even close to what the papers are printing. I haven't even had a report of a cat stuck in a tree! But people are panicking—because of what they're hearing, and maybe worse, they don't see anything that looks remotely like what they're being told."

The Commissioner paused, but it didn't seem like a proper moment for response.

He continued: "So I have detectives check out the water supply. Somebody's surely poisoned it, making half the city delusional.

"But no, the water's clean as ever."

The more the Commissioner frowned, the more frightening grew the diagonal slant of his mustache points.

"On top of that," Knifetongue said, "I learned that patrolmen were quietly being rounded up for some secret investigation. Not by Internal Affairs. No, by the ever-diligent, self-effacing Chief Inspector Jonathan Brewster Uncas—hauling in his own brothers in law enforcement with some covert dragnet answerable to no one but his private command.

"Then!" Knifetongue gestured with an index finger, jabbing the air as though with a blade. "Then! I find out that half the men he's looking for can't be found—they no longer exist! They've been seen at work, but once the dragnet spreads, they disappear."

The Commissioner drew himself up. His stance and rage made him appear taller and wider than the fireplace, and he radiated an attitude medieval enough to hold the battle ax and spear without prompting a chuckle from anyone.

<<I swear I still hear thunder.>>

The Detective cleared his throat.

<<Maybe time to drop Leo Malet on the desk?>>

CHAPTER SEVEN

The trio was interrupted by a buzz from the phone on the desk. Knifetongue answered.

"What? When? Who said? Where?"

He frowned at the Detective and Uncas.

"I'll be there," he said, and hung up.

He strode to the door. "Come with me," he ordered.

Knifetongue didn't say where they were going. They went separately. But everyone was chauffeured.

The Commissioner took his place in the back of his black limousine.

The Chief Inspector rode on the passenger side of a patrol car.

The Detective was driven in a patrol car, too. But he was in the back, where the prisoners usually rode. Whoever had been there last must have tried to rob a brewery—of all its products. A lot of which must have been left on the floor of the patrol car.

The smell was bad enough that the Detective wasn't necessarily unhappy to see his conveyance join a crowd of police vehicles clustered before a bar.

Spotting the Commissioner surging through the crowd of cops was easy—he was head-and-shoulders taller than many of the men who served under his command. The Detective's driver let him out, and he had taken only a few steps toward the curb when Uncas joined him.

The outline of a four-leaf clover accompanied the establishment's name on the sign above the door: THE PADDY WAGON.

"I know this place," the Detective said. "It's a cop saloon."

Uncas nodded. "Natty Brown owns it," he said. "Retired patrolman from the Eight-Three. Tends bar like it is an altar and he is the archbishop of booze."

<<That's almost poetic for a stoic Mohawk copper.>>

The Chief Inspector and the Detective continued to the door and entered past a big Irish cop with the gatekeeper's job.

The place was full of cops, but there wasn't a customer in sight. Everyone here was part of the investigative team.

The ornately carved back bar gleamed in the light from the overhead lamps. It ran nearly the length of the wall, upon which was an array of bottled spirits, signs promoting a variety of local and imported brands, framed photos of cops and politicians. The beer sticks stood at attention in clusters.

A door was open at one end of the bar. It led to a narrow hallway. Within this passage a pay telephone clung to the wall, surrounded by penciled scribblings: names, phone numbers, messages. Three other doors pierced the walls. All were open: one led to a cramped office cluttered with invoices; the second gave way to the toilet; the third offered steps to the cellar.

The cellar—that's where the action was.

Knifetongue was already there, along with five other cops, when Uncas and the Detective descended. The Commissioner towered over everyone in the cellar, but he bent over to keep his head from colliding with the floor joists above.

Everyone sneered against the smell. No one was willing to appear unmanly in the Commissioner's presence by covering his nose and mouth with a hand or handkerchief.

"Rats been at 'em," one of the cops said to the Commissioner. "They been here awhile—a couple or three weeks, maybe." He nodded toward a dark corner that had been hidden by stacks of crates and beer kegs, which had been pushed aside to reveal a pile of bloated corpses, blackened arms and legs in a tangled nest. The stained tarp that had covered the bodies had been pulled away, releasing a cloud of flies.

Another spoke up: "Nobody could smell this upstairs?"

A third replied, "With that toilet and all the spilled beer? I been in here with McElroy, his breath could kill a moose—who'd notice this charnel house?"

Knifetongue frowned. "How many?" he asked.

The first cop hung his head. "Ten. One looks like Natty—still got his bartending apron on."

"All the rest?"

The first cop's shoulders slumped. "Cops."

"*All* of them?" Tamped-down rage smoldered in Knifetongue's voice.

"Yessir." The cop cleared his throat. "The ID we found on some of the bodies—they're cops. Gargle O'Bryan, Matt Finn—"

"Finn was at a precinct meeting yesterday morning!" Knifetongue roared.

"Yessir. All of us, we've seen these guys around the past three weeks. It doesn't make sense."

The Commissioner whirled toward Uncas and the Detective. A wild fierceness appeared ready to take hold of him—the Detective half expected a madman's cackle to erupt from behind that devilish mustache. Or a dragon's bellow of fire.

"Upstairs!" he snapped.

At the top of the stairs, the Detective paused only long enough to scan the notes written on the wall where the phone was mounted. Then he looked along the gleaming bar, where a few empty glasses stood abandoned.

They passed through the barroom. The investigating officers ignored the Detective and Uncas as they followed in the Commissioner's wake. They entered a shoe store next door, which the police had taken over as a remote command center for the crime scene.

Knifetongue went behind the sales counter and stood beside the cash register.

<<Can't resist the seat of power, can he?>>

The Detective sighed.

<<Make sure the Red Goose stays out of his reach. It could be a deadly weapon in his hands.>>

The Commissioner simply glared at the Detective and Uncas for a long, long minute. Then he said, "Explain."

The Detective kept quiet. He knew that in this situation, he was little more than evidence—Exhibit A—to support whatever Uncas said.

Or . . . he would end up a scapegoat sacrificed to Knifetongue's rage.

The result depended on the chief inspector's words.

Uncas began, "These deaths are part of a plot. These men were killed by other men who took their places, impersonating them among the people who knew the dead men. The Paddy Wagon has been open, Natty has been seen tending bar. Because cops congregate here, the impersonators could meet frequently without raising anyone's suspicions. Whoever took Natty's place must have been the person who received news and passed it along to others involved in the plot."

"What kind of plot?" Knifetongue hadn't moved a muscle since demanding an explanation.

Uncas didn't even cut his gaze toward the Detective. "Apparently a plan by a foreign power to invade the country."

The Commissioner raised one eyebrow.

"Says who?"

Uncas still didn't look at the Detective, but he gestured in his direction. "The Space Detective alerted me to what he had learned. Based on the information he shared with me and some . . . physical evidence, I began my undercover round up of suspects within the department."

The Commissioner made a noise in his throat. He'd already made clear how he felt about that.

There had been friction between Knifetongue and the Mohawks in the department from the first day he stepped into the Commissioner's office. Some of this was the result of the normal internal politics that ebbed and flowed within every governmental agency. But some of the bad feelings grew from cultural roots, arising from the often-violent encounters between the Viking settlers and the natives they'd found in their new homeland.

So a wrong step or word could put Uncas in a deep hole, career-wise.

"Why wasn't I informed?" Knifetongue asked.

"Normally, that would have been my first move, sir," Uncas said. "But initially I did not know the extent of the . . . infiltration within the department. From clues gathered by the Detective, here, we determined the characteristics of likely candidates for impersonation. I went about pinpointing those men in the department who may have been replaced. While you are above suspicion, sir, I could not be sure who around you might compromise the investigation, either willingly or inadvertently. As you pointed out, Matt Finn and the others have been seen regularly all the while the real men have been dead in Natty Brown's cellar. No one suspected any of them of anything out of the ordinary. And who would have thought Natty Brown was involved in something of this sort? I took it upon myself to keep the investigation close, undercover, to improve the chances of discovering and capturing the impersonators, and . . . to reduce any chance that bad news about the department might become public."

This last point must have scored with the Commissioner, because his other eyebrow also rose. The fierceness of his aspect lightened slightly, but he still had a face that could intimidate a charging bull.

Uncas paused, awaiting some response.

<<For a man of few words, he can sure get long winded.>>

The Commissioner turned to the Detective. “What clues did you find?”

“I learned about the imposters in the department. Sir.”

“How?”

“I'm working with a . . . federal agency. Two patrolmen were spotted in an unexpected location. I investigated. I found the bodies of the actual policemen.”

Knifetongue's attention returned to Uncas. “That's when your roundup began?”

“Yessir.”

“What about the news reports? Bug attacks?”

The Detective spoke up: “That's part of the federal operation, Commissioner. Disinformation, they call it. The foreign agents are expecting some sort of initial action by, uh, a kind of cockroach. Fierce. After that—the invasion at large begins, apparently. The imposters rally, and the storm troops are let loose.”

“So? There are no bug attacks. What's going on with these headlines?”

“Disinformation, like I said. The invading force thinks its plan is operational and working, to force the hand of those still undercover.”

Knifetongue began nodding. “To catch them with surprise,” he said.

“Absolutely.”

The Commissioner crossed his arms, appeared to study the woodgrain of the countertop. Then he looked up sharply.

“I still don't like any of this. Invasions, internal investigations going on without my say-so. And what foreign power are you talking about?” He glared at the Detective.

“I'm not sure.”

“Does this have anything to do with Berlin?”

“I don't think so. As I said, I'm working for another agency. And I'm just, eh, an employee, so I don't get *all* the information.”

Knifetongue's face turned ugly. “Neither do I.” His glance toward Uncas would have made a Plutonian shiver. In fact, I did. To the extent that I can.

“There is no more secrecy about these imposters,” the Commissioner said. “The news about the find in Natty Brown's bar is already spreading through every precinct in the city. If it's not, my cops aren't worth what the city is paying them. So you can try to dig out any more clues, but I bet the time is past for catching anyone at this time."

Uncas nodded, silent. There was no need for the Commissioner to make clear that he was to be consulted on any investigative decisions.

"You." Knifetongue turned to the Detective. "I consider you a bad influence on my chief inspector. I don't care who you're working for. This is my city. I recommend you consider the hospitality of someone else's city." He cocked his head, a theatrical move that wasn't reassuring. "Consider it strongly."

He stalked out.

In the silence of the store, Uncas leaned on his cane.

The Detective sighed. "Chief Inspector . . ."

Uncas interrupted. "I have work to do. I am sure you have something to do. Elsewhere."

He, too, stalked out.

<<He didn't even offer us a ride.>>

"How safe would you have felt in the back seat of a patrol car after that interview?" He headed for the door. "That's not an offer I would have accepted."

<<You know, I don't think there's a Red Goose in this shop.>>

CHAPTER EIGHT

The Detective had spent some hours in the file cabinet. He had stepped into the Workroom folder and in the wee hours of the morning he spizzled back out into the office like spray from a can of Cheez Whiz. "Get the Studie ready."

He returned to the warehouse storing Ronnie's rocket. He stood staring at the blast buggy several moments before he boarded.

<<So, this is about the red blinker?>>

"Yep. Came to me when Uncas gave me the cold shoulder. The light flashed off that lapel pin he wears, the feather."

<<Uh huh.>>

The Detective placed a box on the control panel where the red light was not flashing at the moment. The box was about the size of a Canasta card tray. Its top surface was matte black and divided in two sections.

"Two components to my box," the Detective explained. "One uses algae from Fezziwig IV to detect any electromagnetic outputs that may be communication or beacon broadcasts. If present, the algae will glow. The other part uses bog mold from the third moon of Borrioboola-Gha XII."

<<I thought the Jellybys quarantined that system.>>

"Apparently there's a black market for bog mold. Black marketeers are very enterprising and entrepreneurial. So here we have bog mold, which, in the presence of radio waves, will pulse in colors. The color from the spectrum will correspond to a particular frequency."

<<Sounds great. But you're sure that's not just a dressed-up Canasta tray?>>

No response. Sometimes my wit is too elevated to be appreciated by my audience.

The Detective sat and watched his gadget. Nothing. The rocket's red light didn't flash, the card tray didn't glow.

<<Did you switch it on?>>

"The light wasn't blinking when we got here. I thought a sensor might detect me coming aboard and activate whatever makes the light work."

We waited half an hour.

<<Maybe something is different. Did you have something with you last time that you don't have now?>>

"I don't—"

The red light flashed. Twice. No more.

The Canasta box didn't do anything.

The Detective stood and stared at the gadget, arms akimbo.

<<Are you sure algae and mold are in there? Maybe someone conned you with parsley and caviar.>>

He watched this static show several more minutes without uttering a word. Then he pocketed the box and exited through the gull-wing hatch.

"Well, well."

An object sat behind the blast buggy's thrusters on the floor of the warehouse. Something big.

<<That wasn't there before.>>

"Nope."

<<Looks like a kid's toy. A top. If the kid is the size of King Kong.>>

"Looks like a whatchacallit . . . a dreidel."

<<Don't those have only four sides? This has, let's see, six.>>

From the tip of its point to the end of its stem or handle, the thing measured about eight feet.

The Detective approached it. He had his bog-algae device in his hand and his arm was extended. Nothing.

<<Do moldy algae hibernate?>>

He put the box back in his coat pocket. He reached out a gloved hand slowly. The tips of his fingers touched the thing.

Nothing.

He walked a circle around it. "You make anything of it?"

<<I don't have much to offer. I've not encountered a space dreidel before.>>

"It's from space?"

<<Makes sense. It appeared beside a space ship.>>

"Anything else?"

<<It's not metal. Cellulose.>>

“Wood fiber?”

<<Yeah, but reconstituted wood, like a wasp nest.>>

He leaned against one side of it. The thing didn’t budge. “Weighs more than a wasp nest.”

<<That was just an example. Actually, I regret mentioning any sort of bug these days.>>

“Is it solid? Does it contain something inside?”

<<I can’t tell.>>

The Detective stared at it. Then he turned and stared at Ronnie’s rocket.

He started walking toward the warehouse door.

<<Now what?>>

“Back to the office. Too much funny business going on.”

PART THREE

Hammer and Hack

CHAPTER ONE

It was Thursday. Rory Hack was being chased by someone with a meat cleaver.

Actually, Thursday had nothing to do with it. Any day of the week, I could check in on Hack and chances were good he'd be on the run from somebody.

This particular Thursday, he'd interrupted a butcher in the middle of work. But what the butcher was working on wasn't a side of beef: it had been the husband of a client who had hired Hack two days ago.

Hack had shadowed the husband to the butcher shop the night before, after the shop had closed. He'd hung around in the dark for several hours, then saw a light come on behind the blinds covering the shop window. It was about three in the morning. Hack had slipped in the shop's back door from the alley—despite his thick fingers, he had a knack for locks—and caught the butcher in the act of dismembering a human body. Hack knew whose body when he recognized the face on the head sitting on the block.

Hack made a noise when he saw the head looking at him. Correction: it looked, but it didn't see anything. The butcher spun around, and Rory hurtled into the meat man—despite the bloody cleaver in his hand. Hack was unarmed, and he pummeled the guy with some solid blows for a few moments. But the butcher regained his wits and swiped with his weapon—it looked for a moment like Hack might live up to his name. So he turned and ran.

That's when the chase began.

Hack was pretty nimble for a rotund fellow. He fairly flew down the alley, the butcher close on his heels.

The alley extended the whole block. It was dark back there, and Hack did his best to avoid tripping on items scattered in his path. Cats screeched and scattered. The pavers were uneven under Hack's feet. His soles clapped loudly as he ran.

But Hack tripped, somersaulted, landed on his knees by a cluster of garbage cans. The butcher charged, his cleaver raised for the killing chop.

Hack grabbed and heaved one of the garbage cans, filled and heavy. The butcher tried to dodge but was clipped by the can. One leg flew up, the other flew out, and the butcher began a cartwheel as he started to squeal. The cleaver tumbled through the air. The butcher hit the ground. The cleaver smacked blade-first into his left forearm.

He squealed in earnest.

While Hack got up to tend to his recent pursuer, I called in an anonymous tip to the closest precinct. The cops would be there soon.

Hack wouldn't be in a lot of hot water. The police knew all about his skill for finding trouble.

But they would hold him for questioning at least until after sun up.

He was a private eye. He worked for the Space Detective.

I mentioned that some Louies don't realize they're Louies. For the Detective, some Louies aren't really Louies, because they aren't really Local Entities assisting against aggressions by extraterrestrial agents. They're just employees.

Rory Hack—and his partner, Pete Hammer—fit into this category. The Detective used them for non-exotic stuff. The address of their office—not that far from Frank Lava's shop, really—was the public address most people found when they wanted to hire Space Detective. After all, he needed an actual private eye business to keep his cover for our activities related to avoiding invasions. No one really questioned how private an investigator could be while wearing a helmet in public. But it seemed to pay off better than running newspaper ads.

The Detective located Hammer and Hack's office near Police Headquarters purely for business motives. The number of people who set out to report a complaint to the police, only to be intimidated by all the official comings and goings at the city's main cop shop, was considerable. Quite a few civilians would veer away from the chiseled steps leading up to the double doors of the New Angoulême Police Department, only to find a more comforting environment at Hammer and Hack's upstairs office.

That's where the Detective went the day after the grisly discovery at The Paddy Wagon.

On the way over, I'd suggested a way to mend fences with Uncas.

<<Why don't you send Van Eckk over to Knifetongue? Tell him Uncas was doing the country a great service.>>

The Detective shook his head. "The Commissioner wouldn't be impressed. Having a federal agent trying to smooth over the situation would be like poking a stick in Knifetongue's eye. He'd only be reminded that an authority besides him also has power in New Angoulême and that Uncas had been serving two masters—not the Commissioner and his city alone—and acting somewhat independently. That might land Uncas in hotter water. I don't want that."

<<Didn't think of that.>>

"Also, it would be completely out of character for any agency to authorize that kind of admission or offering of appreciation."

<<Well, there's that.>>

The office was tucked above a bar and behind a door with a pebbled-glass window that had *Hammer & Hack* painted in black on the glass. That door opened into a common room with a desk and a row of straight chairs along one wall. That row of chairs was interrupted by two doors, also with pebbled glass, that each gave entry to separate smaller offices. The smaller offices were used by Hammer and Hack for private consults with clients. The desk in the common room was intended for a receptionist, but that role was handled by a young lady who also worked in the other office on the second floor, an accountant's operation. Right now, the desk was being used as a chair: Hack sat on it and his feet dangled above the floor. His shoulders were slumped in a tired curve. No one ever accused him of being dapper, but now his knees had scrapes with dried blood visible around the bandages, which were exposed through the holes torn in his pants.

The Detective shook Hack's hand. "Where's Pete?" he asked.

"Meeting with a new client. Got worries about his business partner."

"Rough night?"

Hack shook his head. "Didn't start out that way, but she sure finished up like that."

<<I've heard that lament before.>>

"Lady says her husband's not acting like himself. Angry and twitchy all the time. Drinking more than usual. She thinks something's going on she oughta know about."

"And?"

"I trail the guy twelve days. To work, to the bar, to his poker night. Nothing seems like he's trying something on the sly. Hard worker, hangs out with other hard-working Joes. Yeah, he gets riled up pretty easy, but no worse than lots of guys I've seen."

"So?"

"So poker night, he loses some big pots to this fella runs the butcher shop. I follow him over, I sneak in, next thing I know the shmuck is ready to be tomorrow's cold cut special. Butcher blows up and wants to make finger sandwiches outta me, too."

The Detective walked around the room, looked out the window and down to the street. "Any history between these two gentlemen?"

"Nah," Hack said, then flinched as he shifted his shoulders around. "Think I pulled something in my back when I threw a garbage can." He hardened his jaw line. "It's nothing. No, they grew up together. Neighborhood pals. Sure, they musta had tiffs like anyone, but nothing serious. Both were in the Army. Not together. My guy was infantry, butcher was in an armored battalion."

"The police have anything?"

"Not that they shared with me." Hack shrugged. "We're not that close."

The Detective stood by Hack, picked up something from the top of the desk.

"*Creepy Crime Comics.* A client leave this behind?"

"Nope, that's mine." Hack tugged the issue from the Detective's hands, rolled it and stuck it in his back pocket.

The Detective paused, then started toward the door. He turned before leaving. "See if you can find anything else the victim and the butcher had in common. Tell Pete to call me when he gets in. Be careful." Then he left.

<<Rory isn't the shy and bashful type, but the way I saw him charge that butcher in his shop wasn't entirely a smart move.>>

"Hm."

<<Wondering if he'll trade you his funny book for your Leo Malet

story?>>

"Not at the moment."

<<Okay, so don't drown me with conversation. If you've got a minute, go check out the front of Frank Lava's store. I want another look at that big wooden gun.>>

"Why?"

<<I live in a jar. I got no pockets. I find giant pistols fascinating. Humor me.>>

"Okay, all right."

While the Detective loitered before Lava's door and I scrutinized the big gun, the Detective asked a question: "At the Paddy Wagon, I took a look at the notes scribbled on the wall around the telephone. Did you catch all those?"

<<Sure.>>

"Anything unusual there?"

<<All the numbers checked out to actual addresses. Some were homes, a few were bookies.>>

"Anything else?"

<<Some businesses. One type of business was repeated: three beer distributors. Nothing unusual about that in a saloon.>>

"No."

<<Okay, I'm done here. Unless you want to go in and pal around with your buddy Frank.>>

"No, I want to check on Ronnie."

So he headed for the office.

CHAPTER TWO

Before the Detective could open the file cabinet to visit Ronnie, we had a visitor.

Pete Hammer walked in the door. His outline fizzed around the edges a moment, then he was entirely in the room.

If I were to say Rory Hack was a bit roughhewn, unpolished around the edges, and that he bought his suits off the rack (and often enough didn't first check the size on the labels, so if a coat looked a little tight across his gut, or the sleeves a tad short, no one was surprised), I would also say Pete Hammer was the perfect opposite. He always looked like he'd just stepped from the haberdasher's emporium. Neatly groomed. Mustache carefully trimmed. Nails manicured. Custom-tailored suits with perfect pleats and creases. The finish of his shoes shone like every shoeshine stand in town knew he was the world's biggest tipper.

The differences in the two private eyes meant they could offer services to a wide range of clients. Society types and big-business operators—or their wives—were usually comfortable with Hammer. Working class folks gravitated to Hack.

Hammer normally exuded a sense of calm rationality. Today he looked rather exasperated.

"Hi, Pete." The Detective gestured toward the guest chair. Hammer limped over to it. "Hurt your leg?"

"I'm so sorry to barge in, but I'd wanted to speak with you privately."

"About?"

"Rory." He sat. "But let me catch my breath first. Mr. Sanderson gave me a bit of a surprise. That's where my leg was injured."

"Oh?"

"Oscar Sanderson. We met for coffee at his club, The Coracle. Posh and quiet, rather Old World in its charm. He wants me to check on his partner, Wilhelm Onderdonck. Says he's acting . . . 'erratic' was his word. The two started their business thirty years ago. Architects. Sanderson said Onderdonck had never behaved in quite the manner he's been demonstrating in recent weeks."

"Such as?"

"Raging outbursts toward staff. Screaming at the top of his lungs. Just yesterday he threw an upholstered chair out a window."

"Doesn't sound like normal behavior to me."

"Hmph. When I began questioning Sanderson for details—if there were personal matters in his partner's private life that may be contributing to these scenes, or if something had changed in their business, or if he and Sanderson had some new stresses between them—he charged out of his chair and took a swing at me!"

Hammer had a flabbergasted look on his face I'd never before seen.

"Why?"

"He said I'd insulted him! 'I asked you here to look at Wilhelm, not at me!' That's what he yelled as he tried to tackle me."

"What did you do?"

"A couple of the club's butlers or waiters or whatever-they-are pulled him off me and another escorted me out. I've encountered some strange behavior from clients before, but not usually at our first meeting. At least, nothing quite so violent."

"Well, calm down. Catch your breath."

"I'll be fine." He raised one arm and frowned at it. "But I've scuffed the elbows of this jacket, and I'd ordered the material special from Luigi. It's a shame, really."

"Hm. Okay. So, tell me about Rory."

Hammer's frown was replaced by an expression of surprise, as if a stranger had asked him to name the square root of Pi while he was immersed in the middle of an aria at the opera.

"Oh! Hack. Indeed. As irritating as he frequently manages to be in his pursuit of raising my disdain to ever greater heights, I am truly concerned about him."

"In what way?"

"He's ever more reckless, taking greater risks than are necessary. He's quite good at what he does, and his methods are not my methods, but how he works proves successful more often than not. You know this. That's why you hired us."

The Detective nodded.

"But something seems to be eating at him. To prove something to someone—himself, perhaps? That he's rougher and tougher than anyone. Nothing and no one get in his way as he tracks down whatever he's trailing. It's almost like—obsessive behavior, one might say."

"Such as?"

"The other day we're riding to the train station. Traffic stops. Two cab drivers jump out of their cars and begin an altercation. One bumped the other, I suppose. Rory leaves our car and gets in the middle of it. Both drivers start swinging at him. He knocks one down, the other pulls a gun from his car. Can you honestly believe it? I'm getting out of the car when I see that, the driver puts the barrel to Rory's head. What's Rory do? Spits in the man's eyes, grabs the revolver and pistol whips the man. I get there and restrain him before he harms anyone else in any worse manner. He gave me the gun—grudgingly—and then the police arrived."

"And then?"

Hammer's shoulders slumped. "I'll simply say we missed our train. It was all terribly embarrassing."

The Detective tapped out that same rhythm on the desktop with his fingers I'd heard him noodling with the other day. He asked, "What do you think is causing this, um, untoward behavior?"

It was one of the few times I'd seen Pete Hammer stumped. He shrugged and pointed at the newspaper on the Detective's desk. "It's crazy all over. Maybe Rory has the crazy bug, just like everyone else."

The headline at the top of the page:

> JUVENILES TORCH
> PUBLIC SCHOOL
> *Classrooms now ash piles*

The Detective picked up the paper. "Maybe you're right, Pete," he said. "Maybe you're right."

CHAPTER THREE

"Do you know who Fredric Wertham is?" the Detective asked.

<<I've seen his name in the paper.>>

Hammer had left. The Detective hadn't returned to his planned visit with Ronnie Roquette, but had remained at his desk, tapping out that tune with his fingers as he read all the news stories about the latest juvenile delinquent escapades around the city and state. And in other states as well.

He'd stopped his finger tapping. He picked up the phone and started dialing.

"Miles? Space Detective here. Wait, look, I know you don't want to get caught talking with me, that's why I called instead of dropping by. It's no secret I'm in hot water with the Commissioner." Miles O'Brien was a desk sergeant who would occasionally lend a helping hand. If the political barometric pressure registered in the proper range.

"Look, it's just a question. Just a few minutes of your time. Okay, all you have to say is 'No,' and that's it. No problems for you. How's that?" He put that Smile in his voice again. "Simple enough for you to say 'No,' right? No bad feelings if you do. Just a question." He paused for a response. Then: "Okay, all those juvenile delinquents your men have been hauling in. Among their effects: you collecting a lot of funny books?"

The Detective started jotting a note on a piece of scrap paper. "Okay, nothing funny about them. Crimes and horrors, right? Oh, some funny bunnies and squirrels, too? Okay. Thanks. You're a big help, Miles."

He hung up.

"Let's go."

Past the tobacconist's shop downstairs, a bar, a pawnshop, and a shoe repair shop, to the magazine stand at the corner of the block. Moe's Magazines. Moe didn't work there. His son, Conrad, sat in a chair on the sidewalk. He was twenty-three years old and wore a suit like he was ready to work in the ladies' lingerie department of Macy's, if a store would let a man work there. He was ready to be the world's greatest lady-killer. He could sweet talk any female customer into buying at least two more publications than she had originally intended to purchase. And he never had a single ink stain on his fingers.

<<Do you think Pete Hammer has been mentoring this kid?>>

"Hi, Space!" the kid said.

"Hi, Connie. These funny books—which are your best sellers?"

"Among professionals like yourself, or for kids?" Connie laughed.

The Detective chuckled. "Good question. Any grownups buy these things?"

"A few. Most say they're for their kids, but I think one or two are reading them on the train home behind a newspaper."

"For now," the Detective said, "let's look at what the kids are buying."

Connie picked up some issues with colorful drawings of animals that appeared as characters in animated shorts that played with the film features at the movie theaters. There were also some books featuring cowboy stars and books with exotic settings, like the jungle and outer space. "This is mostly what the younger kids get."

The Detective flipped through the array of colorful newsprint. "And the older kids?"

"You mean like the kids getting in trouble with the cops?" Connie asked. He pulled out issues of a different sort: filled with the type of crime and horror stories that were probably in the issue of *Creepy Crime Comics* that Rory Hack had plucked from the Detective's hand. Compared to the first selection of books Connie had drawn from the rack, these displayed far more lurid cover illustrations: men and women brandishing knives and guns and even axes in threatening poses; women bound to tables beneath the leer of a mad scientist; even a dripping head that had been chopped from its body.

<<Ick. I'll have nightmares. Or I would. If I slept.>>

"I'll take all these, Connie. Thanks."

Back in the office, the Detective flipped through the pages.

<<So, does this stuff give Leo Malet a run for his money?>>

"Not exactly. Remember Fredric Wertham?"

<<Just his name.>>

"Psychiatrist. Or psychologist. I don't remember which. He's been studying these funny books."

<<Somebody calls these funny?>>

"It's a holdover from the funny pages."

<<At least there's something funny there.>>

"Wertham says these books about lurid crimes, evil criminals, and the ads they carry—look, you can order a knife or handcuffs through the mail—are all pushing these young people to commit all these crimes."

<<They read it, then they want to do it?>>

"Something like that."

<<Sounds like a big leap from reading a badly colored fantasy to acting out like that.>>

"I would tend to agree, but with the JD crime rate escalating so dramatically, one has to wonder if Wertham isn't on to something."

<<So this has to do with what? The stuff Pete was talking about Rory?>>

"Maybe so. I'm not sure yet."

<<Rory's a grown man. He has no reason to rebel against authority. He may not come across as the brainiest guy in town, but I find it hard to believe reading some icky funny book is going to make him turn recklessly violent.>>

"According to Pete, something's prompting that kind of behavior. And you said the way he charged that crazed butcher wasn't a necessary risk."

<<Yeah, that's true.>>

"Let's think about this a minute."

The Detective started tapping that tune again.

He plucked up the phone and dialed.

"Hello, Mr. Grieg, this is Space Detective." Grieg ran the tobacco shop downstairs. "No, I haven't yet figured out a way to smoke a pipe in my helmet. But I'll let you know when I do. Is Tommy there?"

Tommy Shaw made deliveries for Grieg after school. Eleven years old and fascinated by the man in the helmet who worked upstairs.

"Tommy, hi, this is Space Detective. Keeping you busy, eh? Listen, you told me your uncle drew funny books. Bill McCarty? Do you know where he works? Oh, you've been there? Can you tell me the address? That's great. Thanks so much, Tommy."

After hanging up, he strode to the door.

<<What about Ronnie?>>

"He'll keep. I know where to find him."

<<Gonna talk to Tommy's uncle?>>

"Yes sir. We're going to learn about the funny business with the funny book business."

CHAPTER FOUR

The address took the Detective to a third-floor room in a hotel that offered weekly and monthly rates. A bed was pushed against the wall. The bed hadn't been made, and the sheets and a blanket were twisted and hanging off a corner. A skinny fellow sat on the tangle of linens, his back to the wall. A board was propped on his raised knees, and he drew with a pencil on a big sheet of thick paper on that board. A cigarette dangled from his lips.

Two other men sat on straight chairs. They also had drawing boards on their laps. A lamp table sat between them. A bottle of black ink and a cup of coffee sat on the table. On the floor by the table was an open coffee tin. It was full of cigarette butts. The coffee came from a pot on a hot plate plugged into the wall. One of the seated men was applying ink to a page with a brush. The other was, like the man on the bed, working furiously with a pencil on a sheet of paper.

The man with the brush responded to the Detective when he said, "I'm looking for Bill McCarty."

"That's me."

None of the three stopped working. But McCarty glanced up before returning his attention to the brush on the page. He had short black hair that seemed to bristle from his head. Thick eyebrows on a jowly face. A dead pipe stuck at an angle from his mouth, and it gave his face an arrogant expression.

The Detective explained that he got McCarty's name from his nephew.

Despite the arrogant appearance, McCarty displayed a friendly charm. "Oh, that Tommy's a fine fellow. What can I do for you?" He looked up long enough to show a quick smile, then bent over his work again. "Sorry, I don't mean to be rude, but we got a deadline to get a book over to our editor today."

"You're all working on it?" the Detective asked.

"Oh yeah. A cowboy thing. Joey," he nodded at the man on the bed, "he draws the figures, but he's no good with horses, so Ray," a gesture at the other seated artist, “does those, and I put ink on their pencils. I do the letters, too.”

“Ah.” The Detective watched this small assembly line long enough for Joey to drop his page on the floor and begin another immediately. A few moments later Ray pushed his hair back from where it had fallen over his eyes, then he lay his fully penciled page on a short pile at Bill’s feet. Next, he picked up the page Joey had just finished. Finished, that is, except for the horses.

“Joey’s real good at drawing girls,” Ray said, then tucked his board into his lap and started drawing horses. His hair fell back down toward his nose.

<<Wonder if there are any cowgirls in the cowboy story?>>

“Um, Mr. McCarty . . .”

“Bill is good enough for me.” He displayed that quick smile again, but didn’t even look up this time.

“Okay, Bill. I’m trying to learn about this funny book business.”

“Sure, whatcha want to know?”

“Do you gentlemen do only cowboys?”

“Cowboys, romance stories, some funny animals.”

“Romance?”

“Joey’s real good at drawing girls,” Ray said again. He smiled as he said it.

Bill continued: “Ray pitched an idea for a jungle man story. We’re doing a book of jungle man stories tomorrow.”

“And a jungle girl,” Ray interjected. “Joey draws it, might be more popular than Roongarah.”

“Roongarah?” the Detective asked.

“The jungle man,” Ray said. “The jungle girl’s named Evie.”

<<A jungle girl can be named Evie, but a jungle man can’t be called Sam or Ralph?>>

Joey stirred from his drawing. He pulled a new cigarette from his shirt pocket, lit it from the butt he’d been smoking, then tossed the butt into the pile in the coffee tin on the floor. All his movements were very deliberate and careful. He looked thoughtfully at the page before him a few moments, then started back at work with the pencil.

The Detective returned to his questioning. “So how about all these crime comics that are making news right now?”

Bill shook his head. "We don't do that stuff. We saw enough horrors fighting Berlin." He stopped moving the brush, looked into some distant image beyond the walls of the room. "All three of us, we worked in the biz before the war. Went off in big ships and marched and fired and got shot at, and dreamed about coming home and drawing stories again. Stories about heroes. Who fought battles but didn't get muddy or bloody. With a clean sense of right and wrong." He looked up at the Detective. "Something different from our days fighting Berlin, watching our buddies die around us."

He was quiet for a moment, then went back to his ink and brush.

The Detective prompted more: "And?"

Bill sighed. He continued working as he spoke. "The market for the super heroes faded when guys came home from the war with their stories about its horrors. The notion a clean-cut hero in a funny suit could take care of villains by flying around in a cape—something didn't click with readers anymore. Even the kids. Everybody lost something inside—their innocence, or a hope that something clean and brave could exist in the world after what happened in Europe."

"But you're drawing cowboys—surely they are heroes in your stories."

"Oh yeah," Bill said and nodded. "But they don't take place in a world like today. Those stories are in the past. After everybody found out how awful the war was, stories about the wild west seem like fairy tales from another world. That's why these space stories are getting more popular, I think."

"You know what people want?" Ray asked. "They don't want heroes today. They want victims and martyrs. Being heroic—that's being stupid and childish. That's what the cynics think."

Bill looked at the Detective. He shrugged. A concession of agreement with Ray's statement was in the shrug.

"Say," Ray spoke up, "is anybody doing a Space Detective comic book?"

"No."

"Might be good for business," Bill added.

Joey raised his head and spoke for the first time: "You got a Space Girl in a helmet back at the office?"

"Um, no."

Joey shrugged, went back to work on the bed.

"So, no more super heroes?"

"Some, a few popular ones from the bigger publishers. But the business has collapsed from the glory days before the war. We work here 'cause it's cheap—this is Joey's room; Ray and I pitch in from what we make to help with the rent. We gotta finish a book a day to get by."

The Detective nodded. "So, what about these crime books?"

Bill frowned. "They're bringing the heat down on all the books, even cowboys and jungle girls. The delinquents are reading those crime books that leave nothing to the imagination, getting in trouble with the law, then every Momma in town is raising Cain about the evils of funny books."

"The outfit you fellows work for—does it publish these crime and horror books?"

"We work for lots of people," Ray said. "Whoever we can beg an assignment out of."

"We're pretty quick, a whole book in a day," Bill explained, "so sometimes they need something quick. We can do that, and what we turn in is pretty good."

"Especially if we can put some girls in," Ray said.

"But every one of the publishers has at least one or two of those titles," Bill continued. "But really, only one company is the leader in that kind of thing."

"Who's that?"

"Go see Eirik Grimsson."

"Think he'll see me?" the Detective asked.

"Why not?" Bill asked back.

The Detective shrugged. "He's probably catching a lot of heat for all these crazy books he's publishing, because the juvenile crime rate is being tied to his books."

Ray perked up. "Grimsson is a sweetheart. He'll see anybody. When he turns me down for work, he practically weeps. But he knows how to make a buck, and if kids are buying his books, he'll keep right on putting them out. Sure, he'll see you. And you'll see what I mean—he'll feel bad that he's never met you before. Mention my name, he'll probably weep about not giving me work, and I won't even be in the room."

McCarty looked up and nodded. "It's true. Guys in this business are hard-hearted about money. Some are fair with the guys who do the work, others are trying to figure a way to cut you out of every penny possible even while they're talking to you. But Eirik Grimsson is a fair dealer. Maybe we don't work for him because we don't want to do his kind of books, or maybe we're not good enough to do his books. But he'll treat me like an old friend when I walk in his door. Go ahead. Ray's right. He'll talk to anybody."

The Detective offered thanks and said goodbye. As the door closed behind him, Ray called out from that one-room factory, "Think about that Space Detective book."

<<I like that idea. Especially the Space Girl part.>>

He was going down the stairs. "How do you look in a dress?"

<<I don't have the legs for it.>>

CHAPTER FIVE

He was headed to Eirik Grimsson's office. The Detective got out of a cab in front of a building on the corner of Seventh Avenue and West Fifteenth Street. It was a turn-of-the-century brick building, essentially a red cube anchoring the corner, nothing particularly distinctive except its brick colonnade. Inside, a clerk at an information desk directed him to the sixth floor.

<<I understand your concern for Rory. But why are you spending so much time on this funny book thing? What about the shapeshifters? The cockroaches? Ronnie and the pirates?>>

"I think it's connected."

<<The JD crimes and an invasion?>>

"Yes. It's like the cockroaches. The juvenile crimes are a distraction, a diversionary tactic that keeps attention off the primary threat the Hyrnavians are working on."

<<Consider me skeptical.>>

"What's wrong with that theory?"

<<Come on. World conquest with kids and funny books?>>

"They tried crazy cockroaches, remember? Bugs. And that was just locally. If these funny books really are tied up in a scheme, just think—they're distributed across the country. These crimes are occurring everywhere, not just New Angoulême."

<<Youth in rebellion. Nothing new. Kids have run away from home. Gone west with Huckleberry Finn. Joined the circus. Or worse. Think of the dame who gave her parents forty whacks.>>

"'Dame?' What kind of magazines are you reading?"

<<Maybe I read your Leo Malet when you weren't looking. Like I said, a little mystery—>>

"Goes a long way."

<<Anyway, sounds like a long stretch. Youngsters run amok as part of a grand invasion plan?>>

"Prodded on, somehow, by these comic books. Pushed to a higher, more dangerous level."

<<Sounds like you and Dr. Wertham should have a chat.>>

The Detective stepped out of the elevator into a wide reception area that appeared nearly bare: there was a desk facing the elevator, three straight chairs, and an Oriental rug on the floor. What once may have been an opulent display of wood detailing had been obscured, for the paneling and trim had all been painted off-white, and the paint was chipped here and there. Three frames hung on the wall behind the desk: Each displayed the lurid cover art for one of Grimsson's increasingly infamous comics.

A young woman with a wave in her dark hair and a flash in her brown eyes looked up from papers arrayed on the desk. The ends of a silver chain around her neck were connected to the earpieces of a pair of black-framed glasses that rode the crest of her sweatered bosom. "You have an appointment?"

"Are you Mr. Grimsson's secretary?" The Detective had the Smile in his voice.

"Nope, I'm the copy editor. And I answer questions from guys who don't have appointments and who don't answer my questions." Her retort had sharp little edges, but she smiled. "I've seen your picture. Interested in having a monthly book at the newsstand?"

"Not exactly, but I'd like to see Mr. Grimsson."

"I'm Hazel." She stood and smiled at The Detective. She placed on the desk the short stack of typed papers she'd been reading when interrupted. She stuck out a hand and shook the Detective's.

The Detective started to reply, but she cut him off. "I said I'd seen your picture. You ever take that thing off?"

"Um, no."

"Hm." She walked to a door in the wall behind the desk. "Come on back. Eirik is just reading. He probably needs an interruption. He may not know it, but he probably does."

The Detective followed Hazel along a hall to an office that had no door. The hinges were in place, but no door was hung there.

"Go on in," Hazel said, and stood aside as The Detective entered.

The office walls were lined with bookcases, all of them filled to overflowing. Waist-high stacks of books and magazines and funny books stood on the floor, leaning like houses of cards ready to tumble.

In front of one wall of shelves was arranged a magazine rack. It was stuffed with the bright colors of the latest funny books—both Grimsson's and those of his competitors.

There was no desk, but a long table was arranged in the middle of the room. Its surface was covered with a jumble of funny books, most of them opened to interior pages. Sitting behind this table, perusing a magazine about talking dogs and cats, was a bookish fellow—yes, I said "bookish"—with wavy black hair and thick glasses. He wore a blue bow tie with a starched white shirt whose sleeves were rolled up above his elbows.

Hazel was gone. The reading man didn't look up. The Detective spoke: "Mr. Grimsson?"

"Ah?" He continued to read, his fingers caressing the paper before flipping to the next page.

"Excuse me."

Grimsson finally looked up, a dazed, unfocused appearance to his eyes behind the corrective lenses. "Oh. Hey. I know you. Mr. Space Detective." He stood and extended a hand. His fingertips were smudged black as though he'd had his prints taken.

They shook. The Detective said, "I'm sorry to come by without an appointment—"

"Hey, no problem," Grimsson waved it away. He sat down again. "If Hazel didn't want you back here, you'd not be seeing me now."

The Detective paused, looked around. "Is the building shaking?"

"Ha! It's okay. It's the presses downstairs. Running the books. I sit down, the presses roll, it's like a massage. Here, have a seat." He looked around. Books everywhere. "Okay, I don't have another chair." He looked at the Detective and smiled, made no effort to go get a chair or to suggest a direction to look for one.

"Uh, that's okay."

"You're here about the book, right?" Grimsson interrupted.

"What book?"

"The Space Detective book. Right?" His lips puckered and his thick brows gathered above his nose. "We're doing a Space Detective book?"

The Detective put the Smile into his voice. "Not that I know of. But I hear rumors that people want to do one."

"Maybe I do. You should meet my artists. I bet Hazel would want to write it. She's been bugging me to let her write a book. She must like you, she let you back here. She says she's tired of editing, wants to write." His attention had seemed to wander somewhere while he talked. Now he looked at the Detective again. "Would that be okay, Hazel writing your book?"

"You might ask Hazel, first."

Grimsson cocked his head. "Is there a Space Girl? Back at your office?"

"Uh, no."

<<Maybe it's time to advertise for some feminine help.>>

"That's okay. Hazel might get jealous if she had to write in a Space Girl."

"Right. Mr. Grimsson—"

"Please, Eirik is fine." He waved his hands again. "Mr. Grimsson is my father. He started this business. Publishing dime novels, then the detective and western magazines." He bent and rummaged in a pile by a corner. The tower of magazines toppled—*SHLUMPF!*—and Grimsson raised and waved a pulp-paper magazine with a bright-colored cover featuring big splashes of red and yellow: *Top Hat Mystery.* The cover painting captured an action-packed scene: a man with a desperate expression, his clothes in rags, held a knife to the throat of a respectable-looking young woman who bit her lips in fear. The man held an automatic in his other hand, firing toward the reader, apparently at attackers arrayed beyond the bounds of the issue's cover dimensions.

<<Where does the top hat come in?>>

"The mystery men got big, you know. Guys in masks and guns. Mad geniuses taking over the Potomac. Invasions." His head tilted to the side as he followed his thoughts. "You know, right before the war, the mystery men got very popular. Lots of paranoia boosted sales. Then the soldiers went across the ocean, and the news started coming out about how awful Berlin really was. The mystery men and their master villains couldn't compete with the real news on the radio."

He shrugged. "Sales plummeted. My father was at loose ends. He asked me for advice. My father, he asks me for advice about his business, that is a man with loose ends, he's reached the end of a map and he doesn't know where the road goes. So I say let's try this funny book business. Keep the presses rolling, the employees busy. He says okay, we start this new business, the old business dries up. My father, Mr. Grimsson, finally says, 'I don't know this business,' and hands it over to me. Our boys come home from Berlin, they want something different, everybody wants something different, the crime movies and the radio shows start up with different kinds of stories, so that's what I do with the funny books." He shrugged again, sat down at his book-covered table. "Sales are good again." His ink-smudged hands lay on the open pages of the dog-and-cat book.

The Detective nodded. "But aren't you creating a lot of friction with these crime books? The newspapers, the police?"

Grimsson made a lazy gesture with his hand. "Oh, everybody. The school boards, the teachers, the mommies and daddies. 'My innocent darling is brainwashed by your shoddy stories.' Okay, let's say a little truth here: One, nobody is innocent. The little darlings are born bad, just like their mommies and daddies, who are blind to the badness in their little darlings.

"Two, if the kids were really so innocent, if their mommies and daddies were so innocent in their teaching their kids, my shoddy stories wouldn't be brainwashing them. They surely wouldn't be brainwashed to go set fire to schools and rob stores.

"Three, my stories aren't so shoddy. I hire the best artists, good writers. Maybe the stories aren't pretty, but bad guys get their just desserts at the end. Real people do wicked things in real life, and that's what you'll see in my stories. Mommies and daddies just aren't used to seeing real life drawn up in a funny book."

"Maybe funny books aren't the right words to use."

"Maybe. And maybe the readers should be older, not little kids. I got no issue with that. But there isn't another distribution stream right now that would be more appropriate, I guess. The newsstand guy can sell what he wants to who he wants."

"So you're just going to keep on making and selling these books?"

"Why not? People buy 'em. Just ask Morrie Cortland, my business manager. My business is to stay in business. To do that, I provide something people are willing to pay for. Sales tell me plenty of people are willing to pay for what I make, no matter what the headlines and teachers say." Saying these words, Grimsson had gotten a bit red in the face.

The Detective reached out a hand. "May I?"

Grimsson handed one of his titles to his guest, *Crackling Crime Comics*. The Detective leafed through the pages. "So who is your nearest competitor?"

"Hah! No one!" Grimsson clapped his hands. "No other company wants to get in this hot water. Don't get me wrong," he said as he waved his hands before his face. "Some folks have tried. Always the second-string guys, the ones who follow trends but don't set them. The art not so good, the stories really scandalous with no redeeming qualities. Bad guys killing people higgledy piggledy and no justice in the end. Evil run amok, shocking stuff. But the quality isn't there. Sales may spike at first—hey, the readers say, here's something new—but then they see what they're buying, they compare that junk to the fine stuff I'm selling, and they drop it. And the also-ran publishers drop the books and move on or go out of business."

Grimsson had grown more animated as he talked about his rivals.

The Detective picked up another magazine, one of the funny animal books from a different publisher. "So, no talking bunnies or mice for you?"

"Bunnies! Mice! Rats!" Grimsson was shouting now, his face red, his glasses steamed so that his eyes were obscured. He waved his arms above his head. "Everybody has a plan, and mine is always the bad one!" He clutched a rolled-up comic in each fist. "Who cares about talking mice? A mouse runs out of my baseboard, says to me he wants some cheese, I'm throwing a shoe at it."

He shot to his feet. The table overturned, and a wave of colored paper surged toward the Detective. "There's nothing wrong with my plan! This is my company! You feel those presses rolling under your feet everywhere you go in this building. That rolling energy of words and ink powering along under your toes. That's my plan! That's my business!"

Grimsson had advanced so that the Detective had backed out the doorless entry into the hallway. A bald man in glasses and a nice suit and tie stood farther along the passage, one foot slightly raised as though he wasn't sure whether to advance or turn and run. Hazel the not-secretary was at the other end, where she had escorted the Detective in to see her boss. A look of surprise mixed with worry worked across her features.

"That's my business!" Grimsson asserted again. He stalked into the hall, and the Detective stepped toward Hazel and the entry, still facing the raging publisher. "You tell him, Morrie!" The bald man in the suit nodded. He remained in place, but still appeared ready to run away. "You think you can do better, prove it, Space Man!"

<<I think he's forgotten your name.>>

"Mr. Grimsson, I'm not sure—"

"I told you, Mr. Grimsson is my father. I'm the boss here! You don't like it, beat it!"

Grimsson swung the rolled comics as if he were swatting a horde of attacking mosquitoes.

The Detective turned, nodded a farewell to Hazel. "Sorry to have caused a rumpus." He started toward the front door of the office.

"I'm sorry, Mr. Space Detective," she said. "I just don't know."

Out on the street, the Detective let out a sigh. "Whoo."

<<Guess that ruins our chances for a Space Detective comic from Grimsson's presses.>>

"Oh, yeah, that's too bad."

<<Yeah, I bet Hazel coulda fixed us up with some real excitement. Not like our real lives.>>

"Watch out, I may start to weep." He waved for a taxi. The two comics he'd picked up in Grimsson's office were still rolled up in his gloved hand.

<<Some reading for the ride?>>

"Research. Clues, maybe." He gave the cabbie the address for Hammer and Hack's office. The car had barely begun to move when the driver pushed hard on the brakes. The Detective was jostled, looked out to see the problem.

Kids.

Seventy or eighty kids. Striped shirts, caps, sneakers, a wave of kids rushing into the street from around the corner, stopping traffic. Cars lurched as brakes screeched. Kids aged from ten years to sixteen or so surged into the lanes, swept around the vehicles, thumping the fenders with sticks, hammers, ax handles. A thrown brick smashed the windshield of a stopped car. A gang of ten attacked one car, one juvenile stomping on the hood, the others rocking it on one side, attempting to roll the vehicle over.

"Call Uncas," the Detective ordered.

He pushed open the cab door against the bodies of the rushing children and teenagers. One nearly tripped him as he got out. Another swung at his head with a tire iron. The Detective ducked; the metal bar clipped an edge of his helmet. He slammed his shoulder into the kid's gut, and his attacker took a sudden hard seat on the pavement.

I put in a call to Uncas.

The Detective pushed against the fighting tide. Hands pulled at his arms, tugged at his clothes. Someone bit his knee. He stood in the middle of the block. He was tackled from two directions. The Detective was pushed, pulled, driven to the pavement. He shoved, tried to roll. He managed to scoot under a car, dragged his way to the other side of the vehicle, scraping his helmet against the undercarriage. He squeezed out from underneath, stood up with his back against the side of the automobile. Another crew representing the city's angry youth—boys and girls—rushed him. The Detective raised one knee, one of the teenagers slammed into it with his chest and fell to the street. A lead pipe dented the top of the Detective's helmet. He staggered, then spun and knocked the five youngsters off their feet. In the moment's respite he pulled a black box—the size of a woman's compact—from a pocket inside his jacket, raised his hand over his helmeted head. When he pressed one of the studs on its surface, there was a moment when each person in the chaotic crowd, despite the racket, could hear just a seemingly distant *ping!* Then everyone on the street—the kids, the people in the cars, anyone on the sidewalks within forty yards—dropped where they stood or sat. Every motor stopped running. The sudden silence that followed all the noise was startling.

The Detective was the only person still standing. He replaced the box in its pocket, dusted off his knees. He walked back to the cab, examined the driver slumped over the steering wheel. He was snoring.

The Detective let a couple of bills flutter onto the seat beside the driver, then trotted across the sidewalk to an office building. He dodged inside, hurried past the elevators and made his way to the freight door in the back. He exited to an alley, ran to where it connected with a side street, then turned and began walking to the next block. He turned again at the corner, keeping a brisk pace. Sirens were growing louder, approaching the now-silent block he was leaving farther behind.

"Too bad we don't have any excitement in our real lives," he said.

<<You betcha. There may be a few questions about what happened back there.>>

"You phoned in an anonymous tip, right?"

<<Just like always.>>

"Then the police won't know I had anything to do with it. No questions for me, fewer headaches for Uncas."

<<What about the driver? He'll remember he picked up Space Detective. Or people who watched from the buildings?>>

"Maybe. If questions come, I'll address them then."

He'd turned another corner, flagged another taxi and was soon riding to Hammer and Hack again.

<<The radio reports swarms of kids running rampant at the subway stations.>>

"Another reason to stay out of the underground stations: I might get trapped there. Probably that crowd we ran into came up from one of the stations. These mobs of crazed kids have easy transport from one part of town to another on the subways."

<<If this JD stuff escalates at this rate, the city will be a mess by nightfall.>>

"Give it a couple hours. Commissioner Knifetongue will have the trains shut down within an hour. Before night he'll convince the mayor to declare a state of emergency. The National Guard will be out to support the police."

<<Think that might hinder your investigation?>>

"Not if I move quickly. Still think I'm on the wrong track?"

<<Maybe not. But if you are, this mess with these kids has to be cleared up before we can get anywhere with the shapeshifters and whatever they were up to.>>

"I still think the comics and the cockroaches—they're connected."

<<Grimsson turned out to be a real pussycat, just like Tommy's uncle said.>>

"He certainly did." The Detective unrolled the comics he kept from Grimsson's office and started flipping their pages. "I wonder if everyone in this funny business is a sweetheart, just like him."

CHAPTER SIX

The Detective went up the stairs to the door that read *Hammer & Hack*. He entered the office.

It was a mess.

The waiting room chairs were scattered, some knocked over. Pete Hammer stood in the far corner, leaning on a black cane I'd not seen before.

Rory Hack stood in the middle of the room, brandishing one of the client chairs in a posture that appeared to be threatening toward his partner.

They both turned toward the door when the Detective came in.

"Am I interrupting something?" he asked.

<<Hack's working on his lion-taming moves for some undercover circus job.>>

Hack's bullying posture faltered a bit, then he dropped the chair. It clattered on the floor. Embarrassment flushed his face. He retrieved the chair, sat it upright on its feet.

Hammer didn't move from the corner, but raised one eyebrow as though bemused. The imminent threat of bodily harm hadn't cost him his usual sang-froid.

He said, "We received a phone call."

"'We' nothing," Hack sputtered with sudden, renewed anger. "You answered the phone before I could get to it."

Unperturbed, Hammer continued: "It was for you," he said, and he indicated the Detective.

Hack looked surprised. "It wasn't for me?"

Hammer's eyelids lowered, half-covering his eyes. "He thinks I'm keeping potential girlfriends from him."

"I never get a chance at the dames," Hack blustered. "Hammer always detours 'em away from me with all that fake charm."

The Detective looked at Hack. "'Dames'?"

<<I had no idea Leo Malet was so popular.>>

Hammer put both hands on the head of the cane. "It was a woman's voice, yes. Said her name was Hazel Byrne. 'I'm not a secretary,' she said."

<<Hazel Byrne. She's got a last name. She must like you.>>

"The number's on the pad by the phone," Hammer added.

"Clean up this mess," the Detective directed. He dialed the number.

Hazel's voice answered: "Great Comics."

The Detective said, "Miss Byrne, this is Space Detective."

"Oh, Mr. Detective, this is Hazel." The cool professionalism in her voice suddenly disappeared into a gush of breathlessness. "I don't understand what happened when you were here. I must apologize."

"You don't have to apologize for your employer's behavior."

"It's *so* strange," she said. I heard an anxious bewilderment in her tone. "Eirik is usually the very nicest guy you'll ever meet. I mean it, really. But lately he's had these spells. I don't know. Well, you saw it. He just gets kind of crazy."

"When did these episodes start?"

"Two or three weeks ago?" She was silent for a moment. "That sounds right. Or maybe I started noticing them then. They've been getting worse. Maybe they weren't so bad or lasted so long at first, but Eirik's been getting more furious, more violent lately when he has these spells." Hazel's voice dropped in volume: "I've been a little afraid. Not for me, but that he might do something crazy, get in trouble somehow."

The Detective opened one of the drawers in the desk on which the phone rested. A nest of comics sat inside. He shut the drawer. "Has anything changed at the office in the past weeks? Problems with staff?"

"Oh no, nothing like that. And business is good. Eirik's always jolly after he goes over the finances with Morrie."

The Detective's fingers drummed on the desktop the same rhythm he'd been playing so often recently. I was ready to hide his radio, but then I remembered: he'd broken it on the cockroach that had attacked Uncas. "How about with the printing presses?" he asked. "Any changes there? Equipment? Supplies?" His fingers stopped moving, and he looked at the tips of his gloved fingers. They were still smudged from scampering in the street with the attacking juveniles. "New ink supplier?"

"No, nothing like that."

"Okay." He reassured her that everything would turn out fine and gave her the number for the main office. “Thank you, Miss Byrne.”

“Please call me Hazel.”

“Um, okay, Hazel.” He said goodbye and hung up.

<<I think she really wants to write that Space Detective script.>>

“Uh huh.”

<<And maybe not just for the funny books.>>

“Uh hum.” He cleared his throat, checked on Hammer and Hack’s progress at straightening the room, then pulled a phone directory from another desk drawer. While he flipped through the pages, he gave orders: “Rory, straighten your tie, go down and get a cab for us. I’ll be down in a moment.”

After Hack had left, Hammer said, “If you want Rory’s tie straight for where you’re going, you should examine your own attire. You look like you’ve been rolling in the gutters.”

The Detective looked at where Hammer pointed the ferrule of his cane: tears, stains, and dark smudges marred his suit. He touched the dents in his helmet. He shook his head. “You might say I have.”

He held out to Hammer the two rolled-up comics he’d collected from Eirik Grimsson. “Take these to Inspector Uncas. See if the police lab can find anything on the pages.”

“Like what?” The dapper fellow looked at the gaudy magazines in the Detective’s hand with undisguised disdain.

“I don’t know. Just ask him to look. Tell him I sent you.” He lay the comics on the desk. “And wear gloves or put them in a bag.”

“Oh, a bag will do it,” Hammer said. “I don’t care to be seen with this trash. Are they from Grimsson’s company?”

“They’re from Grimsson, yes, but only one is published by him. The other is published by a company called National Thrills.” The Detective replaced the phone directory in its drawer. “That’s where Rory and I are headed.” He turned at the door. “Before you leave, check around here. Take an inventory of your partner’s funny books. I’m curious just what titles he’s been reading.”

Hammer nodded, then sneered at the two comics on the desk. The door rang as the Detective shut it behind him.

CHAPTER SEVEN

Operations were rather more formal at National Thrills than at Grimsson's Great Comics.

National Thrills had prestige—of a sort—by having been the first, best-established comic publisher since the first four-color appearance on the newsstands of Mighty Man, a handsome, muscled marvel who defeated bad guys before they realized the battle had begun. Mighty Man had set the tone for a long string of costumed mystery men who appeared from a variety of publishers—some shoestring affairs that disappeared as quickly as the ink dried on their newsprint pages, others making bags of cash for their founders within mere weeks—and gave work to men like Bill McCarty and his two pals in their cramped rented room.

The popularity of the mystery men had suffered, as McCarty had noted. But some—like Mighty Man—still appeared from National Thrills, carrying on despite lower circulation figures, because of the public's familiarity with the character. Mighty Man had stayed in front of the public thanks not only to his dime-an-issue adventures but also through two Hollywood-produced serials, a number of theatrical animated shorts created by one of the top animation studios, and a weekly radio show that had been broadcast for nearly ten years.

So the Detective and Rory Hack had cooled their heels in the reception area for nearly a quarter of an hour before National Thrills' publisher pushed through a plate-glass door to shake their hands.

He was in a tan suit. He had a boyish face that contrasted with his very thin ginger hair. His left arm clutched to his side a slender briefcase of leather tanned to match the color of his suit as he extended his right hand. "Roger Comet."

"Pardon?" The Detective seemed taken aback by the name.

<<Intruding in your realm of nomenclature, isn't he?>>

"Roger Comet. Publisher, National Thrills. Odd name, right?" He grinned, like a schoolboy who's won the spelling bee. "My father, Willem Cortoldt, started the company. Thought the man who brought the world Mighty Man should have a flashier name. Changed his to Comet."

"Ah," the Detective said. "I'm—"

"Space Detective, of course. Everyone knows your name."

<<Saves money on business cards.>>

"My associate, Rory Hack, Mr. Comet."

As the publisher shook Hack's hand, Comet said, "I must apologize, I'm on my way to a meeting, so I don't have much time, but I guess you're here about the Space Detective comic?"

A light flashed in Hack's eyes. "Hey, that's a great idea."

<<Everyone thinks so.>>

"Actually," the Detective said, "no. Not at the moment, anyway. I'm interested in your business, Mr. Comet. Your business has been in the news frequently."

Comet's face brightened. "It's about the Mighty Man movie, right?"

"Um, no. I mean the juvenile crime. The possible connection between the rising crime rate and the readers of comic books."

The brightness left Comet's face. He'd just gone from winning the spelling bee to misspelling *onomatopoeia.* He turned a little jittery. "Those aren't my books. My books are *Mighty Man*, *Maxie Moose*, *Sky Ranger*, *Night Ranger*, *Rawrbazzle*, *Professor Penguin*, *Montgomery Mercury*." A ray of hope seemed to light Comet's features again. "And maybe *Space Detective*?"

Hack's face appeared caught by the same ray. "That's a great idea."

<<Apparently rolling in the gutters doesn't lessen your appeal. Or we need to check your helmet for another breach. You may be radiating confidence again.>>

The Detective cleared his throat. He put the Smile in his voice. "That's a topic for another meeting. Unfortunately. However, these crime books . . ."

Comet's demeanor changed. "That's Eirik Grimsson's trash! Nothing like that would be welcome in my house, and nothing like that is published by this house. National Thrills may seem tame to smut mongers like Grimsson, but we play a role in our nation's culture. In strengthening the character of our young people."

<<Wonder if he's met any of those young people in the subway lately.>>

Comet continued: "Mighty Man and the others—they reaffirm the value and existence of goodness in those boys of ours who went to war with Berlin, had their belief in goodness shattered."

<<You sure touched a sore nerve.>>

"That's commendable. Mr. Comet—"

"Really," he interrupted, "I need to get going."

"I understand," insisted the Detective, "but do you have copies of any of your books on hand?"

"Absolutely! Come along." He led the two visitors through the glass door and along a gleaming hallway. Dozens of doors interrupted the wall, some open, some closed, but a hubbub emanated from every room. Young men darted from one door or another and dodged their counterparts on their ways to other doors.

Comet strode with an air of righteous purpose, and everyone he encountered stepped aside for him. He seemed to zip into one of the open doorways. The Detective and Hack followed into the room in time to hear Comet say to a harried fellow at a desk cluttered with opened comics and character sketches, "Harry! Books! For our visitors."

Harry's face turned red from his chin to the top of his bald head. He slowly put his feet on the floor from where they'd been resting on an open drawer. He raised up from his chair, knuckles on his desk, and glared at Comet. Then he opened his mouth, wide enough for the Detective and Hack to see every tooth in his head: "Stop yelling! Always yelling! 'Books!' I'm working here! There are no books to yell for if I'm kept from working!"

He continued to glare a few moments more. Comet's shoulders sagged. Harry then reached down to the opened drawer, came up with a clutch of comics he thrust at Comet.

"Wonderful!" said the latter. "We'll leave you in peace, Harry. Thanks so much!" Comet shooed his guests into the hallway, then led them back to the lobby. He handed over the stack of books. "Here you go, Mr. Detective, Mr. Hack. Please enjoy these. And feel free to visit again when we can talk about your new comic. Really, though, I must leave now." He clutched the case with both hands tight against his chest.

"Thank you, Mr. Comet," the Detective said. "A couple more questions, please, before we go."

"Please hurry."

"Ah. Do you, Mr. Comet, read the books you publish?"

"Me?" Comet's surprise seemed compounded. "Of course not. I

mean, well. I'm certainly too busy."

"Clearly so," the Detective agreed. "Thank you for your time, Mr. Comet." They shook hands, and he directed Hack to the exit. Comet dashed back through the glass door. The lobby's lights turned the door into an opaque glare.

In the elevator, Hack asked, "Can I carry those comics for you, Boss?"

"No, I'm fine."

Hack kept his gaze on the packet in the Detective's hands until they stepped out of the elevator car.

They crossed the gleaming floor and out onto the sidewalk. A cacophony of car horns filled the air. Taxis, trucks, and buses were halted in the street. A horde of children and teenagers were charging along the lanes normally reserved for traffic. They beat on the vehicles as they passed with stones, bricks, pipes, tire irons. A uniformed cop blew his whistle at the crowd with the same effect he might have had on a stampeding herd of cattle. He dodged empty beer and soda bottles hurled his direction, then he was pulled to the pavement by the rush of kids. Pedestrians pushed up against the buildings, goggle-eyed at the flood of delinquent juveniles.

Hack swore. His face was red, his hands were tight fists. "Those brats! I'll show 'em!"

The Detective hooked Hack's arm, pushed his shoulder into the man's chest and pressed him against the wall of the building they had just exited. "Stop it, Rory!"

Hack glared at his boss.

The Detective ordered, "Go get that cop out of the street. Bring him here!" Just as he could put a Smile in his voice, he could speak in a commanding tone that few people could shake off. Hack glared a moment more, then glanced down like a submissive dog. He shook loose, then charged for the downed cop. Less than a minute later, he was holding up the dazed policeman, who leaned against the wall beside the Detective.

Two minutes later, the swarm of youngsters had passed. Drivers and pedestrians alike stared after their dwindling forms for several moments before driving and walking along once more.

Hack spoke to the cop. "Okay, buddy?"

The cop coughed, nodded. "Yeah. Thanks, thanks a lot."

The Detective asked, “Do you need a ride? Can we call an ambulance?”

“No, no, I just need to catch my breath.”

“Call in to your squad,” the Detective said. “Let them know what happened here. There’s a phone inside, by the cigar shop.”

The cop nodded. “Good idea. Thanks. Thanks again.” Hack patted his shoulder as the man pushed through the rotating door into the building.

Hack waved down a cab. They were climbing into the back when the Detective spotted a black car passing them.

“That’s Comet’s car,” he said. “I saw him in the back.” He dropped onto the bench seat and shut the door. “Let’s see where he’s headed.”

The driver craned his neck. “Where to, pal?”

“Do you mind following that car?” The Detective pointed.

“How often do I get to drive around a movie star? Sure!” He put the car in gear and rolled into the flow behind Comet’s car.

Hack looked at the Detective, his eyes opened wide. “You’re in the movies? I didn’t know that.”

“Me neither.”

Hack shook his head. “Movies and comic books. Gosh.”

<<You'll have to start wearing that helmet just to hide your swelled head.>>

“Hm.”

<<I'm surprised women aren't already mobbing the office, clamoring to be Miss Space Girl.>>

“Is there a way to turn you off?”

The cabbie stirred and looked into his mirror. “You talkin’ to me?”

The Detective sat back. “No. Nope.”

Comet’s car passed Eriksson Circle and entered Central Park. It stopped at the riding stables. Our cab drove past, then parked.

“Wait for us,” the Detective said as he and Hack slipped out. They approached Comet’s car.

The Detective slipped a hand inside his coat, tapped on the driver’s window with his other hand. The driver was startled, dropped the magazine he’d been reading, reached for the ignition. A distant *ping!* sounded, and the Detective removed his hand from his coat. The car’s engine wouldn’t turn over.

Comet glared from the back seat. His briefcase was open beside him. Inside the case was a stack of comics, and in his lap lay open three others. All were crime comics published by Eirik Grimsson's company.

Comet pushed open his passenger-side door. "What's the meaning of this?" His boyish face was flushed and his ginger hair had darkened with sweat.

The Smile was back in the Detective's voice. "I'm sorry to bother you, Mr. Comet. I'd said I had a couple of questions. I asked only one."

"What is it?"

"Do you print your books at National Thrills?"

"In the building?" Surprise shone on the publisher's face. "Goodness, no. Delta Printing, across the river in New Nederland. It's in Vreeland. They print our books."

"I see. They started just recently?"

"Oh no, they've been running our books for years."

"Thank you, that's all I wanted."

"What about my car? What did you do to it?"

"It'll be fine and start right up in about five minutes. Unless your driver floods it by continuing to press the gas. Tell him to rest, go back to his magazine. Then it'll start right up." He waved. "Good day, Mr. Comet."

Hack and the Detective returned to the cab.

"That was weird," Hack said.

"Maybe," the Detective said. "Let's go back to Hammer & Hack."

CHAPTER EIGHT

Hammer and Hack made faces at one another while the Detective called Uncas.

The chief inspector was not thrilled. “I am terribly busy. What do you want?”

<<Everybody wants a friend like that. Someone who'll drop everything just to hear the sound of your voice.>>

The Detective turned on the Smile. “Have your lab boys found out anything?”

“About what?”

“The comic books. Pete Hammer brought them over for me.”

Uncas sighed. “I am running an investigation. I am not running errands for freelance troublemakers. And I have my hands full with rampant gangs of children who are running amok like rabid dogs.”

“Look, Chief Inspector,” the Detective said, “those books tie in to your investigation.”

“How?” When Uncas said the word, it didn’t sound like a question. It sounded like “Prove it.”

“The kids are reading these books. The ones I sent over. And these, I have some more.”

“So?” It sounded like “You haven’t proven anything yet.” That Uncas can pack a lot into one word.

“Have your lab check out those books. And these. I’ll have Rory Hack deliver them.”

Uncas cleared his throat. “Please, not Hack.”

“Okay, Pete Hammer.”

“What is the lab looking for?”

<<He doesn't sound very enthusiastic yet.>>

“I’ll admit, I don’t know,” the Detective said. “But I think there must be something. All these kids are running around with these books. And I’ve encountered adults acting irregularly, too. I know some of them have been reading these same books. I think it’s connected, and your lab can help find that connection.”

"This sounds far fetched."

"Look, send a couple of your detectives over to the house of the guy Rory was tailing. See if he was reading these funny books. And the butcher who chopped him up. If so, you'll know we're on the right track."

"Your track, not mine."

"Fine, my track. But what can it hurt?" No answer. "You're not finding any of those missing imposters from the department, are you? You won't. They've gone into hiding. I think these juvenile crime sprees are tied to the murdered cops and the cockroaches."

"Oh good grief."

"No, listen—"

"No, you listen," Uncas interrupted. "Those cockroaches are at large."

"I thought we got 'em all!"

"Here, yes." Uncas sighed. "But in other cities—Los Angeles, Chicago, St. Louis—reports are coming in. Cockroaches—apparently similar to the one you showed me—are causing havoc among the populations there and other large cities."

"So I was right. Don't you see?"

"My concerns right now have to do with shut-down subway stations and roving bands of crazed children and their frightened families."

The Detective thumped the desk. "Then have the lab check out these books. What can it hurt? If your crew finds something, maybe they can find a way to combat what's happening with the kids. If they don't find something, you've eliminated one possibility. Look, when did all this kid crime start?"

Uncas considered. "The first reports? Four months ago."

"Great." The Detective flipped through the copies he'd gotten from Comet. "I have issues that are cover-dated here from six months ago. If there's a difference in some element between the older issues and the new ones, you'll be on the track of . . . something."

"What are you looking for?"

<<Finally sounds a little interested.>>

"Like I said, I don't know. But maybe something on the pages? Some sort of image hidden in the art that makes the reader crazy?"

"Oh."

<<Sounds like you lost him with that.>>

"Look, I think there's something different with Grimsson's Great Comics and Comet's National Thrills. Grimsson's crime and horror comics seem to be inciting all this craziness. Maybe your lab can find out what's so different."

Uncas must have thought it over, because after several moments of silence, he said, "All right. Send them over. I will direct the technicians to search each of these books." He paused. "I hesitate to ask, but what are you going to do next?"

"I'm going to visit the printing plant in New Nederland that churns out National Thrills' books. Want to come?"

"I have no jurisdiction across the river. Stay out of trouble."

After he hung up, the Detective directed Hack to go downstairs and hail a cab.

"Why do I always have to get the cab?" Hack appeared ready to pout.

The Detective used the Smile: "What cabbie would dare to pass you by?"

Apparently this question did the trick. Hack left.

The Detective directed Hammer, "Take this stack of books from Comet to Uncas. Again, use a bag or gloves."

"Don't worry. Here's the list of Rory's funny books I found. My expectations were borne out by the low-brow caliber exhibited in my esteemed colleague's reading material: two knife-and-ax crime and horror celebrations from Great Comics and eight talking animal books from National Thrills."

<<Think Hammer reads Leo Malet?>>

The Detective asked, "Pete, what opera did you attend last week with that exiled Walloon princess—Miss Delvaux?"

Hammer frowned. "*Tosca.*"

"That's really just a shocking melodrama dressed up with lots of dancing and singing, isn't it?"

"Really, Space," Hammer shook his head, "the artistry, the composer's mastery—"

"Dashiell Hammett composes in a more straightforward key, I think. Rory is good at what he does. You both are. Let's try to get along while we tackle this case."

Hammer snorted in a way I doubted he displayed his derision to his society clients. "This is a case? Someone's paying us?"

The Smile was back in the Detective's voice. "If we get out without our skulls cracked—for now, that's payment enough for me." He left Hammer standing by the desk, poking at the stack of comics with the tip of his cane.

CHAPTER NINE

The cab dropped the Detective and Hack at the main office, where they loaded into the Studie and headed for the Singstad Tunnel. They'd picked up a newspaper on the way, and Hack read the headlines from the passenger seat.

"It's just like the papers were saying here a few days ago—bugs are attacking people all over the country," Hack said. He flipped through the pages. "But there's nothing in here now about bugs attacking anyone in New Angoulême."

"We cleaned up the bugs here in the city before they had a chance to start their big cockroach chaos kick off."

"We?"

"Uncas and me," the Detective explained. "I found out about the bugs, and his squads rounded them up."

"So what about the news stories about the bugs here in town?"

"A diversionary tactic to confuse the people who planted the bugs in the first place."

Hack went back to reading from the columns of type. "People are evacuating their homes, leaving the cities. The cops are searching everyone at roadblocks—they won't let any trains leave or planes land, in case some bugs are smuggled aboard and try to infest another city. It sounds pretty ugly."

The Detective nodded.

"I'd half thought these bugs were a distraction, a diversionary tactic in themselves," he said. "But the craziness they're causing—the fear and disruption of authority—I may have underestimated just what they could cause."

<<Maybe that's part of the plan.>>

"Hmm?"

<<Civilization starts to topple, brought down by bugs. The Hyrnavians swoop in with a way to shut down the cockroaches, they stomp out the threat, then the population and the government hail them as heroes. They receive a big welcome, then before you

know it, they're in control of everything.>>

"Possibly."

Hack looked confused.

"Just thinking out loud," the Detective said. "Anything in the paper about bug reports from Europe?"

Hack searched. "British Isles," he answered. "But I don't see anywhere else mentioned. Not that they might reveal that kind of news, anyway."

"Perhaps."

Hack had found nothing else of interest in the paper by the time the Detective parked the Studie in the lot of the printing plant in Vreeland. It rose before them like a massive slab of brick and concrete whose walls were interrupted by a single door along the front and a single row of small windows near the roof line. Deliveries of paper and ink were clearly made around the corner, where one large truck after another passed from sight as others appeared from the back and turned onto the highway for destinations out across the country.

The Delta Printing building was only one large structure among a community of sprawling manufacturing plants. Scores of tall smokestacks spewed clouds into the air, keeping the sky bound with a roiling darkness.

<<So this is the happy home of Maxie Moose and Mighty Man.>>

They entered. The reception lobby was not so posh as that of National Thrills, nor did it show signs of having an earlier elegance painted over like Hazel's realm at Grimsson's shop. Here at Delta Printing, everything was strictly functional: The floor was covered with worn but polished linoleum tiles the color of mashed pinto beans, metal shelves along the walls were heaped with catalogs and sample books, and a metal desk with a big dent in the front was the largest item in the room. (The dent and the chipped green paint suggested the desk might have been salvaged from wartime use.) There were two chairs. One behind the desk, one in front.

The one in front—ostensibly for customers—was metal with chipped black paint, no padding. There was no way to tell if the chair behind the desk was padded, because most of it was obscured under a massive fellow who sported a crew cut and a face that looked as dented and chipped as the furniture. He wore a plaid short-sleeved shirt whose most prominent color was red. Other than that—big, ugly, mostly red shirt—the man was hidden behind untidy stacks of paper on the desk and two black telephones, each acting as paperweights on two of the shorter stacks.

A toothpick waggled in the man's lips as he spoke: "Whadda ya need?"

"Hello, I'm Space Detective—"

"I know who ya are."

"—and I'd like to meet the plant manager."

<<He didn't ask about a Space Girl. Think that's a good sign?>>

The Toothpick nodded his chin toward the empty chair. "Have a seat."

<<Think twice about that. Sit in that chair and you'll be in danger of getting swamped by that tide of paper on the desk.>>

The Detective didn't have to sit, because a swinging door on the back wall opened for a man who looked completely out of place: His black hair was pomaded, his mustache points were waxed, and he wore a three-piece suit—it might not have met Pete Hammer's criteria for quality, but it fit perfectly and was a nicely cut off-the-rack piece of fabric.

"Mr. Detective? I'm the Delta Printing plant manager, Gerald Contour." He shook the Detective's gloved hand. "How may I help you?"

"I'm interested in learning how your plant works, and how you print comics for National Thrills."

"My pleasure. Come on back."

Contour led the Detective and Hack through the swinging door to a short hallway. Two doors interrupted both walls, left and right, and Contour continued through a heavy metal door at the end of the hall. When the door opened, the visitors were struck by a roar of mechanical noises.

Through the door, they stood upon a concrete landing overlooking rows of massive presses arranged on a vast floor twenty feet below. Ranks of giant rolls of newsprint were lined against one long wall. Along with the noise, Hack took in the smells of paper and ink that filled the air, and he pinched his nose a few moments, then shook his head and gave it up.

Contour nodded, and the trio descended the steps to the manufacturing floor. Workers in ink-stained clothes moved about the presses, touching dials, adjusting levers—concerned with the machines like acolytes tending giant metal gods. No one hurried, but shifted from location to location like visitors to stations on a pilgrim's journey.

Massive rolls of paper spun to feed the clattering maw of the presses. The mechanical thrumming sounded like a fleet of trains rushing past all at once, each train of cars stretching to the horizon. The roar was too loud for talking, so Contour gestured for the Detective and Hack to follow to the opposite end of the press floor. They walked through a large exit—its overhead door pushed up—into a slightly quieter area. Here, printed sheets were folded and trimmed and stapled into the form familiar to newsstand customers. Stacks of the colorful publications were bound with twine and tossed to a loading platform near another overhead door used by freight trucks.

For all the noise dedicated to publishing these radiant, action-packed books, the factory workers went about their business methodically, slowly, as though daunted by the size of the machinery and the operations surrounding them.

Contour stopped outside on one of the concrete docks, beside a delivery truck being loaded with tied bundles of comic books. The air was finally clear enough of sound he could be heard: "There's not a lot to our operation here, but there's a lot of it." He smiled.

The Detective nodded. "I'm sure you go through a lot of ink in a day."

"Indeed," Contour said, and he pointed to tanks arrayed within a chain link fence behind the far corner of the factory building. "We receive new deliveries every two days. There's one now, in fact."

A large truck swept around a corner into the graveled lot. *Van Bruggen Inks and Distillates* was painted on the door of the truck cab, along with a local telephone number.

<<Shall I check out this ink operation?>>

"Indeed," the Detective said.

"Pardon?" Contour asked.

"Sorry, but are all these books for National Thrills?"

"Oh no," Contour said. He smiled again, patted his hair. "Some are for Mr. Comet's operations, and in fact, he is our largest customer. Others are for other clients, such as Courtlander Funnies, Goossens Galactic Entertainment, Exciting Publications, and Funny Stuff."

"Wait a minute," Hack said. "You print funny books for all those guys?"

"Oh yes," Contour said. "We print books for . . . well, for all the comic publishers."

"All of them?" the Detective asked.

"Yes, well, no." Contour frowned. "Not for Great Comics."

"Eirik Grimsson's company?"

"That's correct. He has his own presses."

"So everybody but Grimsson who puts out comic books is your client."

"Indeed." Contour tilted his head. "So are you quite satisfied with your tour?"

The Detective nodded. "I think so."

"Which of our clients will you be working with?"

"Pardon?"

"For the Space Detective book?" Contour smiled again. "Will it be National Thrills, or someone else?"

Hack looked at his boss with an expectant gleam. But his expression fell when the Detective answered, "Um, that's still in negotiation."

Contour nodded. "If I can be of further assistance, please let me know."

<<He's certainly a clean, well-dressed fellow for such a noisy, inky operation.>>

The Detective and Hack walked around the building to where the Studie was parked. As Hack climbed into the passenger seat, the Detective said, "I think it's time for a drink."

Several blocks away, he parked beside a brick building, *Yesterdays Bar & Grill.* "Go on," the Detective said. "I'll be there in a minute."

He watched Hack enter the bar, then sat in the car tapping his fingers on the steering wheel.

<<When does your other career begin?>>

"What other career?"

<<The musical cabaret.>>

"Oh." He chuckled. "Something from the radio. Just stuck in my mind."

<<Kinda like me?>>

"Something like that." He steepled his gloved fingers. "What about the ink company?"

<<Appears to be clean. Owned by a family for years and years.

All the employees have been there for years, too. Which got me to thinking.>>

"About?"

<<I started checking out Delta Printing. They place a lot of help wanted ads.>>

"So?"

<<At least one a week, for the past four or so months.>>

"Business seems to be good. They probably need lots of help getting Maxie Moose on the racks."

<<That's reasonable. Until I compared the frequency of the ads with missing persons reports.>>

"Ah, you're starting to make music, too."

<<Yep. Nearly all the missing persons reports in Vreeland and the surrounding communities for the past four months have been employed at Delta Printing.>>

"No one has seen this connection?"

<<Maybe the local cops are really a bunch of mandrakes from Demeter X.>>

The Detective was silent a few moments, then nodded. "I've heard stranger things."

<<You've said some of them.>>

"So what do you think about my snooping around the funny book business now?"

<<Maybe I'm a little more convinced.>>

"But it doesn't make sense. Grimsson's books aren't printed here. He prints his books on his own presses."

<<Maybe he's in league with the Hyrnavians? He sure didn't seem to be acting like people expect him to act, or how they say he usually acts. Maybe he's an imposter, too. Hey, Uncas is calling into the office.>>

"Let's go call him back." The Detective went into the bar.

"Welcome to Yesterdays!" shouted the bartender. He stood in the open center of the bar, which surrounded him in a rectangle situated in the middle of the bar's large room. Tables and chairs—empty at the moment—and a jukebox hugged the walls, which were adorned with beer and booze signs and photos of sports teams. Hack was leaning against the bar beside two other patrons. All three were turning up mugs to their mouths.

"Phone?" asked the Detective.

The bartender pointed to the back wall, where a payphone clung to the knotty pine paneling alongside a doorless doorway to a short passage leading to a restroom and—most likely—the office.

The Detective dialed. "Hello, Inspector. Any news from your lab boys?"

"The laboratory conducted tests on those books you had delivered. The titles from Great Comics—"

"Eirik Grimsson's books."

"—were clean. Nothing but printer's ink on cheap paper."

"Really?"

"So I had the other books tested."

"And?"

"The inks have been adulterated. Something has been mixed into them. The laboratory technicians could not identify the compound. Perhaps your friends at those federal agencies may have an idea. But my men tested the ink with some mice. Whatever is in that ink induces violent psychotic episodes in the mice. The mystery component is apparently absorbed through the skin."

"I'll be a monkey's uncle."

"I have never seen your face, so I cannot put forward an opinion about that."

<<Hey, the stoic Indian is cracking a joke. Maybe he's an imposter, too.>>

Uncas continued: "I have more. The older issues your man brought in—they did not have the doctored ink. So the time frame fits the beginning of the juvenile crimes."

"Ah."

"One last thing: Both the butcher and his victim—the ones your man Hack encountered—had been reading these tainted books. We found copies at the homes of both men."

"Thanks, Inspector. I think I know where the stuff is coming from." The Detective explained what we had seen and learned.

Uncas gave a warning: "Be careful. I have no jurisdiction there. And what you have said suggests the local authorities may be infiltrated by these hostile agents you continue to bring up. One other thing: All of your suppositions are based upon no hard evidence. What we have uncovered is still, one might argue, circumstantial."

"True," the Detective admitted. "I'll try to rectify that part of the equation. Thanks again, Inspector." He hung up and walked to the bar.

"Hey, Mr. Space Detective, it's an honor." The man tending the beer sticks was rotund enough that he'd joined his apron's strings behind his back by tying another length of string between them. "We don't get famous folks here so often." He extended a hand across the bar. "Tommy Bouchoux, proprietor, at your service. What'll you have?"

The Detective studied Bouchoux's wares. All the beer taps were labeled Pluto's Pilsner. "Looks like I have only one choice."

"Ah, that's all anybody wants around here anymore. But I don't touch that stuff. I got my personal inventory here, if you want." He brought up a bottle of sour mash bourbon from below the bar and added two glasses. "Took a trip out west once, came back with a taste for this stuff."

"None for me, thanks," the Detective said.

"Your loss, but more for me." The bartender poured a glass and raised it. "Cheers." He sipped and then smacked his lips. "Ahh, that's the stuff."

Both turned their attention to the other customers. Hack had pushed away from the bar, and the other two men were both swinging their empty mugs, looking for an opening to bash the detective's brainpan. Chairs were knocked over, tables clattered. Hack swung his own fists and blocked his attackers' swipes with his forearms.

For a stout bartender, Bouchoux was through the bar's drop-gate and swinging a hickory ax handle before the Detective was around his corner of the bar. While one customer blocked the handle with a chair, the Detective yanked Hack off his feet, threw him to the floor. Then he ducked as a beer mug flashed past, and grabbed his assailant with both hands. A surge of electricity crackled through the gloves—the fighter jittered around and the fight flew out of him as he fell to the floor.

The Detective stepped over to Bouchoux's dancing partner and zapped him, too.

The bartender leaned on the ax handle as if it were a walking stick. "Now that's a heck of a trick!" He mopped sweat from his face with a handkerchief. "Say, are they dead?"

"No, just stunned. They'll wake up with headaches. Big headaches." The Detective had pulled Hack to his feet. He put the commanding tone into his voice: "Rory, you'll get the same treatment if you don't straighten up!"

"I'm sorry, Space." He scrubbed his face with both hands. "It all just came over me."

"My apologies, Mr. Bouchoux," the Detective said. "My employee, Mr. Hack, hasn't been himself lately."

"Hey, no problem. It's been happening in here a lot lately." He picked up one of the downed men's feet. "Help me haul 'em outside? I'll call their wives to come get 'em."

After Bouchoux had returned to his station behind the bar and, at the Detective's direction, served Hack a tall tumbler of water, the Detective asked, "Lots of fights by your customers?"

"Oh, yeah. This used to be a calm place, the most violent thing happening was somebody stuck a dart in his hand. But lately?" He shrugged and sipped his bourbon.

"How long's this been going on?"

"A few months?" He waved his hand. "Everything's nuts these days. Kids running around like hopped-up vandals, their old men fighting like kids in the playground at school. I put bars over the windows because of the kids. Nuts."

"Most of your customers are from the factories?"

"Yep. Every factory crew has a favorite hangout. The Delta Printing guys, they come here."

"Ah."

CHAPTER TEN

It was dark when the Detective and Hack left Yesterdays. Workers from Delta Printing were starting to drift into the bar, their shifts over for the day. After asking permission from Tommy Bouchoux, they left the Detective's Studie parked in the back of his lot, behind the building, and started walking.

<<Where to?>>

"Delta Printing."

"Pardon?" Hack asked.

"Where we're heading."

"Oh. Think we can get some samples?"

"I doubt it. The business office should be closed by now, and taking samples without permission would be stealing."

"We don't steal. We're the good guys."

<<Keep saying that, Rory.>>

"That's right," the Detective said.

Back at the plant, the two avoided straying into lighted areas, instead skirting the property until they were at the back of the building near the fenced-in vats that fed ink to the reservoirs within the building that supplied the presses—the roar still came from within the building.

At the gate in the fence, the Detective pulled a key from a pocket. It was a Corbel Key—related to the technology that protected the locks of the warehouse holding Ronnie's blast buggy, this device could open the tumblers of any lock. He slipped it into the padlock, twitched the key, and the lock popped open. He and Hack slipped inside the fence. They examined the vats with a small but intense beam of light that originated from a tiny dot on the Detective's helmet.

"Everything looks okay here," Hack said. "All the tanks are clean, the paint still looks shiny, like somebody's waxing the finish every so often. I've seen cars with duller paint."

"Check the connections for the lines that run from the tanks to the building. See if you notice anything out of place."

Hack began tracing the metal conduits. He ran his fingers along their surfaces. He was walking around one of the larger tanks when he stopped and said, “Hey.”

The Detective joined him. “What is it?”

Rory pointed. “All these tanks have Van Bruggen’s name on ‘em. But this line taps on here,” and he gestured at a large-gauge conduit from one of the massive tanks, “and runs into this box.” The box was metal-sided, tall as a man, and sat on a concrete pad separate from the one the tanks rested on. “Look here at the color of this pad,” Hack noted. “The color is different from that one. This concrete under the box was poured a lot more recently than that one for the tanks.”

“Right you are, Rory.” The Detective examined the box. “Here’s a door.” He used the Corbel Key again. A hatch opened on the side of the box, revealing a connector.

“Looks like it’s for a pressurized hose,” Hack said.

“Must be how they fill the tank.” The Detective closed the hatch. He had swabbed the connector with a square of cloth that he tucked into an envelope that he poked into his jacket pocket.

<<Rory seems okay when he’s doing his job. He’s on the ball.>>

The two left the enclosure and the Detective locked the gate. He gestured, and they made their way through the shadows back to the front of the building. The door they had entered earlier in the day was locked. The Corbel Key turned out to be very handy during the excursion to Delta Printing.

The lobby was dark.

They tip-toed through the swinging door into the hallway. It was dark, too, but light from the door of one of the offices projected a bright trapezoid into the passage.

The Detective and Hack crept to the doorframe, peered in. No one there. Empty but for a desk, file cabinet, and overturned chair. They entered.

Hack went behind the desk. His eyes widened. “Hot rocks from hell!” he hollered.

The Detective stepped up, put a hand over Hack’s mouth. “Shush! But probably no one could hear you over the presses.” He looked down. Stretched on the floor in a widening crimson pool was the ugly man who had met them in the lobby earlier. The toothpick still stood out from his lips. But a desk spike—the sort used for spiking invoices—had been slammed into his skull, and its base stuck up from his head like a parody of a unicorn's horn.

"Another one," said a voice from behind the pair, and they turned to see Gerald Contour standing in the doorway in his three-piece suit, the fabric marred now by a splotch of blood. His hair was tangled like a disarrayed halo, and his mustache points drooped. Black tears, like watery ink, streaked his face.

"Always more disagreements these days," he said. "It's hard to find good help. I keep hiring, but something always comes up, and I have to let them go. Are you here about the position?"

The Detective nodded. "Uh, sure."

"Wait a minute." Contour's focus sharpened. "I haven't run the ad yet." He raised his hands, and each one held a glittery-sharp box cutter. "You're just more trouble."

Before the Detective could move, Hack shouted and vaulted the desk to smash Contour into the hallway. The Detective dashed out of the office. Rory was pounding Contour with his fists. Contour was trying to slash his attacker with the cutters.

Another roar. A crackly, un-mechanical-sounding roar.

The Detective looked toward the lobby's swinging door.

Two ink-smudged factory workers approached.

And then their clothing stretched and shredded.

Torn by the spikes that began to grow from their enlarging forms.

<<Shapeshifters!>>

The Detective pulled Rory away from his human punching bag, then kicked Contour in the ribs. The plant manager tumbled to the floor and groaned.

<<Think Contour manages those plants, too?>>

The Detective pushed Hack toward the door at the end of the hall. "Go!"

The shapeshifters charged.

The Detective and Hack had nearly reached the door to the manufacturing floor.

<<There are even more of 'em that way, you know.>>

"But it's too noisy for them to know what's going on up here."

The Detective fell to his knees.

One of the shapeshifters had knocked into him. The Detective slid and rolled onto his back. The monster charged, talons reaching. The

Detective snatched the Model 6 Rigelian Hand Zapper from its holster, aimed, pulled the trigger. *POM!*

The beast blossomed into a shower of splinters and shreds of moss.

<<Hah! Who needs defoliant?>>

Contour and the other shapeshifter were nearly at them. Hack helped the Detective to his feet and headed to the door.

They burst out onto the landing high above the press room.

"Rory, climb piggyback onto me and hold on—"

Hack was gone.

He had vaulted the railing and sailed out with a yell that couldn't be heard over the train-engine roar of the presses. The Detective watched as Hack went down and slammed into a clutch of workers who had gathered at the corner of one of the giant presses.

The Detective swore.

<<You'll never find a Space Girl with sweet talk like that.>>

The workers were scattered and stretched on the floor like a dropped deck of cards. Hack rolled to his feet, picked up a garbage bin and threw it to crash into two more workers. Others on the press floor couldn't hear what was going on, but some were starting to notice Hack and his volatile and very unfriendly activity, and a crowd was starting to form and head his way.

The Detective reached into his pocket. He was going to retrieve the Ping! thing that had dropped everyone on the block during the juvenile attack. But that's when the hallway door crashed open. The surviving shapeshifter swarmed out and smacked into the Detective. Its claws raked sparks from his helmet.

He spun, grabbed the thing with both hands. Electricity crackled blue through his gloves. The monster roared that breaking-spaghetti noise as black smoke twisted from its spikes. Then it swatted the Detective away. He stumbled down a few of the steps, and was pulling the Pinger out. The creature swung forward, and the talons of one hand pierced the device. The little machine blasted apart, blowing the monster's hand into a cloud of pollen. Light bulbs in three rows along the ceiling shattered and blue fire arced between the fixtures. The presses howled like angered giants as they began to spin even faster, and dust roiled up from cracks that appeared in the concrete floor as the throbbing machines started to wrench loose from their anchors.

The monster stretched for the Detective, but he had out the Hand Zapper again, and the shapeshifter was quickly blasted into smoldering mulch.

Gerald Contour stood on the landing. The Detective ignored him, turned and jumped over the railing.

Unlike Hack, he didn't fall to the floor.

He flew.

He sailed over the mob surrounding and pummeling Hack.

He swooped, picked up a three-foot-long spanner and winged over the crowd, knocking them aside with blows to their bodies. Their shouts and yells couldn't be heard over the presses' howling, and the noise was so great the entire scene almost seemed to occur in complete silence.

Once Hack was free, he staggered and nearly collapsed to the floor.

The Detective landed, pulled Hack to him, and wrapped his arms around his trunk. "Hold on!" he shouted.

Rory nodded, but whether he heard wasn't clear. He hugged his boss, and the Detective took to the air.

Contour remained on the landing above the rocking presses. Black tears again flowed from his eyes, stained his ruined suit. He still clutched the cutters.

His lower lip jutted out below his mustache in a pout.

His mouth moved, but no one heard him: "I hope you never get that damn comic book deal, Space Detective!"

The Detective and Hack flew through the open freight doors and out into the night air. Their ears rang with the racket they had just left.

Two dozen workers chased after the two detectives.

<<I don't see any shapeshifting going on. They might all really be human.>>

One block away, the Detective settled to the ground when he reached the street. "The shoes' charge is almost gone. We gotta hot foot it, Rory." He looked back and saw the screeching crowd getting closer. He saw the bleeding cuts on Hack's face. "Can you make it?"

Hack nodded, grunted. "Let's go, Boss."

The Detective hefted Rory to his feet, got an arm around the broad-shouldered man.

Then they ran.

They didn't try to dodge into the shadows. They ran straight down the middle of the street, their pursuers getting closer.

When they reached Yesterdays, they rushed inside and fell to the floor. Tommy Bouchoux ran forward and threw the locks as the first of the factory workers slammed against the door's outside surface.

The Detective pushed to his feet and spun around, looking for more attacks from the bar's patrons. But he, Hack, and the bar owner were the only people in the building.

"Where is everyone?"

Bouchoux shrugged. "One of my factory guys got a call, he listened, then hollered for everybody to follow him, and they all ran out the door. A few minutes later, here you guys show up."

Something smashed one of the front windows, and a neon beer advertisement crashed to the floor. But the bars over the windows kept everyone out. The men in the bar heard shouts and yelling, but no discernible words. Just animal-like roars of rage.

The Detective drug Hack over to lean his back against the bar while he sat on the floor, then the Detective slumped onto a bar stool. "Afraid we've turned your customers against you by holing up here."

Bouchoux waved the thought away. "They'll be back. They can get beer anywhere, but the ambiance and the snappy patter? There ain't nowhere else in town like Yesterdays." He leaned over Hack. "You been pickin' more fights, buddy?" He looked up at the Detective. "Maybe you, too?"

The Detective's clothing showed more rips, was prickly with splinters from the monsters he'd destroyed, and his helmet was dented and scratched. "Maybe me, too," he said.

He took off his Flying Florsheims, sat them on the floor. "Flying makes the feet hot."

Bouchoux gave him a puzzled glance.

The bar owner shrugged, went to the back of the room. "I got a first aid kit back here in the office. I've needed it a few times lately. Looks like your buddy needs it now."

Another window smashed; glass shards showered to the floor.

The Detective took the kit from Bouchoux and began tending Hack's injuries. Nothing too serious: minor cuts, bruises, scrapes. Amazingly, he had escaped being sliced to bits by Contour's box cutters.

"I think he needs a drink of the good stuff," Bouchoux said, and he ambled behind the bar.

"What about the phone?" the Detective asked. Hack winced as his boss swabbed a cut.

"What about it?" Bouchoux replied as he poured bourbon into a glass.

"Will this crowd outside tear out the wires, try to cut us off from help?"

"You haven't seemed in a hurry to call anybody so far," Bouchoux said. He approached with the drink. "It'll be okay. As much as they'd like to be unreachable to their wives while they're in here drinking, they'd never hurt the phone. They need to be able to call their bookies."

He handed the glass to Hack.

The building shuddered. Signs fell from the wall. Glasses and mugs crashed to the floor.

Then the sound of a roaring explosion blocked out all other noise.

The three men hunkered down as the rest of the windows flew out of their frames.

CHAPTER ELEVEN

The Detective looked up from where he'd covered Rory with his body. "You okay?" Hack nodded.

Bouchoux shook his head. Splinters of glass flew like water from a shaking dog. "Damn."

"What?"

"I wasted my good bourbon on the floor." He stood up.

"You've got some small cuts on your arms. I can clean those for you," the Detective said.

The bar owner looked out the empty window frames. The bars were intact. "Your crowd of close, personal friends has disappeared." He craned his neck. "There's a hell of a fire down the street."

"Delta Printing," Hack said.

"If that's true, I better clean this place up," Bouchoux said. "There'll be an outta-work mob in here tomorrow drowning their sorrows."

Hack shook his head. Then he groaned and held his head. "You don't sound too worried."

Bouchoux placed on the bar the bourbon bottle and another glass. "They may be out of work, but the tips'll be great." He poured two drinks. He looked at the Detective, who turned down the offer. The bar owner brought the glasses around and handed one to Hack. "C'mon, this deserves a toast."

Another crashing explosion sounded down the street.

<<That may be all your evidence going up in smoke.>>

The Detective shrugged. "It may also be the end of those contaminated comics."

<<There are still plenty in circulation and in the distribution channel.>>

"Might get Van Eckk to pull some strings, get a mass round-up of whatever's out and about. And I'm sure some outraged parents and crusading intellectuals will gladly start a few bonfires to save western civilization from the threat of brain-rotting entertainment that incites antisocial behavior."

<<Okay. So you're ready to put an end to this funny book investigation?>>

"Don't rush me. I need to think about this a bit before I say one way or the other."

<<Oh, that's right. You'll need to salvage the comic book industry from the indignant rage of the rampaging mobs so you can still get a Space Detective funny book deal.>>

"Oh brother."

Tommy Bouchoux approached. "You okay, Mr. Detective?"

"Just thinking out loud."

"Ah. I've been known to do that too, but it's early yet." He looked at the back wall. "Well, the clock's broken, but it feels early. Cheers."

PART FOUR

Jupiter

CHAPTER ONE

It was nearly ten in the morning following the Delta Printing investigation—a word I use loosely here—before the Detective finally sat down in one of the visitor chairs at Hammer & Hack. Rory Hack was settled in a hospital for injuries he sustained at the factory, and Pete Hammer remained close by, a worried expression occasionally appearing on his face between his episodic rants of condescension regarding his partner's idiotic determination to do more harm to himself than to the people he attacked.

<<Do you think Rory saw the shapeshifters?>>

We had discussed the night's events while the Detective made his way from the hospital to his employees' office.

"No, I think he was so intent on punching Gerald Contour into jelly that he barely noticed the two guys coming down the hall even before they shifted to their battle aspect. I had him turned around toward the other end of the hall by the time they had shed their work clothes."

<<But he still may have seen them. Or he may realize what he saw after he has time to rest and think about the night.>>

"True. He helped me up after I blasted the first one in the hall." The Detective sighed. Although Hammer and Hack worked for the Detective, they weren't privy to all the particulars of his work. "We'll address that as it comes up, if we need to."

Inspector Uncas had joined the Detective not long after Space sat down. They were meeting here for two reasons: The Hammer & Hack office was close to police headquarters and convenient for Uncas; and if Commissioner Knifetongue was having one of his staff keep an eye on the inspector, dropping in on Hammer and Hack was less damning than a trip to the Detective's office.

Uncas had surveyed the Detective's bedraggled appearance and, instead of remaining standing as he usually did, he also sat in one of the visitor chairs. "I am surprised the dapper Mr. Hammer would allow such an untidy member of society to loiter within his domain."

The Smile was in the Detective's voice: "It's a domain he shares with the perennially untidy Mr. Hack. So I get a little leeway."

"Ah, I understand." A rumor of a smile—not even a hint—might have been visible on the inspector's face if the light were just right.

"Tell me about your night," he said.

The Detective filled him in—minus some details about shapeshifters from Demeter X—about the missing employees, the discovery of the dead Mr. Toothpick, and Gerald Contour's apparent volatile dementia.

"So your only real clue was a box of—something—tapped into the ink tanks? And you were attacked by murderous factory workers, a point that would be swept away by any worthwhile attorney for the printing company, because technically you were trespassing—not to mention breaking and entering—and the workers may be said to have been attempting to apprehend a threat to their business. But perhaps those concerns are moot at this point, because all that potential-if-questionably viable evidence went up in fire and smoke?" Uncas tapped his cane against the toe of his shoe.

<<Does he work for the cops or for the DA?>>

"That sounds about right," the Detective said.

Uncas sighed. "I will report the murdered man you found. I will see whether anyone knows if Gerald Contour escaped the explosion and fire." He stood and leaned on the cane. "Do not suppose you are making my job any easier."

"Hey, I'm a concerned citizen, inspector," the Detective said. "A potentially corrosive influence on the impressionable minds of our nation's youth has been, ah, well, stopped."

<<Ooh, that was snappy and poetic.>>

"Perhaps," Uncas said. "These books with the contaminated ink are still in circulation. We are not sure how long the effects last, nor if the influence of the chemical eventually dissipates from the older copies of the books, which will likely be read and re-read, especially if there is a gap in the publishing schedule because of the loss of the primary printing company."

"Well, no new copies with the bad ink will be showing up soon. Because Delta Printing handled nearly all the funny book business—except for Grimsson's Great Comics—no other company is really able to get up and running to fill the vacancy."

"Meanwhile I still have tribes of underage thugs running rampant in my streets." Uncas moved to the door. He turned before leaving. "I have found none of the imposters who infiltrated the department. Reports from other cities say the problems with the attacking bugs are growing worse. I do not know what, exactly, I am dealing with. I am not even sure that what you uncovered at Delta Printing is actually the source of the juvenile crime wave. There is more left unanswered at this point that concerns me than what is solved." He paused.

"Is there something specific you want to ask me, Inspector?" the Detective asked. "Or to tell me?"

Uncas appeared to chew something for a moment, then to swallow. "I do not know. I am simply stating a few thoughts. If you have other thoughts that may help to settle some of these concerns, I would be willing to receive them."

"Naturally I would offer whatever I have, Inspector."

"But I would request that you be judicious and discreet."

"I understand."

Uncas performed a barely perceptible bow of his head—the enameled feather pin on his lapel winked in the light like a flash of warning—then he exited.

<<He's a very polite fellow. When he's not busting your chops.>>

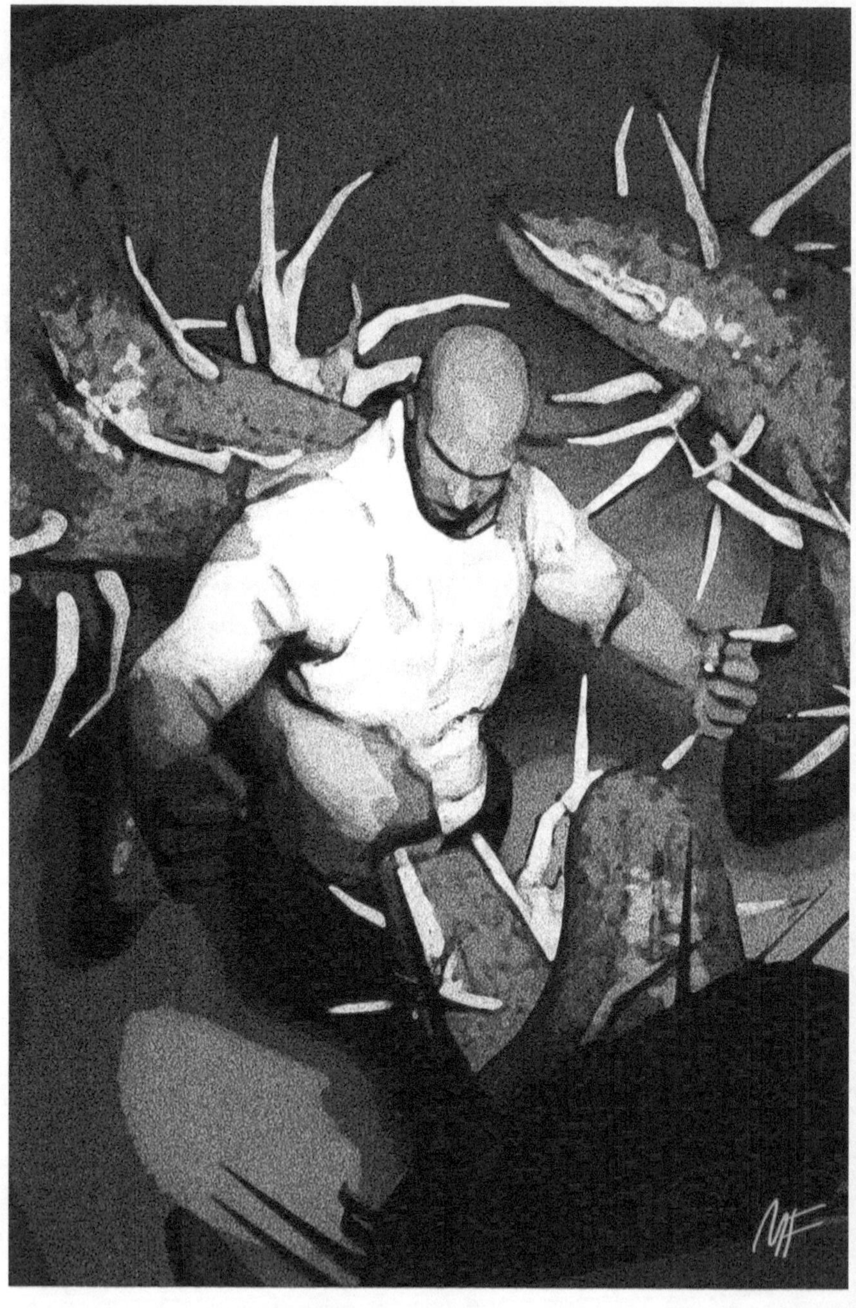

CHAPTER TWO

"What are we missing?"

<<What do you mean?>>

The Detective was back in his proper office. He wore a fresh helmet and suit. He'd been reading the newspapers' accounts of the bug attacks in other cities (along with questions about what had happened to the reported bug attacks in New Angoulême) and the explosion that had destroyed Delta Printing. Regarding the latter, no fatalities had yet been determined, but some employees—as yet unnamed—remained missing.

"I mean this: We've shown the connection between the comic books and the rise in violent crimes. And we found the connection to the Hyrnavian Pirates with the presence of the shapeshifters."

<<So you say. There is no evidence left to support those claims. And even if the connection between the printer's ink and the crimes is absolute, the presence of the critters from Demeter might be coincidental.>>

"True, but unlikely." He tapped that familiar rhythm on the desk. "Let's say the connections are all correct, and the Hyrnavians used the comic book crime spree for a reason."

<<Okay.>>

"Okay. So, what's the reason for the connection?"

<<That's a mystery, all right. Maybe the Hyrnavians have been reading the same magazines I was talking about.>>

"The ones about keeping some mystery in a relationship?"

<<Yeah.>>

"If you have a subscription, I'll cancel it now. And if I hear you mention it again, I'll make you read Leo Malet."

<<I hear and obey.>>

"So you have no more notion about the reason for the comic book plot than I do."

<<Correct. The only thing I can think of is to stir up chaos.>>

"Makes sense. But that's what we thought the cockroaches were for."

<<The bugs *are* stirring up chaos.>>

“True. So we have two kinds of chaos going on simultaneously, and now we’re waiting for the other shoe to drop.”

<<I don't wear shoes.>>

“Ronnie doesn’t know what’s next. I visited him after I retrieved my new helmet.”

<<Has he reformed?>>

“Not quite. But he’s certainly on the track.”

<<What about the Billy Goat?>>

“He was just delivering goods for Ronnie. I’ve checked him out again. He knows nothing except he was supposed to be paid for delivering Ronnie’s cartons.”

<<What will you do with him?>>

“I’m about ready to release him to Uncas. But maybe I’ll just wipe some targeted memories of this whole episode from his consciousness, then release him back out to the world at large.”

<<Might be simpler than turning him over to Uncas.>>

“Agreed.”

<<But we're still missing something, right?>>

“Right.”

<<So, you know what I'm thinking?>>

“Yep. There’s something more to come.”

<<Maybe I'm wrong.>>

“I don’t think so.”

<<Darn.>>

CHAPTER THREE

Billy Goat's head lolled. Then he snapped awake. His eyelids fluttered rapidly—like he was having a fit. Then he settled down and stared at the Detective.

They were in Billy's apartment. Billy sat on the little sofa. The Detective stood by the door.

"You're lucky, Billy."

The delivery man looked around, waiting for a punchline. "Howzat?"

"I'm letting you go. The cops don't even know you were a part of the trouble, so you're pretty lucky."

"Yeah, that's me. Lucky."

The Detective took a folded newspaper from under his arm and tossed it to Billy. It flapped open in midair and dropped into Billy's hands to reveal one of the headlines about the cockroach invasion.

"That's what you helped make happen, Billy," the Detective said. "The cops don't know you were tied up with that. But I do. Think about that before you accept another easy job."

Billy stared at the paper. The Detective left.

CHAPTER FOUR

"I have a report on the fatalities from the explosion at Delta Printing."

Twilight was soon to push away the day with darkness. Inspector Uncas and the Detective stood on the path from the parking lot to the Central Park riding stables. The site had proven productive for the Detective's investigation earlier when he had cornered Roger Comet, so he wanted to meet Uncas there. The near-night timing was the inspector's preference, in case his superiors at the department cared to shadow him about the city following his seeming disloyalty to the brotherhood of blue. A nighttime meeting, when shifts were changing at most of the precinct houses, meant less likelihood of being tailed. Or, if being followed, the cop doing the dirty work would be near the end of his shift and probably tired, a bit bored, and easier for the inspector to spot.

Here he was, so apparently no one was trailing him around the city streets.

Uncas still had his cane. He also carried a brown kraft envelope clutched between his arm and body—it stuck out from that big dark coat he wore, and looked like a bookmark in a bulky, man-sized tome. The inspector pulled it out, removed two photos from inside. He showed the first to the Detective. "Know him?"

The photo was grainy, like a blown-up portion of a newspaper photograph cropped to show the head and shoulders of a single figure.

The Detective nodded. "Gerald Contour." The photo showed a slightly younger Contour than we had met, but he still looked dapper in a three-piece suit, even in a bad picture.

Uncas tucked the photo back into the envelope. "He is dead. This one?"

This one looked little better than a booking photo from the police department. It probably had come from an employer's file. It was Mr. Toothpick.

"The dead man I found in the factory office."

"Then your report is confirmed on that account." Uncas put that one away, removed two more photos. He held them up in one hand, like a magician showing the audience two cards for a trick. "How about these two?"

The Detective shook his head. The quality and poses in the pictures suggested they also were employer's photographs.

Uncas glanced at them, tucked them away with the others.

The Detective asked, "Did they die in the explosion?"

Uncas looked out at the darkness gathering about them. Globes atop lamp posts began to flicker to life. "Their bodies were found in the basement of the apartment house they both lived in. They had been dead a few weeks, at least. But statements from other Delta employees say the two men were both seen at work recently." He turned a fierce look toward the Detective. "This matches our findings with the dead policemen and their imposters. So perhaps you are vindicated in your adventure outside the city. The dead men who have not been dead at the Delta plant and the missing cops—they seem linked by the similarity of the circumstances."

"Agreed."

"I shall speak candidly. I am not sure that I find this discovery reassuring or cause for greater worry." He stopped talking when a figure came into view as it crossed the parking area: a man carrying a rolled-up newspaper in one hand, a paper bag in the other. He reached the roadway and sat on a bench. He was just beyond the reach of the lamp-post light.

Uncas looked at the Detective, then slowly strode to where he could better see the stranger. He returned to the Detective's side. "He has a flashlight and is studying the Racing Form." He shook his head. "And drinking a beer from a bottle in a bag."

The Detective shrugged. "Nice night for that, I guess."

<<Maybe the horses in the riding stables whisper tips for a sip of his bottle. What do you think?>>

The Detective leaned against a railing along the path. "What now?"

The lamp light highlighted the wrinkles in Uncas' face as he frowned, the rest of his features melded into the night's darkness. "You have been the one to have all the ideas and clues. You have followed your instinct for trouble from one dead man to another. Actually, from one pile of dead people to another. Have you reached a dead end?"

<<Was that a joke?>>

The Smile wasn't in the Detective's voice when he answered. "Perhaps. I know something's probably going to happen—something connected to everything else that's been going on—but I don't know what. Or when."

Uncas leaned on his cane, one fist atop the other where he gripped the crook. "I understand authorities in every state are confiscating comic books. As best they can, where the bug attacks have erupted."

The Detective grunted in reply—not quite approval, just a basic acknowledgement.

"Samples of the ink and paper from the press rooms of Eirik Grimsson have been taken to the police laboratory. They will be tested to see if any contaminants similar to those in the books from Delta Printing are present."

"Good idea."

<<I wonder if Grimsson was a teddy bear when he got that visit?>>

The Detective asked, "Find anything at the Paddy Wagon?"

"No." There was a sound, like a sigh of disappointment, from the inspector, but it was too indistinct to identify clearly.

The Detective crossed his arms. "There were notes written on the wall. By the phone."

<<I told you before—beer distributors, bookies.>>

"They were checked. Some backroom bookie parlors, a few residences, and beer distributors. None of them are unusual for jottings in a bar."

<<Just what I said.>>

"Hm."

Silence then. The sound of a deep-gut belch from the guy on the bench.

Uncas straightened. "I must go. If something in the range of the unusual should come to your notice, call me."

"Sure." The Detective stood away from the railing and turned to leave.

Then something happened in the sky.

Or to the sky.

In the dark above the buildings—although in New Angoulême, the dark above the skyline was never truly dark, but lit from below by the city lights, the darkness appeared to be a sort of vaporous curtain draped overhead—a lightness flickered and twisted.

<<It's like the aurora borealis.>>

Uncas and the Detective stared up at the sky.

And what had been a flickering thread overhead expanded in a snap, broke the sky apart, fractured it into ragged slashes of yellow and purple.

There wasn't a sound.

But there was a blast.

Soundless but violent.

The Detective and Uncas were blown off their feet.

And then both men lay flat on their backs, unconscious.

CHAPTER FIVE

<<Wake up! Wake up! *Wake up!*>>

"Okay, I think I'm awake."

<<Don't move.>>

"What?"

<<Don't move.>>

"You said that."

<<A tiger is licking your helmet.>>

The Detective lay on the ground. The sun was up.

A tiger was licking his helmet.

The animals—some or most or all, I didn't know—had been released from the zoo, and a tiger had appeared a few minutes ago, settled beside the fallen form of the Detective, and began to lick his helmet.

"A what?"

<<Tiger.>>

"Okay."

<<Don't move.>>

"Got it."

The beast was massive. Even not counting the tail, its length from nose to the beginning of the tail was greater than the height of a man. It had licked the Detective's helmet, then hunkered down beside his form to continue enjoying whatever tactile or flavorful pleasures that activity provided. Whatever jungle gave birth to this beautiful monster was a far cry from the open grassy field of Central Park where it now lay teasing the Detective's helmet with rasping licks from a tongue as wide as an outspread hand. At home, its color effectively hid it amid the green and black and stripes of sunlight that broke through the canopy; here, stretched on civilized public grass, the tiger's orange, white, and black hide was no more hidden than a roman candle's explosion in the night sky.

<<You're probably wondering why I wanted you to wake up, since you can't move. No, don't talk. I was afraid you'd stir to consciousness and that would trigger the tiger to attack.>>

A rattling purr—or a growl—rolled out of the big cat's gut.

<<I don't think your electric grip will faze it. It's bigger than the Demeter shapeshifters, that's for sure. And I don't think the Florsheims will fly you away quick enough before it could tear you up.>>

Keeping the Detective informed that I was considering the various angles of this problem would reassure him. That's what I thought, anyway. Besides, I knew he wouldn't answer me while a jungle cat used him like a lollipop.

I didn't have to carry my one-sided discussion any further. From the stables came a rumble, then a stampede of horses. They charged across the roadway, whinnied and turned as a group to run away from the tiger, whose scent they caught. New Angoulême stable horses might not know a tiger from a horsefly, but they knew the scent of a predator.

The tiger ceased its licking. It got to its paws and bounded after the small herd.

The Detective rolled to his feet.

Uncas came around the stable into sight. "Are you all right?" he called as he ran to the Detective's side.

"Yes, thanks." The Detective shook his head. "Whew. Are you okay?"

Uncas nodded. He looked up at the sky. The sun was above the trees. "What happened?"

The Detective looked around. "I don't know. Something big, I guess, if the tiger is out of the zoo."

"Not just a tiger. I saw a bear and some wolves earlier. I woke up by the stable. I saw the tiger over here with you, so I thought setting loose the horses might attract it away from you."

"Thanks. Thanks again."

<<I wonder what flavor helmet tastes like to a cat?>>

"Why are all these animals loose?" the Detective asked.

Uncas gestured, and the two started along the roadway.

Sitting on the bench where he'd taken his seat last night was the same man with the Daily Racing Form still open in his lap. He waved for the inspector and the Detective to approach.

Uncas asked, "What happened last night?"

The fellow on the bench—a balding man in his late fifties, whose jowly face hadn't met a razor in a few days—looked up at the inspector like a man who had just heard a parrot say his name. “Can’t say. Could be anything, you know? Or can you know?”

The Detective asked, “Why do you say that?”

“That’s just the way things are. Or are they?” He spread his hands, then brought them together as if he were going to say a prayer over the racing news.

“Who are you?” Uncas demanded.

Again, the man gave him a baffled look. “I am the God of Incalculable Variables.”

<<Not how I ever imagined a god. Kind of bedraggled.>>

He continued: “You could be on your way to see your sweetie. Got a ring in your pocket, already called the justice of the peace, gonna get hitched this afternoon. Then a bird lights in a tree that hasn’t been swayed by a hundred years of storms, and the roots give ‘way and the tree falls and splats you flatter than a bug on a windshield. If you could predict that, you would have made other plans, gone another way to meet your sweetie. But who could know that, really? Not me, and I’m the God of Incalculable Variables.”

<<Indeed.>>

“All the possibilities are there—” he tapped the newspaper, “and unless your horse has run in the rain, you don’t know if she’s a mudder until the heavens open up. So you lay down your bets and the sun is bright and the track is fast, and your four-legged deliverer from slavery to the pawn shop can’t make it to the money.”

The Detective leaned forward. “What’s your name, sir?”

“I told you,” he said and grinned. His feet danced a little jig, kicking a paper bag from which the brown-glass neck of a bottle was exposed. “I’m the God of Incalculable Variables.”

“Were you here all night? Did you just sit here while that tiger was over there?”

“That was a tiger? I thought it was a butterfly that had found its desired form.”

“Where do you live?”

“Right here. I’m not moving from this bench. The more you move around, the more you invite the other variables to descend upon you. Who knows what could fall from the sky?”

<<He’s got a point there.>>

Uncas plucked at the Detective’s sleeve. As the two stepped away, an empty Hell Gate bottle rolled out from under the bench warmer's feet, bouncing through a nest of dead cigarette butts.

The Detective followed the inspector along the roadway. "We will come across a patrolman, let him call in someone to get the fellow to some medical care," Uncas said.

They didn't come across a patrolman. Instead, they found an abandoned Ford stopped diagonally across the roadway, blocking any traffic that may have come along. The driver's door hung open. Uncas put a hand on the hood.

<<He's a big one for checking engines for fever.>>

"This car has not moved for hours." The inspector looked around. "Why has it not been towed? There should be a traffic jam here."

The Detective looked back the way they had come. "Was anyone working at the stable?"

"No."

"Come on."

They continued toward the edge of the park.

"You seem to be relying on that cane more today than last night," the Detective noted.

"You move as though you were attacked by a gang of ruffians with brass knuckles," Uncas replied.

"Whatever hit us hit pretty hard," the Detective admitted. "Look how long we were out of it—all night, most of the morning."

They came across a few more empty cars. As they approached the entrance to the park, they heard a sound in the bushes beside the roadway. The inspector pushed aside the leaves. He jumped back, his face red.

<<Oh boy.>>

A man and woman—both naked as the days they were born—were intertwined in a very intimate knot. The inspector's interruption didn't create enough motivation for them to pause for their surprised audience.

<<I don't think they even noticed.>>

Uncas' mouth moved, but nothing came out.

The Detective took Uncas by the elbow, pulled him along. "Let's find that cop. He's going to be busy."

They reached the street.

It was filled with cars—no engines running, doors hanging open, left parked this way and that, facing opposing traffic lanes. A few had a tire rolled up onto a curb.

People were everywhere. Some gathered in knots, singing or laughing. Others drifted about, moving from group to group.

A woman in a ballerina's tutu pirouetted along the sidewalk, circling lampposts, hopping over people squatting around chalked-out areas for playing marbles or dominoes.

A man sat on the curb, caressing and kissing a fire hydrant.

A group of men and women sat in a circle around a bonfire blazing in the middle of an intersection. Each held a stick and roasted marshmallows over the flames.

Two old men competed to see who could spit the farthest. One kept hitting his rival's shoes.

A gang of women played stickball in the street. The youngest looked to be in her sixties.

People danced. Couples waltzed. A group appeared to be in the middle of a furious jitterbug contest. A large circle of people clapped in time for a frantically spinning number of dancers moving in response to the squawlings of an old man.

<<What is that?>>

"I think they call that square dancing."

A handful of men—some in business suits, others in pajamas—collided during a game of tag with another group playing leapfrog and Simon Says.

Uncas and the Detective walked along the sidewalk—dazed by the sights surrounding them.

"Where are my cops?"

"What has happened to New Angoulême?"

<<The other shoe has dropped.>>

A woman in an elegant evening dress carried a bucket. She stopped occasionally to reach into the bucket, then flung a handful of mud behind her before continuing her march along the street.

<<Ah. The cops.>>

A clutch of Mohawks in Police Department blue sat cross-legged in a ragged circle around one of their fellows who stood and juggled half a dozen batons.

Uncas started to charge the group, but the Detective held him back.

"They're out of it—just like everyone else."

Uncas scowled.

The Detective said, "They're men, just like everyone else. Just because they're cops—whatever has happened, has happened to them, too."

Uncas turned, furious. "Then why not us?"

The Detective looked around. "I don't know."

Although the scene displayed a sort of chaos compared to the typical city scene one might encounter on a normal day, the crowds were relatively orderly and causing no harm.

Then, disorder arrived.

A stampeding herd of juveniles—from the age of six to eighteen or so—charged through the adults. The youngsters wielded staves and pipes and broken bottles and stones, and they hurled these and batted bystanders as they hurtled along the pavement, breaking up the games and singing and dancing.

Uncas reached into his coat for his shoulder holster, but the Detective grabbed his arm and pushed him against a building wall. "They're in no more control of themselves than the adults. We know that. You want to assert control, I know, I understand. But shooting those kids won't help protect anyone. We've got to find out what's happened, see if we can reverse it."

The mob of youthful anarchists roared past, leaving moaning and crying adults behind. Other adults, left untouched by the horde, went back to their previous play, apparently oblivious to the harm done to their neighbors. They seemed to have no memory of the chaos that had just swept through their ranks.

Uncas gritted his teeth. "Unhand me."

Released by the Detective, the inspector shrugged his coat back into place. "All right."

They went into the street.

A man in a fetal curl moaned. Crimson ran from his nose.

A woman lay on her back—one hand and one foot twitched infrequently. Bruises already began to show on her limbs.

One man held the hand of another. The second lay with his eyes closed, the back of his head laying on a flat pillow of blood.

The Detective kneeled and gave comforting words to one, moved to another. Uncas used a woman's head scarf to tie a sling for her arm. He stood and walked to another, then another. Then he stood. He surveyed the scene before and around him. Although several were injured, those who remained unharmed by the hit-and-run assault continued to amuse themselves with frivolous games. Others had resumed their dancing—waltzes, minuets, tangos.

The Detective bent over a woman who was hyperventilating.

<<I've put in calls to all the hospitals in the city. No one is answering. At any of them.>>

Uncas trotted to a call box on a lamppost. He picked up the receiver, but couldn't raise anyone.

The Detective waved away a chattering group of men and women who wanted to show him yo-yo tricks.

Uncas stepped to where the Detective was wrapping a sleeve torn from a shirt around a man's two arms, held before the man's abdomen, one arm acting as a splint for the other. The inspector touched the Detective's shoulder. "There are too many."

The Detective sighed.

"The One-Four is this way." He stalked off toward the nearest precinct. He didn't look back to see if the Detective was following.

He was.

CHAPTER SIX

<<This is not encouraging.>>

The Fourteenth Precinct was abandoned.

The same confusing scenes of carefree insanity had filled the streets all the way to the precinct. As the inspector had led the way up the steps to the entrance, an old man sitting on the bottom step smiled a black smile as he juggled his two dental plates. He greeted them, "Welcome to Piano City."

<<Was that supposed to make sense?>>

"What does?"

The Detective followed Uncas as the inspector slammed through halls and offices, up and down stairs, all in a vain attempt to locate anyone who worked for the department.

They ended up back in front of the sergeant's desk at the entrance to the precinct.

"Where are they? *Where are they*?" Uncas stomped around the room.

<<The inspector is going to lose his title of Mr. Control soon.>>

The Detective spoke, a calming tone in his voice: "Inspector, they are outside with everyone else."

"They have abandoned their post! They are sworn to protect their city—but they have abandoned their post! People are hurt, they are out of their minds in the streets!"

"Clearly they are no more immune to whatever happened than anyone else, Inspector. Simply because they are members of the Police Department doesn't mean they are no longer human."

Uncas spun toward the Detective with a snarl. "*We* were immune. *We* aren't dancing in the street! Why?"

"I don't know."

"Why?!"

Before the Detective could respond, one of the phones on the sergeant's desk rang.

Uncas snatched it up and answered: "Fourteenth Precinct."

"Who is this?"

"I am Chief Inspector Jonathan Brewster Uncas."

"Uncas! This is Knifetongue. I've called precincts all over town. You're the first to pick up."

"Commissioner, what has happened?"

"I don't know. Who's there with you? Anyone?"

"Eh, Space Detective."

"You're both normal?"

"Yes sir. Where are you?"

"Headquarters. I'm alone here. Everyone else is insane in the streets. Or maybe some are hiding indoors, I can't tell."

The Detective interrupted. "How do I get in on this call?"

Uncas said, "Commissioner, hang up. We'll call you back in a moment."

He gestured for the Detective, dashed down a set of stairs to the communications room in the basement. He paused long enough to pick up a pair of headphones at the empty radio desk. Not a single signal came through the speakers. He moved aside, sat before the switchboard. He plugged in some wires, donned the headphones, handed a telephone to the Detective, who pulled up a chair beside the inspector. Uncas dialed a number. The Commissioner answered.

"What is going on?" he said.

The Detective asked, "Commissioner, are you all right?"

"What have you done? Is this your doing? What have you done to my city?"

Uncas interjected, "He has done nothing to cause this—whatever it is. I was with him all night. We were together when—when the sky erupted."

"What?"

The calming tone was back in the Detective's voice: "We don't know what happened, but somehow all three of us haven't been affected. Maybe we will be, but it hasn't happened yet. Or maybe there's something about us that kept it from happening. Something we have in common."

"In common?" Knifetongue bellowed. "*Us*?"

"Do you have another answer, Commissioner?"

Uncas' eyebrows slowly rose on his forehead as Knifetongue's silence stretched out.

He asked, "What could it be? Something in the air?"

The Detective shook his head. "Everything I breathe is filtered through this helmet. You two breathe the same thing as everyone else in the city. But you aren't running loose in the streets."

"Ah," Uncas said. "It is not just that we have something in common. Everyone out there, affected by whatever it is—they all have something in common, too."

"Agreed," Knifetongue said.

<<So—what is your common denominator?>>

"*They* all eat," Uncas said. "*We* all eat."

"Well," the Detective said, "not really. Not like you eat."

Uncas looked at him.

Knifetongue gurgled something irascible. "So," he said, "do you *drink*?"

"Um, no."

"Wait a minute," Uncas said. "Do you drink *any*thing?"

"Not exactly," the Detective said.

"What about alcohol?"

"No, not at all."

"Nor do I," Uncas said.

<<Not surprising.>>

Knifetongue chimed in: "Me, neither."

<<Now, that's surprising.>>

Uncas had a look on his face that would have launched laughter among the ranks he commanded if conditions outside the precinct hadn't been so dire.

"Wait now," the Detective said. "None of us drinks any alcoholic beverage."

Knifetongue answered, "That seems to be true."

In the silence that followed, I noticed that the Detective had begun tapping his fingers on the desktop before him. The rhythm followed that same tune he'd been knocking out for days on whatever flat surface he encountered during moments of concentration.

"Do you remember what the bar looked like at The Paddy Wagon?" the Detective asked.

Uncas looked puzzled. "What?"

"Just thinking out loud."

<<Yep. I remember.>>

He'd stopped tapping his fingers when he asked me that first question.

"There were liquor bottles behind the bar, right?"

<<Yes.>>

He nodded. "What kind of beer was on tap?" Uncas had an expression of discomfort on his face by this time.

<<Let's see, there were four or five sticks. Four. And they were for Hell Gate, Pluto Pilsner and Cold Day.>>

"That's three."

<<Two were for Hell Gate.>>

"And all those are Hell Gate Brewery products, right?"

<<Yep.>>

"No Pabst, Ballantine, no other brands?"

<<Hell Gate is a local brewery. It's popular. Maybe other brands were for sale in bottles only.>>

"I wish I'd had a look in the cooler. Do you remember the markings on any of the items we saw in the cellar?"

<<Yes. Come to think of it, there were no boxes or barrels in sight marked with anything other than Hell Gate brand names.>>

"What about the liquor bottles?"

<<Huh?>>

"Behind the bar."

<<Oh. Four Roses, Jim Beam, Bushmills, Old Crow, Canadian Mist.>>

"Beer and whiskey. Simple menu."

<<Technically, some of those whiskeys are actually bourbons.>>

"Right." He started tapping out the music again.

He stopped. "Were they open?"

<<What?>>

"The bottles on the back shelf."

<<Oh.>>

I went over the images I'd collected from the Detective's pass through The Paddy Wagon.

<<No. They still had the tax stamps glued in place. None had been broken open. All the bottles were full as new.>>

"Ah."

He was quiet for a long time. Quiet except for tapping out that music in his helmet onto the top of the desk.

Uncas looked ready to pull his gun.

"Is there a phone book around here?" the Detective asked.

Uncas rummaged in a drawer, pushed a thick directory across to the Detective.

He flipped through pages, put his finger to a number. "Plug me in another line, I gotta make a call."

He disconnected the call to Knifetongue, dialed the number he found in the book. He waited, got no answer, hung up. He flipped through the directory again, dialed another number.

"Joey?" he said. "Space Detective. Are you okay?"

The Detective nodded. He put a hand over the speaking piece. "Joey Vanderclokk. Runs a beer distributorship. Not one on the wall at The Paddy Wagon. He deals in hauling spirits, but doesn't drink 'em." He spoke again to Joey: "What's going on around your neighborhood? Yeah, same thing here, all over thc city. Just hang tight, Joey, we'll get it straightened out. Keep a watch on your family, try to get them safe and out of the way if you see any of those kid gangs come running into the block."

The Commissioner piped up to Uncas, "What is this all about?"

The Detective continued: "Joey, what's been going on with beer sales lately? What have your customers been ordering? Hell Gate products only? What about the other brands? Orders have been falling the past six months. Okay, thanks, Joey. Be careful."

He hung up, looked at Uncas, who reconnected the Detective's line to Knifetongue.

"Explain," the Commissioner directed.

"I think that's it," the Detective said. "It's like the comic book ink. Something is in the Hell Gate beer products, something that keeps people coming back to those beers and no others, something that's made everybody lose their minds and go dancing in the street."

Uncas frowned. "That sounds far fetched."

"Think about it," the Detective urged. "The Paddy Wagon—only Hell Gate beer in stock and being consumed. The bar we holed up in when we visited Delta across the river—Yesterdays—the owner said the only thing any of his customers wanted was Hell Gate. I bet you can find the same story in nearly every bar in town. Package stores, too."

Silence from Uncas and Knifetongue.

The Detective rapped the desktop. "It makes a crazy sense, and we're dealing with something crazy here. It follows the same sort of strategy as the comic book crimes. But the targets are adults, while the comic book ink was targeting kids. Well, mostly."

Knifetongue spoke up. "For the momentary sake of argument, let's say you're right. Now what? What can we do about it?"

Uncas nodded. "If you are correct, everyone out in the streets has been drinking this tainted beer for weeks or months. Something last night triggered their dramatic change in behavior. How do we change them back?"

Knifetongue said, "All of New Angoulême has gone wacky. All but three or four of us, apparently. How do we bring an entire city to its proper senses?"

The Detective sighed. "I don't know. But there must be some sort of antidote. It would only make sense. What benefit does it have for someone for an entire city to be lost in a childish fog, like the adults, or rampaging in gangs, like the kids?"

Uncas thumped the desktop. "We have to protect our people, somehow."

"Wait," Knifetongue said. "I didn't call the Other Precincts."

"They can help," Uncas said.

"I'll call back," the Commissioner said, and broke the connection.

"What did he mean," the Detective asked, "by the Other Precincts?"

Uncas looked at him. "He means those that report to the Black Commissioner. In Harlem."

CHAPTER SEVEN

The part of the island called Harlem was known as Muscoota to the Manhattan Indians who lived there when the Dutch settled the southern end of the island and named it Nieuw Amsterdam. As the Dutch settlement spread northward into the Indians' fertile farming country, Muscoota's native identity was lost as it was renamed Nieuw Haarlem.

During the passing of generations and the ebb and flow of economic prosperity and collapse, the land's fertility dwindled and plots were sold off until what had been farms was given over entirely to residential communities. With improvements developed in transportation, these communities eventually united into neighborhoods of the larger city, New Angoulême.

Descendants of old Dutch and Walloon families still called the place New Harlem. But the people who called it home called it simply Harlem.

Nearly every Harlem resident was black-skinned, although the shades of that blackness varied as greatly as the colors of flowers in a field. They were the descendants of laborers for the Dutch. They were children of indentured servants and freedmen and runaway slaves. They were sons and daughters of slaves emancipated during the War Between the States.

Nearly every black person who called New Angoulême home lived in Harlem and its immediate environs. "We are citizens of New Angoulême," said Samuel J. Battle, the first Black Commissioner. Many subsequent elected and cultural leaders would echo him: "We are members of the human race. We are the Black people. Yes, we are citizens of New Angoulême. Harlem is our home."

More than one newspaper and magazine writer described Harlem's self-sequestering tendencies as similar to a sovereign nation within a nation, like Cahokia in the West.

This cultural semi-isolation within the larger body of New Angoulême is what led Commissioner Knifetongue to call Harlem's five precincts for help. For the cultural pride of Harlem's citizens moved them to support locally owned businesses—such as Harlem-based breweries over New Angoulême's competing breweries. That's not to say that people living in Harlem completely abstained from drinking Hell Gate products, but most would be loyal to Harlem-brewed beverages like Sugar Hill Pilsner and Hamilton Hill Ale. But if Hell Gate products were somehow linked to the cause for the population's delusional behavior, Knifetongue figured a chunk of the population that didn't drink Hell Gate's output might be a source of help for dealing with the current crisis.

William Battle—Samuel's grandson, popularly called Battlin' Billy—sat with Uncas and the Detective now. He did so in his role as Chief Inspector of Harlem—Uncas' counterpart who reported to the Black Commissioner.

Battle and Uncas sat at a table with the Detective in a basement room of Police Headquarters. Each had a tablet of paper, making lists, scratching notes.

<<Is algebra homework next?>>

"All right," Battle said. His face was square and given character by deep smile lines. His skin was the dark color of roasted coffee beans, and the fluorescent light gleamed highlights across his forehead, nose and cheek bones. His broad shoulders supported the image of a man who could carry great burdens. "The church associations and other teetotalers have been organized and sent out. Those who can operate bulldozers and tow trucks are clearing streets and major arteries for emergency vehicles. Medical staff from Harlem are making contact with their counterparts in the rest of the city—those not affected by whatever's going on. So at least emergency medical needs can begin to be addressed."

"We will have the uniformed strength from the Harlem precincts spread out to deal with immediate problems as they arise," Uncas said. "In most cases, that may be the roaming bands of juveniles. But one squad is assigned to round up any released zoo animals. And all of the squads will also be watching for fragile citizens who already are vulnerable because of age or health conditions and are unable to take care of themselves because of the mania that has swept the city."

"How many cops are we talking about here?" the Detective asked.

"Fewer than two thousand from the five Harlem precincts," Battle answered.

<<For the whole city?>>

The Detective shook his head. "Commissioner Knifetongue must be chewing the draperies in his office."

"Perhaps not," Uncas said. "He is a very optimistic leader. I have heard him say, 'With five New Angoulême patrolmen, I can keep this city safe against any crime wave.'"

"We're not far from that now," the Detective said. "What about water traffic?"

Battle spoke up. "Obviously there are some problems. Nearly all the craft operated by local crews are at risk of wrecking or sinking. Or perhaps being lost at sea, if they head out from the harbors. Ships with crews from other localities have, for the most part, set out for other ports."

"Aren't other cities having similar problems?"

"Strangely enough, or perhaps fortunately enough, only a very few."

Uncas said, "According to the radio reports we have been able to receive, only three cities have been struck by this mass . . . whatever it is."

"Oh?"

"New Angoulême, New Orleans, and San Francisco."

"Really?" The Detective tapped out what was becoming a familiar rhythm on the table. "If our surmise about the brewery is right—"

"Which brewery?" Battle interrupted.

"Hell Gate," Uncas answered.

"It makes a sort of sense," the Detective continued. "Each of the three cities has a local brewing tradition with a great popularity among local customers. But why those three cities? Why *just* those three cities?"

<<What do those three have in common?>>

"Port cities. There may be others," Battle said.

"But those are the only ones we are aware of at the moment," Uncas said.

The Detective brought up another point. "What about food?"

Battle looked at him. "You're hungry?"

"No, the people in the streets or hiding in their homes. If they aren't able to protect themselves from the JDs, or even offer simple first aid to people around them, how do we know they can feed themselves?"

"Ah," Battle said. "Once the major streets are clear, trucks with food from schools and warehouses are going to start setting up at strategic points across the city. We hope the instinct for preservation—at least where eating is concerned—will still be great enough to draw people to the distribution points once they learn where they are located."

"We have a recorded message that will be broadcast over the major radio stations, if anyone is listening and we can find staff to man the microphones," Uncas said. "Our resources are a bit thin."

"You guys work well together," the Detective said.

"Indeed," Battle agreed. "Why have we not met before, Mr. Space Detective? Do your cases not take you into Harlem?"

"On occasion," he said, "but not too often. And when I've needed police help or information, I usually just call Inspector Uncas."

"Feel free to call on me as well," the Harlem inspector said.

"So I shall. But as I said, the two of you work well together. Why do you separate yourself from the rest of the city?"

"Essentially, Commissioner Knifetongue is commissioner for the Harlem precincts as well. Commissioner Washington—or the Black Commissioner, if you will—ostensibly reports to Commissioner Knifetongue, but is the leader of the Harlem police force."

"Okay, I sort of see that," the Detective said, "but why do the people of Harlem separate themselves from the rest of New Angoulême?"

"It must be the Curse of Ham," Battle said.

<<Does he mean Genesis 9:25?>>

The Detective said, "'And he said, Cursed be Canaan; a servant of servants shall he be unto his brethren.' There is no Curse of Ham. Noah cursed Ham's son, Canaan. Noah's son, Shem, is the ancestor of Abraham, who became the patriarch of the Israelites. And the Israelites eventually bested the Canaanites again and again."

Battle grinned at Uncas. "This one is very astute. He not only has the name Detective, he even knows a few things." He clapped his hands in a momentary expression of delight that jolted everyone with surprise after they had focused so much attention on the dire situation in the streets.

Battle turned his square face to the Detective. He still showed a smile, but his gaze was very hard. He tapped the table with one strong finger as he spoke.

"Many people in many places for long ages have used the so-called Curse of Ham to formulate all sorts of rationalizations to determine the destinies of the Black people," he said. "No matter our freedoms now, there are plenty of people I encounter more frequently than you might imagine who still would like to impose Ham's supposed curse as a justification for putting one or another project into place."

Battle smiled a smile that displayed no humor. "We sequester ourselves, if you care to call it that, so we may blaze our own path—not a trail laid out for us by anyone else. We have no wish to be patronized, paternalized, or partitioned artificially to fit someone's imagined paradise."

Battle's smile warmed a little. "As for sequestering someone—to use your word—how about you?"

"Me?"

"Yes, Mr. Detective. You're always inside that helmet. It keeps you separate from everyone else, no matter how personable or interesting you may be. Aren't you sequestered, too? Perhaps by choice, perhaps not, I don't know. Why, you may well be a Black man under there, who would know?"

Battle grinned. Uncas sat staring at the Detective, his eyebrows raised.

The Detective shrugged. He answered, "I guess we all three separate ourselves from everyone else, in some fashion. But to keep outsiders from taking advantage of your constituents, or forcing unwanted plans on them, why not get the government involved?"

Now Battle laughed. "Again, the government, no matter its intent, is an outsider. Why turn our destiny over to someone else, whether that someone else is a person or an organization, or an elected representative group? Look, the human race began with paradise in Eden—but they couldn't keep it. Everything since then that a human has created—even this or that utopia—is flawed. Because anything created by a flawed creature is going to reflect that flaw: something flawed cannot create something perfect.

"So, a governing body is created by men, and run by men—those who created it were flawed, those who run it are flawed, and what they do as a group is, eventually and in some fashion, flawed.

"Now, I'm not saying I'm perfect. The people I represent and the law officers who report to me aren't perfect. We're all just as flawed as everyone else. But we'd rather forge ahead with our own flaws, dealing with our own mistakes, instead of compounding those troubles by turning our future over to some other flawed individuals and organizations."

The Detective put a Smile into his voice. "Nicely put. I understand now."

"Understand this!"

The rough voice of Commissioner Knifetongue rolled through an open door just before he stepped into the room, followed by the Black Commissioner, Roland Washington. Both men wore crisp uniforms, and although their expressions displayed fatigue, their eyes were lit by a fire of determination—that of leaders facing a challenge.

Knifetongue thumped the table with his fist. "We're not just facing the matter of feeding and protecting our citizens from whatever dementia has claimed them. Truckloads of beer—Hell Gate beer," he said, and he looked at the Detective, "are being delivered, I guess you'd say, to a variety of points throughout the city. We've had radio calls from some of our patrols. The beer is being unloaded at a number of busy intersections. The crowds are making for it, perhaps because they're hungry or thirsty, perhaps because there may be some sort of addictive agent in the brew that makes these poor souls crave what's killing them."

Uncas nearly snarled. "So there is some agent promoting this situation? Someone is trying to bring down the city in an active, aggressive manner?"

The Detective shook his head. His fingers tapped rapidly on the tabletop, like symbols of his mental activities speeding through the problems facing these men who had vowed to protect New Angoulême. He looked up at Knifetongue.

"Commissioner, I'm here to help if you'll have me."

Knifetongue glared at the Detective. "I'll take your help. But you'll take Inspector Uncas with you."

"Done. Gladly."

"Very well. Commissioner Washington, Inspector Battle and I will lead the efforts we've already launched, and see if we can get some more help from outside the city. Uncas, pull together four or five men—we can't spare more than that—and get to work. I want this brewery business shut down." He thundered out, Washington beside him.

Battle stood. He pointed at the Detective's moving fingers. "What is that tune you keep tapping?"

"I don't know." The Detective stopped the play of his hands.

"Something from the radio."

"I thought so," the Inspector said. "It sounded familiar, but not quite. I kept thinking it was like this." Battle leaned toward the table and tapped out a rhythm. "But it was different, somehow."

<<His is reversed. It's your tune, but backwards.>>

"Oh well," Battle said as he walked to the door. "In times of stress, we're easily distracted to keep from dwelling on what we know is so awful." He turned and saluted. "Good fortune and good work, gentlemen."

"Thanks," the Detective said. "Let's go, partner."

Uncas sneered a bit. He led the way out.

The sun had retreated to the west. The last light was dwindling from the day and darkness was advancing over the city.

The Detective stood on the steps outside the doors of Headquarters. "Just twenty-four hours ago, we were conspiring in the Park."

Uncas stood beside him. "Perhaps *you* were conspiring," he said. "*I* was serving my city."

<<Ah, so that's what that was.>>

"I see. I must've had something in my eye, couldn't quite make out what was happening. My apologies."

"None necessary." Uncas smiled and went down the steps.

<<Heck, he kept you from being a tiger snack. He deserves to play by his rules every now and then, right?>>

The Detective joined the inspector on the sidewalk. "Okay, let's go get a beer."

CHAPTER EIGHT

Chief Inspector Uncas selected four men to join the trip to the Hell Gate Brewery. This place was determined to be the target based on the Detective's deductions from the types of products found at The Paddy Wagon crime scene and from Tom Bouchoux's comments at Yesterdays during the raid on Delta Printing.

"Will four men be enough?" the Detective asked.

"Resources are already stretched thin," Uncas said. "And we will be going in two cars. Two with you and me. Two in the other car."

"Four and two?"

"You cannot have three in a car. That would either leave one alone in the back—which, according to the culture of the uniformed men, would not be acceptable among peers—or it would put two in the back, so that the driver would appear to be chauffeuring the other two, which also is not acceptable among peers."

<<Gosh, these guys are sensitive.>>

"Okay, okay."

<<I guess it's good to be careful with the feelings of sensitive guys—especially when they carry guns and badges.>>

The Hell Gate Brewery was named for Hell Gate—imagine that—where the conflicting currents of the East River, Harlem River, and Long Island Sound collided. The name came from the Dutch *Hellegat*, a *hell hole* or a *bright gate* or *bright passage*. Take your pick. I was thinking that if the brewery turned out to be the source of the city's current corruption, *hell hole* might be appropriate.

We headed from Headquarters at Center Street along Lexington Avenue. The brewery had been established, according to its ubiquitous ads, in 1867. It still stood where it had started, between Ninety-second and Ninety-third Streets and Second and Third Avenues.

Based on the chief inspector's explanations, the Detective and Uncas sat in the back of the lead car with two of Chief Inspector Battle's Harlem cops in the front. Two more Harlem cops followed in a second car. Both vehicles were officially marked with the shield of the New

Angoulême Police Department on the doors of the two-color Plymouths: White on top, blue-green on the bottom.

The men marveled at the destruction as the vehicles moved along a wide but uneven path cleared by bulldozers earlier: autos and trucks piled at the sides of the streets, pushed out of the way for emergency vehicles to have access. Tangles of metal and twisted chrome sat in pools of broken glass, results of the strange calamity that had struck the city.

Citizens wandered into the policemen's path, bewildered or inexplicably cheerful. Some congregated in groups of varying size, all chattering, none listening. Occasionally the driver for Uncas would stop the car so the others could herd aside the people who blocked the way—honking did no good—like two-legged cattle.

The brewery came into view. It looked like a medieval castle: a big building made of dressed stone blocks, an arched gateway in the center of the front.

<<All it needs is a moat.>>

This was the original building. And its intimidating appearance might suggest to an impressionable mind that it could serve as an actual gateway to Hell. Over the years, additions to the brewery had been constructed, and now most of the work occurred in the large structures and lots behind the castle, which extended down to the riverside.

A lot of activity seemed to be whirling around the brewery. Trucks of all sorts—regular Hell Gate delivery trucks, flatbeds, pickups—wheeled into and away from the plant.

"Busy supplying the thirsty crazies out in the streets," the Detective said.

The place was lit up like a Hollywood theater for premiere night. But there was no red carpet, no reporters or photographers.

Uncas' two cars had stopped far enough away to remain unnoticed for the moment. The two cops from the other car got out and came up to the chief inspector's window.

"We will circle one side of the complex," Uncas directed, "and you," he pointed at the Detective, "go with them," he gestured at the cops from the other car, "and check the other side. Stay out of sight and trouble. We will meet back here."

The Detective got out, climbed into the back of the other car, and the two vehicles separated.

Half an hour later, they met again. Everyone exited their cars and leaned against the hood of Uncas' vehicle.

The chief inspector looked to the Harlem cops.

One from the Detective's car spoke up: "We counted thirty or so men on our side of the building."

"Forty, maybe fifty on our side," said Uncas' driver.

<<Doesn't sound like good odds.>>

Uncas nodded.

He looked at the Detective. His eyebrows went up.

<<Your turn.>>

The Detective looked toward the castle, then looked at Uncas. "My math skills aren't the greatest, but when I look there, then I look at us, I think the odds don't look so good."

Uncas shrugged.

He said, "Resources are—"

"I know," the Detective interrupted. "Stretched thin."

"So?"

<<When did Mr. Strong, Silent, and Deep pick up the Socratic thing?>>

The Detective leaned one hand on the car hood. He looked at the brewery. His other gloved hand went up, began tapping that same recurring rhythm on his helmet.

<<What is it with the tapping? I thought you were a detective. Are you really just a frustrated musician?>>

"I don't know about the musician part . . ."

Uncas looked puzzled. "What?"

"We need to see what's going on in there."

<<Thinking about Delta Printing?>>

"Hm."

Uncas still looked at him. "And your suggestion?"

<<All of a sudden, the questions just don't stop with this guy.>>

The Detective stopped tapping. He looked around at the Harlem cops, then to Uncas. "We go in."

Uncas shook his head.

<<Huh.>>

"What?"

Uncas looked at the Detective. "What?"

<<You're not going to believe it.>>

"What?"

Uncas thumped the car hood. "You said, 'What?' I said, 'What?' Now you say, 'What?' again!"

<<That.>>

They heard the sounds. The group turned as one.

Galloping along Lexington Avenue from the direction the Plymouths had driven came a horse.

Massive. Thirty hands high, easy.

White. White like no other white horse any of the men had ever seen. Light flowed along the lines of its rolling muscles as if it had been curried in oil.

The clatter from its gallop was tremendous.

The pavement cracked under its hooves.

Uncas and the Harlem cops were speechless.

Not the Detective: "Oh man."

<<Yep.>>

The huge beast stopped by the parked cars, reared up. Its forelegs flailed the air above their heads.

Then it dropped back down to the street with a thud that shuddered the cars on their shocks. The cops almost went to their knees with the vibration.

The cops couldn't utter a word. Not so the horse:

"Hello, Detective."

<<Jupiter.>>

CHAPTER NINE

I mentioned earlier the Detective and I belong to a far-flung network of agents who try to rein in the more egregious efforts of greedy spacers to annex unwilling planets. In the case of Earth, the planet isn't even ready to join the community of space-faring races. The people here don't even know there is such a community.

Jupiter has been a member of The Reseau so long, his records are buried in archives too deep to recover. No one in the network even knows any more his true name or planet of origin.

He's known as Jupiter now because he was stationed near Earth for so long. His station was located in a capsule of sorts—like the Detective's file cabinet, Jupiter's capsule contained more real estate than seemed possible—that floated snug as a bug in the Jovian red spot. The station remained protected from the giant storm continually swirling within the spot by a type of stasis field that kept everything about the capsule calm and serene. Everything, that is, but Jupiter himself.

Jupiter's sense of adventure was a frequent cause of reprimands. He loved to dally with the ladies—well, really, with anything or anyone—and cross-species intimacy was a particular fetish for him. All those Greek and Roman tales about Zeus and Jupiter romancing women in the form of animals or normally inanimate objects? That was *our* Jupiter. Taking a little Earthside R&R.

Buried in the agency's lost archives was the information about Jupiter's shape-changing abilities. Was he born or hatched or . . . whatever . . . with those abilities? Or did he acquire them in some fashion? Unlike the plant-based shapeshifters who had posed as the murdered New Angoulême cops, Jupiter didn't hail from Demeter X. We don't know where he's from, but we know he's not from there.

But Jupiter would change forms with abandon, with a joy simply for the sake of transforming and for tweaking one's expectations.

Did the Detective know what Jupiter's true form looked like? I didn't know; I bet he didn't, either.

So there he was, prancing before Chief Inspector Jonathan Brewster

Uncas and his Harlem cops. A giant, beautiful stallion.

A giant, *talking* stallion.

"I would have been here sooner, but I have been tied up with something," Jupiter said. "Hitched, you might say."

Uncas finally spoke: "What is this?"

"This?" Jupiter rumbled. "*This?!*"

"This," the Detective interrupted, "is, ah, Jupiter. He's a magician, illusionist. Does a lot of stage work."

Uncas had regained his composure. "I doubt that, as I doubt so many things you tell me. However, continue your explanation. Please."

"Well, you're working all the time," the Detective said. "You probably aren't fully informed about all the entertainment world's performers these days. Anyway, you rely on informants and a variety of folks to support your efforts to keep the city safe and secure, right? Jupiter provides help to me from time to time. His particular skills—" he gestured at the stallion— "can come in handy in, ah, particular situations."

Uncas stared at the Detective, deadpan, for several moments. Then he stared at Jupiter. "Like the current situation?"

<<Just like!>>

"Yes."

Jupiter belched. "Pardon. Are introductions in order? Or should we get right to whatever needs doing?"

"Introductions," the Detective said. He performed his role as the host who knew everyone at the party, and so gave a name to each person gathered about the Plymouths. The Harlem cops had stopped showing their molars, but they simply nodded in response to the Detective giving their names. None of them said a word, nor did they take their eyes off the stallion.

The Detective also explained the set up concerning the brewery. He further noted that Chief Inspector Uncas was in command of this sortie.

"Indeed," Jupiter said. He tossed his head. The stallion's mane glittered. "Tell me, Chief Inspector, do you accept recommendations from your subordinates?"

"So long as my subordinates are not insubordinate." Seeing Uncas discuss points of strategy with a giant talking horse with all the nonchalance of one plumber talking pipes to another was worth getting harangued about the Studebaker's heat sink.

"Noted," Jupiter said. "We are a small force against a larger force. To our benefit, the larger force is unaware we are here and preparing to take action against them. So, as I see it, we have two options."

Uncas glanced toward the brewery, then back to Jupiter. "And they are?"

"One, we sneak in.

"Two, we barrel straight in and scare the hops out of them."

"There may be a third," Uncas suggested.

"A third?"

Uncas nodded. "We do both."

CHAPTER TEN

The squad had divided into two points of attack. The Detective was on the backside of the brewery with one of the Harlem cops, Ed Johnson. The rest were on the opposite side, not far from the main gate. The plan was to charge through that gate, raise a disturbance, while the Detective and Johnson entered in a quiet manner to provide a surprise flanking maneuver.

There had been some terse discussion about the division of labor. Inspector Uncas clearly wanted to keep both the Detective and Jupiter in sight and under his command. But Jupiter was such a new and unknown variable, Uncas planned to stick close to him. He knew the Detective well enough to trust him to follow through on the planned job. Jupiter, however, probably needed more tending.

<<He just doesn't realize what a big chore tending Jupiter can be.>>

"He'll find out," sighed the Detective.

"Before we separate, I need a word with Mr. Jupiter," the Detective had said to Uncas.

The inspector had arched an eyebrow.

<<That is a three-hour conversation for Uncas.>>

"Don't worry," the Detective had responded. "I'm just sharing a word of wisdom to make sure he follows your orders, Inspector."

After the two had moved beyond the patrol cars, the Detective had used two stiffened fingers to tap Jupiter's long, graceful neck. "I know you work more independently than the rest of us in The Reseau," the Detective said, "but my role here is already teetering toward the precarious. I've built an uneasy relationship with Uncas. It's an important one to keep intact if we really are dealing with Hyrnavians and a broad network of Louies."

<<*Uneasy relationship*. I was thinking *queasy* relationship would be a better description.>>

"So?" I'd never heard a horse sound sarcastic. Well, I'd never heard a horse speak English.

"So don't mess it up."

In some ways, Jupiter was like a big, irrepressible and enthusiastic child instead of an ancient intergalactic agent. The Detective had learned from others in our organization that a solid, parental-style reprimand could go far to keep Jupiter's antics in check. To some extent, at least.

Sometimes.

The Detective had turned and stalked back to Uncas and his men. He turned to Johnson, asked, "Ready?"

"Yes sir."

"Let's go."

As the two left the group, Uncas had eyed Jupiter suspiciously before gesturing for the giant horse to join him.

So now the Detective and Johnson faced the back of the castle.

A single door interrupted the imposing stretch of the wall. Boxes and bins spilling garbage made clear the purpose for the door, which appeared from the outside to open by rolling upward on tracks instead of being hung on hinges.

The yeasty smell of brewing beer lay heavy in the air. The Detective and Johnson kneeled in the shadows of an alley across the street from their objective. On one knee, the Detective tapped out a rapid tattoo of the familiar rhythm that became the unconscious soundtrack of those minutes he was deep in thought.

<<Nervous?>>

"Not yet."

Johnson looked at him. "No, I don't hear anything."

Then they did.

On the other side of the building, a stream of trucks entered and exited the main gate, delivering Hell Gate goods to various drop-off points in the city. When a gap appeared, Jupiter was to charge, stirring amazement and fright, while Uncas and his cops were to race their patrol cars to the brewery and block the entrance.

Incoming traffic would be kept out.

But our little squad would be trapped inside.

The Detective heard car horns and a muted clatter from the direction of the main entrance.

"Let's go."

He and Johnson charged across the street to the overhead door.

They ignored the button mounted on the wall for the call buzzer. Instead, they put their fingers in the slight gap between the door bottom and the concrete threshold.

And tugged.

The door rattled upward—unlocked.

Inside, the two closed the sectioned door, then the Detective shot home the dead bolts on either side of the frame.

<<Now you're committed.>>

"If anyone tries to escape that way, they'll be slowed down by opening the bolts."

Johnson grinned. "That may be us." He was slender and sinewy, and his face carried a hard expression, made more severe by the creases at the corners of his mouth and eyes. But entering the brewery and securing the door had lit a flare of joy in his eyes.

"Were you in the war?" he asked.

"No," the Detective answered, "not the Berlin war. Why?"

Johnson's expression changed. "This reminds me of those days."

"Then I have a good partner," the Detective said. He gestured, and they moved forward.

They were in a vast room filled with wooden pallets stacked with barrels and fat bags of ingredients for making the Hell Gate products. A large doorless opening faced them. The Detective moved to one side of the door, Johnson to the other. They peered through.

Massive steel vats were arranged in rows in the next room, tended by fellows who looked like stevedores—sleeves rolled up or cut away to reveal bulging muscles and hairy arms. They wore baggy work clothes that were none too clean.

<<I have a hunch.>>

"Me, too," the Detective whispered, "but let's see."

A glance at Johnson's expression suggested that the Harlem cop had a notion similar to ours about the beer makers.

Johnson hissed, whispered, "They're all wearing plugs in their ears."

The Detective nodded. "It's not as loud here as a lot of other places I've been in."

<<Still, there's no noise from the front of the brewery, where Jupiter and Uncas should be stirring up trouble. Some kind of communication devices?>>

"Hmm. Maybe not. If they are, why hasn't anyone called them away to help with Jupiter and Uncas?"

The Detective signaled with his hands. He pulled the Model 6 Rigelian Hand Zapper from its shoulder holster. Johnson held his Police Positive Special .38 in one hand. At a moment when all the beer workers had their backs to the door, the Detective and Johnson darted into the room, found cover from sight.

Each began an independent sweep along the walls, sticking to shadows and behind cover, the Detective on one side, the cop along the other.

The workers, unaware of the intruders, kept to their business: moving fresh barrels or bags into the room, checking pressure and temperature gauges.

The Detective hunkered down in a nook between two of the massive vats. "Here we go," he said.

On the side of each vat was mounted a pressurized tank. From its valve a flexible pipe fed its contents into the mixture inside the vat. The shine and lack of wear apparent on the framework supporting the tanks—compared to the condition of the vats—made clear that these were relatively recent additions to the vats.

<<What do you suppose?>>

"I think this is how the ingredient is added—the one making everyone act wacky if they've been drinking these beers."

<<Remind you of anything?>>

"I don't need your help thinking about Delta Printing."

<<Or the disaster there?>>

"You are a remarkable source of encouragement and support."

<<I'm here for you.>>

"Hmm."

<<Hey, just what you'd expect from a helping hand . . . >>

"If only you had hands, yeah, yeah."

A low *Boom* sounded from elsewhere in the brewery and sent vibrations through the vat room. The workers—who had, all this time, performed their tasks without speaking—halted in mid-stride, looked at each other. One of the group—displaying nothing on his clothes that signified he held any greater authority than the others—pointed at three of his fellows. The four exited through the door into the rest of the brewery. That left six vat workers, who returned to their duties in the same placid manner they had shown all along.

<<Three to one. Not bad odds.>>

"For someone not physically in the room, you count pretty well, not having fingers and toes."

<<I learned to count in my spare time between mounting cameras and heat sinks.>>

"Gotcha."

The Detective stood, walked up behind one of the workers. He poked the barrel of his zapper against the guy's spine.

The man spun like a top, swatted the handgun away, and slapped the Detective twice, knocking him to his knees.

<<Placid but fast.>>

The gun lay two yards away. The Detective started to move toward it, but his opponent darted forward, grabbed him by the arm and back of the collar. He heaved the Detective up, around, and tossed him against the side of a vat.

<<Ooh, strong. And fast.>>

"Ungh."

The Detective fell to the floor.

The other workers went about their business, either oblivious to the Detective and his thwarted attack or simply ignoring it. Johnson came out from hiding and waved his gun. He shouted for the workers to stop moving and get face down on the floor.

They ignored him, too.

He glanced at his partner, then started toward the worker who was again approaching the Detective.

"No!" the Detective croaked.

Johnson backed away, just as the worker grabbed the Detective—who, in turn, grabbed his attacker.

Electricity crackled from the Detective's gloves. Blue fire arced and danced around the worker's form. He remained silent, grimaced, and tightened his grip on the Detective.

Smoke began to rise up from his hair. His muscles contracted, a blue-fire rictus widened across his face. His eyeballs burst, flame jumped from his empty orbits, and his flesh bubbled.

All this while, Johnson had hollered at the other workers in vain. Now the crew turned and noticed the tangle between the Detective and their colleague, who was in the midst of slowly combusting. As one, they began to stride toward the duo.

Johnson continued to shout: “Stop! Stop!”

When no one heeded, he started pulling the trigger.

First, he hit each of the five in the torso with a single shot.

Each figure staggered, but kept to his feet. One continued toward the Detective. Four turned and approached Johnson.

“Hell’s bells.”

He fired until he emptied the cylinder, stepped backward while he punched out the still-smoking shells and reloaded. The cop snapped the gun back together, voiced a warning, then emptied the gun again.

The four staggered again from the projectiles thudding into their bodies and blasting an exit wound in the back or ribs of each, but did not stop.

Their approach got quicker.

<<This isn't going so well.>>

The fingers of the Detective’s attacker finally had gone crispy as over-cooked bacon, and they had broken away. His body burst into flame and collapsed in a burning heap as the leg muscles shattered into chunks that fell from the bones and no longer supported the creature’s body.

As the turning-to-ashes form of one worker dropped to the floor, another attacked.

The Detective fell back, rolled away from the new threat’s grasp.

“Any word from Jupiter?”

<<I've had no contact with him since he first showed up. Something is blocking the link I would normally have with him. But you're still coming in strong.>>

“I’m gonna fade fast if something doesn’t turn around quick.”

Besides the distinctive helmet, the Detective wore a suit. It looked like a normal set of clothes that anyone on the street might wear—although the color scheme or pattern was sometimes a bit garish—but its innermost layer actually was constructed to act as a containment suit. In some ways, it served as a sort of second skin for the Detective.

From the office, I activated one of the suit’s features—an energy *pop* that flooded the Detective’s system with a rush of power equivalent to an elephant-sized jolt of adrenaline.

The worker bent over to grab the Detective. The latter pushed up, punched the creature's gut so that the Detective's gloved fist mangled his attacker's internal organs and burst through his spine and out his back. His attacker flailed, flopped backward, and dropped to the floor like a bag of wet sand.

<<Johnson needs help.>>

The cop had seen how ineffective his bullets had proven against these brutes. He had moved to get some barrels and equipment between him and his pursuers. The workers were simply pushing aside these barriers or latching onto them and tossing them aside. Johnson didn't have the stamina or physical resilience of the Detective, and he wouldn't last long against them.

He didn't have to.

With his strength and reactions punched up by the suit, the Detective leaped from his side of the room to slam into Johnson's attackers, sending them sprawling like ten pins. Before they were up, he'd grabbed one by the heels, spun him so that he bashed that one's skull against another worker's head. The Detective flung aside that one, and kicked another who was starting to rise. His shoe connected with the fellow's ribs, and the brute flew up and crashed into one of the beer vats. He slid to the floor, his limbs zigzagged in unnatural directions.

The two other workers were up by now, charging the Detective from opposite sides. Before they reached him, his hands flashed out, grabbed the two by their throats, and slammed them together at an even greater velocity than they had achieved. The resulting sight wasn't pretty, but the two attackers were down for the count. Permanently.

The suit's accelerating effect doesn't turn off like a switch in the same way it can be initiated. It has to wear off, as the Detective's biology metabolizes the agent introduced by the suit.

His heightened senses required only half a second to determine that Johnson was upright and relatively unharmed. Then the Detective dashed out of the room, on the way to create more mayhem.

He doesn't rely on the accelerating agent very often. Its results tend to be a tad violent.

The Detective attacked the room—that's the best way to describe it. His fist bashed the jaws or ribs of the brewery workers he encountered—all of them burly fellows like the ones working the vats—and each crumpled to the floor, out of the fight. He nabbed a two-wheeled dolly, swept it about like a bludgeon, destroying barrels of ale, casks of beer, and wrecking equipment all along his path.

Johnson took one look from the doorway, his eyes got wide, and he stepped into the room more slowly than he'd approached the entry. His gun was up, and he was alert for any movement from any suddenly appearing brewery workers.

The Detective rushed from room to room, a juggernaut who slammed down brewery workers on their way to the racket from the front of the building before they were aware someone was rushing them from behind. He left mangled brewing equipment in his wake, plus surges of beer spilled from cracked containers that flooded the floors with foam.

The noise he caused in the bottling room sounded like thunder from Ragnarok. Islands of shattered glass stood up from amber waves of ale rushing toward the floor drains.

The Detective arrived at the front entrance hall of the building.

A remarkable battle was in progress.

Uncas and his Harlem cops were tangled in hand-to-hand combat with a small mob of sturdy brewery workers. They had already emptied their handguns during the fight, and now they used their Police Specials as clubs, hammering at the brutes attempting to throttle and break the attacking policemen. The cops were a valiant group: they were battered and bleeding, but they kept up their share of the havoc among the brewery's defenders.

A larger crowd thronged about a giant naked warrior—Jupiter. The workers swarmed and leaped onto the pile of their fellows like a colony of ants working to overwhelm a single scorpion. Jupiter bellowed and sang like some operatic gladiator. He reached, gripped one worker by the belly, and swung the figure like a rag doll to bludgeon the other battlers. He roared, slammed about, slapped and slugged. His attackers fell back, flew into the air, collapsed and were trampled by their peers. The thump of blows and the sound of cracking bones could be heard over the uproar and Jupiter's shouts, but all the while the brewery crew remained voiceless.

The Detective rushed to Uncas and the cops. He pulled the brewery brutes away two at a time and pummeled them senseless. He slapped and swatted away the last of them off the cops. One broke his legs when he struck the wall. The Detective kicked another and stove in his ribs. A roundhouse broke the jaw of the last of the small giants, who staggered away from the fight with blood streaming from his nose. He trotted back into the brewery's interior.

The Detective helped the cops and Uncas to a wall, where they leaned to catch their breath. All three used the opportunity to reload their guns, keeping their eyes on Jupiter and the main event.

"Thank you," whispered Uncas.

The Detective sagged, his shoulders slumped. "You're welcome," he gasped in reply. The energy burst had been depleted. "Whew."

Uncas nodded toward the melee surrounding Jupiter. "What is he?"

"He, uh—"

<<Magician. You said he was a magician.>>

"Stage musician. Magician. He's a stage magician."

Uncas glared at the Detective. "You just saved my life." He paused. I didn't need the Detective's analysis of Uncas' personality to know how difficult it would be for the chief inspector to admit an obligation to someone with whom he shared such a problematic relationship. "But if he is a magician, I am a Viking."

<<Oh yeah.>>

The Detective looked back at the destruction he'd left on his rampage through Hell Gate. "Where's Johnson?"

<<Nice diversionary tactic.>>

As though awaiting his cue, Johnson appeared from the recesses of the brewery. He pushed a two-wheeler on which he toted one of the tanks that had been mounted to a brewing vat. He paused when he saw the mad scramble going on around Jupiter. Then he spotted Uncas and the others against the wall, who waved him over.

Johnson's left cheek was swollen so that his eye was nearly closed. Blood dripped from his nose. He huffed as he settled the two-wheeled dolly and its load, then turned to watch Jupiter like the rest. His uniform trousers were wet to the knees, and smelled like . . . well, a brewery.

"Is everyone okay?" he asked.

Uncas answered for the group: "We are fine."

Johnson watched Jupiter for a few moments, then asked, "What is going on over there?"

Uncas spoke again. "Our new friend is breaking the spirit of some angry men who do not speak. He also is singing off-key. He seems to be having a thrilling time."

Johnson watched a moment more, then nodded. "Okay." He took a seat beside one of his companions from the Harlem precinct, a man named Jones.

"Ed," Jones said, "you look like you tangled with an irate husband."

"Not that bad," Johnson said. He didn't take his eyes off Jupiter. "But Mr. Helmet here kept it from getting worse."

"That is another question," Uncas said. He was getting his wind back, and his voice was getting stronger. "Just how did you manage all those remarkable feats against those several men who were attacking us? We were having difficulties as a group, yet you swept in and tossed them aside as if they were truant school boys."

<<Clean living and a balanced diet.>>

The Detective cleared his throat. His voice was raspy. "Adrenaline, maybe. Perhaps the continual anxiety from the general situation of the last few days, and the particular condition of the city today—some sort of physical release in the fight, boosted my reaction." He didn't look at Uncas, but he didn't have to do so to know the sort of expression the chief inspector had turned on him. "I guess."

<<That was certainly one of your better performances. Should you pull Leo Malet out of your pocket now?>>

Ed Johnson said, "He really is naked, isn't he?" He referred to Jupiter. There was a tone of awe—and perhaps incredulity—in his voice.

Jones asked, "What did you bring us?" He pointed his chin at the two-wheeler.

Johnson answered, "Tanks like this were hooked up to the brewing vats. Thought it might tie in to whatever's going on with the people out in the streets."

Uncas nodded. "Good work. You actually brought in evidence. You might have the makings of a detective."

Johnson grinned despite the blood and injuries.

"Speaking of detecting," the Detective said as he staggered to his feet, "I wonder that no one else is showing up from inside this castle. It's big enough to hold a lot more than just this crew of bruisers throwing themselves at Mr. Jupiter's fists."

Uncas pushed up to stand by the Detective. "Let us go." He glanced at Jupiter. "He does not need any help."

The pair headed toward the center of the complex. They kept a lookout for any threats. Uncas carried his pistol in his hand.

At a staircase, they ascended.

Behind a door at the top, a reception area funneled to a hallway lined with offices. The place was apparently abandoned. The office doors hung open.

The two checked through the offices, finding little but order forms and notepads with cryptic jottings. In the largest office at the end of the hallway, they found records of shipments. For the past few months, according to the files, orders for Hell Gate products had been increasing.

Uncas dropped the sheaf of papers to the floor. He frowned, sniffed. "Notice the dates on the forms? No one has been in this office for . . . days? Weeks?"

The Detective pointed at a calendar on the wall. The top half depicted a half-dressed young woman sitting on a shiny motorcycle. The bottom half carried a grid of dates for the preceding month. Only the squares for the first week of days had been marked with an X for each date.

"Looks like you're right."

<<From the clues, looks like he deserves his rank.>>

Uncas blew out a long breath.

"None of those workers attacking your friend even tried to use a weapon," he said.

The Detective nodded. "That tank Johnson brought out. If that's what we think it is, and they've been exposed to it long enough . . . maybe they aren't thinking very straight."

Uncas didn't answer, didn't even gesture a response. He looked around the room once more, then stalked out into the hallway. "Where are the rest of the men we saw when we reconnoitered?"

<<They skedaddled somehow.>>

The pair snooped around the factory on other levels, in other sections of the structure that had been added to the castle over the years.

"Nothing." Uncas frowned at the Detective.

<<That frown is starting to look like it may be a permanent feature on his face.>>

They returned to the opening of the brewery, where Jupiter was huffing and puffing beside the pile of vanquished workers.

Uncas said to the Detective, "Tell your magical musician to cover up."

The Detective pulled a tarp from a stack of barrels, hauled it over to Jupiter. "Get decent," he said.

Jupiter responded with a puzzled expression. "Decent?"

<<Tell him he's scaring the locals.>>

Jupiter—a giant next to the Detective—wrapped the canvas around his shoulders like a cloak. The Detective asked, "Can't you tell him?"

<<Nope. Something must be interfering with our comm link. I can't hear him; he apparently can't hear me. The reason I didn't know he was going to show up.>>

"Remember," the Detective said, "you're a magician."

Jupiter grinned. "I've heard that more than once. I remember one night . . ."

"Not now."

The Detective joined Uncas, who kneeled by one of the unconscious brawlers.

"You know what I think?" the chief inspector asked.

"Yep."

The cop pulled aside a torn shirt on the torso of the worker to reveal the man's left breast.

"Hm."

<<Great.>>

Revealed was a scar, evidence of a long-healed branding. The brand depicted a broken rune.

"That was a glorious beginning to what can be a truly wonderful night," Jupiter said. Displeasure made itself evident on Uncas' face as he turned toward the giant. "But don't you have a horrible headache yet?"

Uncas' frown deepened. "What are you talking about?"

"That continual thrumming. Aren't your ears ringing?"

<<Maybe he got hit a few times too hard on the head?>>

The Detective stepped forward. "What do you mean?"

"This, this," Jupiter said.

He held one palm up, tapped out a rhythm on it with the fingers of his other hand.

It was the opposite of the rhythm the Detective had been tapping out for days.

CHAPTER ELEVEN

The Hell Gate Brewery burned.

The Detective stood beside Uncas and watched the flames shoot up into the sky. Uncas shook his head.

"You are no good for my luck," he said.

<<Maybe time to pull out that Leo Malet book?>>

Uncas had entered the brewery again to locate a telephone to call Commissioner Knifetongue for assistance in securing the building and in hauling their prisoners to jail. Before he had gotten more than a dozen yards from the yawning doorway and its pile of brewery battlers, the castle had shaken with multiple booms.

Knocked down, the chief inspector had scrambled to his feet. He pointed at the prisoners—still sprawled in unconsciousness—and began to yell: "Grab them! Get to the street!"

But another blast behind him blew him out the door with a flash so bright the men went momentarily blind. Uncas tumbled against Jupiter, who threw the chief inspector over a shoulder and picked up Jones and Johnson, one under each arm. The Detective pulled the other two cops to their feet, half-dragged one of them, and the group got back out to the street. Jupiter deposited his burdens by the patrol cars. The Detective leaned his cops against one of the cars.

Another explosion—massive, nearly deafening the men, knocking them to their knees and slamming cracks into the cars' windows—caused a large portion of the castle to collapse. The men Jupiter had battered were buried by tumbling debris. Gone.

<<Hell Gate certainly fits its description now.>>

Uncas pressed his lips together so tightly a white ring began to expand across his face from the sharp line of his mouth.

The Detective touched the chief inspector's arm. "There."

<<His luck's not dead yet.>>

The Detective gestured, and Jupiter bounded forward. He lost his improvised cape.

The giant darted past the tangled remains of the fencing, scooped up the tank that had rolled forward with the blast wall, and hauled it back to Uncas and his cops.

<<Now that's magic.>>

Jupiter set the tank on the cracked pavement before Uncas: *tunk*. A small dent was visible near the top of the tank, a few inches from the valve, but the container hadn't been breached, and the entire item appeared intact.

The chief inspector's face relaxed. Slightly.

He spoke to the Detective: "Tell your magician to make some clothes appear. On him."

Jupiter grinned, clearly delighted at the disturbance his lack of apparel caused the police officer. "Chief Inspector, my position is not so exalted that you may not address me directly." He raised one hand, rubbed together the thumb and forefinger in the gesture citizens of New Angoulême would recognize as meaning *gelt*, and without a sound Jupiter's appearance changed: He wore a black tuxedo with white tie, and patent leather loafers. Moreover, his skin now had a pale blue color, his shoulder-length hair turned green, and the irises and whites of his eyes became one color—orange.

He still stood head-and-shoulders over the rest of the men, but Uncas' glare was likely as cold as my home planet's summer, and the chief inspector's ire dwindled not a single notch before Jupiter's stature. The chief inspector stated in a flat tone, "Thank you for retrieving the evidence. That will be helpful. However, I think I do not like you. Magician."

<<Gonna take more than Leo Malet to build this relationship.>>

The Detective spoke up: "Let's get this tank to your police lab—see if the Commissioner has any chemists who aren't under the influence of Hell Gate brews. And we can figure out what's up with this music Jupiter is hearing."

"Not just yet." Uncas shot a withering glance at the Detective. "Your efforts to distract me from learning about your friend are starting to irritate me." He waved at the two Harlem cops the Detective had pulled away from the brewery. "Can you drive?"

The men responded simultaneously: "Yes, sir."

"Take this tank to headquarters. Report to Commissioner Knifetongue. Explain that my investigation continues. Find a doctor, have your injuries tended."

The two left in one of the patrol cars after Jupiter loaded the tank into the Plymouth's trunk.

"Now." Uncas stared at Jupiter, but his words clearly were directed at the Detective. "No more evasion, no more dissembling. Who is Mr. Jupiter? Explain."

Jupiter's eyebrows rose. His smile would have been perfectly suited to the face of a bemused cherub. A blue cherub.

<<Truth or dare?>>

The flames from the brewery flashed light and flickers across the Detective's helmet. A boom sounded every few minutes from the depths of the ruined structure. The scene was eerie—a major fire in the city with no sirens in the air, no fire trucks and hoses in sight. But the conflagration appeared to be restricted to the brewery's compound. Amazingly, no flames were carried to other structures in the neighborhood.

The Detective put his arms akimbo, and one foot began to tap the pavement—the usual tattoo he'd been touching out recently.

He pointed at Jupiter: "He's a bug-eyed monster."

Fleeting incomprehension on Uncas' face. "Pardon?"

"He's a spaceman. A creature from the black lagoon of interstellar wastes. An alien from any number of other worlds." He gestured at the giant. "Look at him. He's a monster."

Jupiter smiled. Charming.

"He's a cop. Like you and me."

Uncas squinted. He stared hard at the Detective, then at Jupiter. Then back at the Detective. "Explain."

"You're a cop," the Detective said. "So is he. So am I."

I wondered if he was going to tell some story about working undercover for the government. Or something else.

Uncas continued to stare. Unspeaking.

"Whatever has been going on with this case," the Detective continued, "and everything lately has been all one case . . . the cockroaches, the murdered cops, the doctored beer, and whatever knocked us on our feet over by the zoo . . . this is not your typical investigation with bank robbers or kidnappers or con men. The runes on the brewery workers—an obvious sign this isn't just a local criminal operation."

"You mentioned an invasion."

"Yes. From space! You're an earth-bound fellow, Chief Inspector, but your people's traditions embraced the cosmos before the Vikings showed up. We're dealing with invaders, but they aren't from across the border, just offshore, or across the ocean. We're talking about invasions from other planets, other stars far beyond the Sun."

Uncas stared at the Detective. A frown slowly clutched his face.

<<Where are those reporters who call this guy a cold-hearted stoic? You've dredged up more expressions and emotions from Uncas in the past week than anyone's imagined he might have for a lifetime.>>

"You," Uncas said. A cold fury colored his words: "After what we have encountered together, all the favors you have asked of me, after the ways in which you have exploited my position at peril of the trust placed on me by my superiors . . . you disdain me so greatly to continue treating me like a gullible fool. I had suspected you might be a special operative for a government agency. The tricks your colleague, Mr. Jupiter, demonstrates in his extravagant manner, merely solidifies my conclusions. And yet you still will not speak to me truthfully. Instead, you conjure this ridiculous fantasy and serve it up with all sincerity as if I were an idiot, a child to be entertained by fairy tales."

Several moments of silence followed.

<<You think he knows *stoic* doesn't necessarily mean *chatty*?>>

Uncas glared.

Jones and Johnson watched, unmoving, silent.

Jupiter continued to smile. Blue. Cherubic.

Uncas spoke: "If you are unable to reveal your true position, your responsibilities, I can understand that. You may simply state that, and I will accept that. But do not feed me foolish lies."

The Detective shrugged. "All right. We understand each other. Can we check out this music thing, now?"

CHAPTER TWELVE

They looked for dogs.

Jupiter heard music no one else in the group could hear.

It matched a rhythm the Detective had been playing unconsciously for several days—in reverse.

The tune Jupiter heard apparently was the same one William Battle had tapped out for the Detective earlier in the evening.

"Let's try the radio," the Detective had suggested.

Jones opened the Plymouth and switched on the dashboard radio. He turned the tuning knob this way and that. Mostly he picked up a mixture of static and dead air.

"Whatever has laid low most of the city has done the same for the folks in the studios," Johnson said.

Jones nodded. "Sad world without music."

"Mr. Jupiter, here," Johnson said, "he hears music. Slide through that dial again."

Jones began turning.

"Slow," Johnson demanded.

Jones complied.

Uncas and Johnson leaned in at the open passenger door. The Detective and Jupiter had their heads by the rolled-down driver's window. They peered at the lit radio grid in the dash as though they could read an answer, even if they couldn't hear one.

"Stop." The Detective pointed. "Roll it back a tad, right there."

Static again. But while the other frequencies had a continuous, unwavering fuzz of sound, the static varied slightly. "Like a pulse," Johnson said.

"A rhythm," the Detective said. "Very subtle."

"It's the music," Jupiter said. "It's what I hear."

"You hear static?" Uncas asked.

"No," Jupiter explained. "It's the same beat as the music I hear."

The chief inspector prodded further: "You hear it now?"

"Yes, yes, I've heard it all night. Since I arrived—" the Detective poked him with an elbow, "in town."

<<I don't hear it. I don't pick up anything like that from any of our communications equipment, either.>>

Uncas pointed at the Detective. "You keep tapping out that tune."

"No, mine's different," the Detective said. "Like this." He demonstrated on the car hood.

"Reversed."

The Detective nodded.

"So," Uncas said, "maybe you hear it, but don't realize it. Maybe you're hearing it and just getting it mixed up inside your helmet, and you tap it out backwards."

"Why can I hear it, and no one else here can? Except Jupiter."

Uncas straightened and eyed the giant. "Mr. Jupiter has demonstrated he has a number of inexplicable and interesting talents. Skills, perhaps. Maybe he is sensitive to the music in a way that we are not." He turned to the Detective. "You have an assortment of tricky gadgets. I know that from surveillance. Perhaps your helmet is not just a disguise or gimmick. Perhaps it is full of gadgets. And perhaps you hear the music, too."

<<The chief inspector seems to keep close watch on you. He must be your biggest fan.>>

The Detective remained silent for a moment. Then he said, "It's being broadcast. Apparently it has been broadcast for some time before the event that turned the city upside down. Maybe for weeks before."

Uncas nodded. "The Black Commissioner had heard it."

"As an instrumental piece on the radio, like I had," the Detective said.

"Camouflage," Jones interjected. "Whoever is sending out the signal wanted to make sure everybody heard it, so if you hear a piece of music on the radio, you can say, 'Oh, that's why that tune is stuck in my head.'"

"It's being broadcast," the Detective repeated. "But everyone who's been doped by the Hell Gate beer is out in the street acting goofy. No one is listening to a radio."

Jupiter frowned. "So? I can hear it without a radio device."

"We've already made the point that you're . . . different," the Detective said. "But the people wandering the streets. What do they . . ."

"The beer," Johnson said.

"The beer," Uncas said. "If the beer was, indeed, tainted in some fashion, resulting in the population's current behavior . . . perhaps they can hear this music."

"Without radio," Jones said.

"Aye." Uncas nodded. "The music and the beer together have reduced or changed the mental capacities of everyone who is wandering the streets."

The Detective was tapping the car hood. Uncas and Johnson looked at him. He grew aware of what his fingers were doing, and he stopped. "We have to find out who's broadcasting this stuff."

"Where?" Jones asked.

<<How do you track a sound you can't hear? Not even a bloodhound would work for this.>>

"Dogs," the Detective said.

Uncas looked at him. "What?"

"Dogs," he repeated. "Everyone—nearly everyone—is running around crazy in the streets. They aren't feeding themselves; they aren't feeding their pets. But havc you seen any dogs running around loose?"

"Just those packs of crazy kids," Johnson said.

"No dogs," Uncas said.

Jones tapped the steering wheel, then stopped. "Dogs hear things people can't. Maybe the dogs hear this music."

The Detective nodded. "Find the dogs, find the place the music comes from."

The chief inspector looked around, focused briefly on the blazing ruins of the Hell Gate castle.

"How will we find all the dogs in this town?" he asked. "We will have all of New Angoulême to search."

"Listen for the howls and barks," Johnson said.

Uncas scoffed. "The city is huge. The music may not even be broadcast from the city."

Jupiter laughed. "I know how to find the dogs," he said.

Then he barked.

CHAPTER THIRTEEN

Jupiter bounded along the street.

He had started trotting away from the burning castle in the direction from which he had arrived earlier. He passed into a cone of darkness between two streetlights—one broken and unlit from the Hell Gate blast—and emerged changed in the light from the next lamp.

Jupiter was a dog, massive as a normal-sized horse and rushing along, the tuxedo gone. But the animal's coat was blue and glossy.

"Easy to follow a blue dog," Jones said, a bit of awe in his voice.

"Keep him in sight," Uncas ordered.

They filled the car. Jones drove. After a three-point turn, the Plymouth wheeled along Jupiter's trail.

Uncas and the Detective sat in the rear of the car. The chief inspector stared hard at the Detective, who pretended not to notice by sitting forward and peering through the cracked windshield.

"Look at that dog go," Johnson said.

Jones whistled. "I'd bet on him in a race."

"I thought you weren't a betting man," Johnson said.

"I'd allow a change for that blue dog."

The beams from the car's headlights hopped across tangles of wrecked automobiles and debris pushed aside following Commissioner Knifetongue's order to clear routes through the city. Shadows thrown from these heaps by the Plymouth swooped across the face of darkened buildings.

Johnson twisted his head around, following something from the corner of his eyes. "This is all like some giant haunted house."

Jones nodded. "Where's the Army? How can this happen with nobody noticing?"

"Maybe there's a blockade," his partner said, "and they can't get in."

"Can't blockade a plane."

<<It could tie in to the reason I can't communicate with Jupiter as I should.>>

"A jamming device, blocking communications," the Detective said.

"That might be part of it."

Uncas grunted.

"Listen," Johnson said.

The windows were down, and a sound could be heard over the noises of the engine and tires and the whipping wind. It grew louder.

"Damn," Jones said. He glanced at the Detective in the rear-view mirror.

"Howling."

Uncas sat up, leaned forward. "Dogs."

Thousands of them. All shapes, sizes, colors. All baying and howling and barking.

Uncas shook his head. "Every dog in the city."

<<This must be the place.>>

The car slowed and stopped on Broadway between Forty-ninth and Fiftieth.

The canine crowd surrounded one building.

<<Lindy's.>>

Johnson goggled at the sight. "You think they all want a pastrami sandwich?"

The four exited the Plymouth. A giant blue dog trotted over to the Detective: Jupiter.

Johnson jumped back when Jupiter spoke: "Whatever it is, is coming from there." He shook his head. "It's a pulsing sound—I can't really describe it."

"Like this?" The Detective tapped out the usual staccato on the car fender.

"Yes—no," Jupiter said. "Like that, but different. Backward."

Jones whispered to Johnson: "He's a hell of a magician."

Johnson agreed. "Talking dog. I'll go see his show when all this is over."

"Why a restaurant?" Uncas wondered.

<<Not Lindy's. The radio station upstairs.>>

"WJUG." The Detective pointed to the blinking broadcast tower atop the building. "Let's go."

The men waded into the clamoring crowd of hounds. Jupiter led the way, snapping at curs, growling as needed. Some of the dogs tucked tails and cowered, others bristled, but backed away before the giant blue brute. The Detective, Uncas, and the two Harlem cops had their guns out in case the pack practiced bad manners.

At the doors to Lindy's—still, remarkably, intact and closed—Jupiter turned, growled and barked in a ferocious display that cleared space for the men to get through the entrance and into the business.

Johnson locked the door after Jupiter followed him in. The dog bounded for the kitchen, where a cloud of foul smoke poured into the dining room and bar. When Jupiter returned a few minutes later, he was in human form again—seven feet tall now, and his skin was bronze, his eyes orange. He wore chef's whites, minus the toque. "Fire's out," he said, "and so are the stove and ovens."

He joined everyone at the bar. The Detective hefted a bottle of gin. "All the liquor tags and seals are unbroken. The rest," he gestured at the beer sticks, "all Hell Gate products."

Uncas turned slowly, surveyed the overturned tables and chairs, the unfinished meals and drinks arranged on serving surfaces.

<<The Chief Inspector is certainly quiet since leaving the brewery.>>

"Hm."

<<Maybe all that loquaciousness set him back to his stoic mode awhile.>>

"Hm."

<<You're sounding a bit stoic yourself.>>

The Detective nodded. Jupiter pointed, and the Detective looked down at his own fingers. They were playing out a rhythm on the back of a bar chair.

"Okay," he said. "Upstairs."

<<Jupiter's quiet, too. Very untypical. Think it's whatever music he's hearing?>>

"Yes," the Detective said, and he opened a door in a hallway behind the kitchen. A set of stairs ascended to the left. On the right, a door: metal, with a deadbolt rammed home. Its small square window revealed an alley behind Lindy's.

The Detective hustled up the stairs. The others followed.

<<Very strange. Normally I'd say either Uncas or Jupiter would have insisted on leading the way.>>

"The music," the Detective answered.

<<That explains Jupiter. He's hearing, I know, and maybe it's

tangled his thinking some. But Uncas?>>

"Confused."

<<Are you okay? You're not usually a one-word sentence kind of guy.>>

"Hear it?"

<<No.>>

"Pounding." As the Detective climbed the steps—slowing as he ascended—he began to lean against the wall, peering up, sliding along the faded wallpaper. One hand held his blaster. The other moved—from the wall to his thigh, then to the handrail—the gloved fingers continually tapping, tapping.

<<You're picking up the music through your helmet.>>

"All along."

Uncas squinted up at the Detective. The Chief Inspector had heard him speak, even though the Detective had whispered within his helmet.

<<It's not simply radio waves.>>

"No."

<<That's why Jupiter can hear it—heck, he probably experiences varieties of synesthesia we can hardly imagine. I bet he *smells* gamma rays.>>

"Yes." The Detective was going still more slowly.

<<And the people in the streets . . . they hear it, too, even without radios. You think the beer ingredients—somehow they let people hear what the tower is broadcasting because of the Hell Gate brews?>>

"Uh huh."

He'd stopped at the landing before a plate glass door. Painted on the glass in gold and black:

WJUG
Radio For The People

The others joined the Detective on the landing. Jupiter's head bobbed, following some tune the cops couldn't hear.

The room beyond the door was dark. But the bulbs in the stairwell would reveal the newcomers to anyone who may have been waiting inside the unilluminated station on the other side of the glass. Like targets.

Uncas took over. "Spread to the sides."

Everyone crowded to either side of the door in the small vestibule.

The Chief Inspector nodded, and Jones stepped up, pushed the door.

It opened.

Jones' hand snatched up, grabbed a dangling bell hung at the top of the door frame before it jangled.

He pushed the door wider, and the visitors swarmed in, then drifted away from the entrance so they wouldn't present a bunched, easy-to-hit target for any potential ambusher.

Both the Detective and Jupiter could see in the dark. But Jupiter's head bobbed more vigorously than it had in the stairwell, so the Detective stepped to a hallway at the back of the room: the dim light coming through the glass door made visible the thicker darkness of an open door to the passageway facing the intruders.

A soft light sprayed out from atop the Detective's helmet to reveal a series of closed doors—four lining each side of the corridor. The fingers of the Detective's free hand continued to dance.

<<You've been hearing the music for weeks—through the helmet, maybe not even aware you were hearing it.>>

"Uh."

<<The tapping—you've been tapping the rhythm backwards—unconsciously—to undo the effects of the sounds.>>

"Uh."

A band of light lined the bottom of the last door on the left side of the hall. The Detective's fingers stopped twitching. He clutched the doorknob. Before turning it, he looked back at his companions.

And the seven other doors slammed open, each releasing a spines-up shapeshifter who bounded into the hall.

CHAPTER FOURTEEN

<<Oh. It's a trap. Of course.>>

The cops fired their service revolvers. This succeeding only in showering everyone with splinters and didn't slow the Demeter crowd at all—despite its strength and the mass it appeared to carry, a shapeshifter's malleable cellulose had little more density than papier-mâché, so the bullets whisked through their bodies with no real results.

That Uncas and the Harlem partners had time to fire shots demonstrated how slowed Jupiter's responses had turned thanks to the debilitating effects of the music. The Chief Inspector, Jones and Johnson emptied their guns, then Jupiter roared and dove into the clutch of shapeshifters. His fists smashed one into sawdust. His other arm swung like a scythe, caught up one creature and flung it into another, whose spikes tangled with those of the first.

Jupiter's starched white clothes quickly turned to shredded scraps. He battled, naked and gleaming, while the cops reloaded their weapons.

Jupiter's orange eyes glowed, then his hands burst into flame as he again morphed his body to fit his will. He grabbed two shapeshifters, whose crackling shrieks tore at the hearing of everyone in the hallway. Uncas covered an ear with one hand, aimed and fired at the head of one of the remaining attackers. Jones and Johnson added their firepower to that of the Chief Inspector, and the creature's face exploded into chips. Jupiter released his hold on one of the flaming bodies, and it collided with the headless beast, and the two burst into flame. The confined space filled with acrid smoke. Three monsters left.

The Detective had given only a glance to the seven ambushers. He knew Jupiter would swing into action: the mysterious space creature's love of battle was legendary among our corps of operatives.

Instead, the Detective focused on opening the door before him.

<<Kick it in.>>

He ignored me. He pulled a Corbel box from the lining of his jacket, attempted to unlock the door. No good.

<<Kick it.>>

He returned the gadget to a pocket, aimed the Rigelian Hand Zapper and fired. Blue flame zigzagged around the knob and frame of the door. Nothing.

<<Kick!>>

The Detective raised his foot, drove it forward, and the sole of his shoe slammed into the panel near the jamb. The door flew open.

<<Science is overrated.>>

He darted in while the door shuddered on its hinges.

The room wasn't large, but it held a big surprise.

<<Ick.>>

The Detective fell back against the door. "What . . . that . . ."

<<I don't know what its real name is, but I call it a Sklug.>>

I don't know what the Detective imagined he'd find behind that door. Maybe a bank of mixing boards dotted with sliders and little glowing bulbs and dials and black plastic knobs. Maybe some wires, a microphone, and some turntables.

What we found was none of that stuff. Okay, there were some cables and wires. But the rest? Nope.

Instead, he walked in on a Sklug.

It was the size of a sofa. A big, overstuffed, seat-the-whole-family-including-the-inlaws-and-second-cousins-sized sofa.

It was massive, filling most of the room.

It was essentially shapeless, a giant, gelatinous mass.

Skin gray like a corpse. But glowing spots blinked and flowed just under its skin. Or surface. Okay, skin, if you think about the stuff that forms on the surface of gravy that sits in the pot too long.

The glowing lights that moved across its shape were red, yellow, and green—so perhaps they made up for the bulbs that would have been blinking on a technician's board. Two thick cables snaked out of one wall. From the cables, strands of individual wires were unbraided and lay tangled about, but the ends were sunk into the Sklug at various points on its body.

The thing didn't have eyes. At least, not eyes like anyone on Earth would recognize. However the Sklug sensed the world around it, there were no visible clues to the organs involved.

I'd only seen a picture of a Sklug. This was the first one I'd encountered in the flesh. Flesh-like stuff. Aspic.

Sklugs came from somewhere far, far away. They communicated silently—or at least in some fashion no other space-traveling race had been able to identify—so interactions with the Sklugs had been minimal since they were first encountered during some exploratory voyage generations ago.

Clearly—clearly to me, anyway—the Sklug was the source of whatever music or noise was being received by the New Angoulême populace who had been made sensitive to it by the tainted Hell Gate beers. Apparently someone had figured out how to communicate with a Sklug. Because here it was, contaminating the skulls of people all over the city.

Including Jupiter and the Detective.

The latter lifted his blaster. But the Sklug must have done something with its music, because the Zapper wavered in the Detective's hand, then the Detective doubled over as though he'd been kicked in the gut. One hand still gripped the Zapper. The other twitched in a staccato that would have made a professional telegrapher proud.

<<C'mon, get up.>>

"Rrgle."

<<You can do it. Focus.>>

"Gick."

I heard Jupiter roaring in the hallway. The sounds of his fight had subsided, but the rackets he made now were sounds of agony. The Sklug's noises were getting to him, too.

<<C'mon! Tap-tap-tap that thing. Backwards! Come on!>>

The Detective's fingers stopped twitching. They curled into a fist.

<<That's it! Focus on the pain. It's a ball, like a tennis ball. In your head. Squeeze it. Squeeze it down to a marble.>>

"Rrch."

<<Don't puke in the helmet!>>

"Gullllk."

<<Squeeze down that marble until it's a dot. Hold it in your fist.>>

"Uh."

<<It's yours, now. You control the pain. You have it in your fist and you can do whatever you want to with it.>>

The Detective panted a few moments. Then he raised his head, whipped up the Zapper and pulled the trigger.

The spots of color disappeared from the Sklug's skin. It began to glow red. It began to quiver, and whatever agonies it felt were communicated through its strange broadcast. The Detective groaned and leaned to the side, but continued to fire his gun. I heard Jupiter's fists pummeling the floor outside the room.

A fog filled the room. Then sparks danced across the Sklug's mass, and it suddenly deflated.

A big puddle began to cover the floor.

The Detective shouted some incomprehensible syllable and fell forward into the ichor spreading on the floor.

Uncas and Jones dashed into the room. They looked at the smoking mess connected to the wires, then bent and pulled the Detective into the hallway.

A ceiling light now illuminated the space. One of the cops had found its switch after Jupiter had destroyed the shapeshifters. The floor was splintered from the pounding Jupiter had given it. The giant alien lay splayed in the middle of the hallway. Johnson kneeled over him, checking for a pulse at the naked warrior's throat.

<<Wrong spot to look for that.>>

There were shards of crushed cardboard scattered about. I realized this was all that remained of the shapeshifters. Jupiter had done a very thorough job on their attackers before collapsing.

"Ugh." The Detective shivered, then shifted to the side of the hall. He sat up, leaned his back against a wall.

Uncas stood over him. Jones squatted beside the Detective.

"You all right?" the Harlem cop asked.

"Hm."

Jones nodded. He glanced up at the Chief Inspector, then returned his attention to the Detective.

"Still hearing that music?"

Several seconds passed before the Detective answered. "No." A sound of relief was evident in his croaking voice.

"Good, good." Jones cleared his throat. "So. What the hell is going on here?"

<<I love the delicate dance steps in interrogation techniques.>>

Jones stared at the Detective. So did Uncas.

<<Before you answer that question . . . >>

"Before I answer that question," the Detective wheezed, "we need to make sure there are no back-up systems. Something that will kick in now that the broadcast has been interrupted."

"Bombs," the Chief Inspector said. "We need to check for bombs. Places have a habit of exploding when you have been around." He managed to say that without the least trace of ironic iciness in his voice.

<<Are there degrees of *stoic*? 'cause I think he's the tops.>>

The Detective pushed to his feet, his back sliding up along the wall.

"I think he's dead," Johnson said. He still was bent over Jupiter. Even with Demeter sawdust powdering his face, his concern for the giant stretched out on the floor was evident.

"He's not dead," the Detective reassured him. "It's a trick. He's a magician. He practices his tricks even when he's asleep."

Johnson looked puzzled. Jones' face was blank of any expression. Uncas' eyes might have narrowed one hundredth of an inch.

"Listen," Jones said.

Everyone was silent and motionless for a moment. "No howling," Jones explained.

Uncas stepped across the hall and into the room in which the Detective had encountered the Sklug. The puddle had turned to a sticky goo.

"Jones," he directed, "go downstairs, check for anything that looks suspicious." He put his hands on his hips, shook his head. "Including bombs. Johnson, go with Space Detective. Make sure he doesn't fall down."

Jones trotted off down the stairs. The Detective and Johnson went into each of the rooms lining the hall, one on the left side, one on the right.

They met at the lobby. "Anything?"

Johnson shook his head. "Empty, but a chair in one, these papers in another." He rattled the sheets in his hand. "Invoices from Hell Gate

Brewery. You?"

The Detective shook his head. "A pencil, a paperclip, and a shoe with a stain. The stain may be blood, I don't know. It stinks, though." He rubbed his fingers together. "I left it all where I found it."

<<The shoe might be all that's left of whomever the shapeshifters did away with when they moved in.>>

"'*Whom*ever'?"

"What?" Johnson asked.

"Nothing."

<<That's right. Magazines have taught me about keeping the mystery in my relationships and the importance of good grammar. And I'm building my vocabulary every month with *Reader's Digest*.>>

The Detective nodded to the door. "Let's find a way to the roof. Might be worth checking the JUG tower for any other surprises."

"Right."

Uncas stepped back into the hall from the Sklug's room. "Did you find a telephone?"

The Detective glanced around the lobby. "There's one here, where we came in."

"I will call the Commissioner. He will want to know what we have found." He made his way to the phone, picked up the receiver. "I do not know if he will want me to explain what we found." He looked sharply at the Detective.

"We're going to the roof."

And out the door he went with Johnson.

A narrow set of steps brought them to a door, through which they stepped out onto the roof. It was covered with shingle sheets. The Detective paused, held Johnson back before the cop advanced farther onto the roof.

The Detective had been through a lot since waking up to find himself a tiger's lollipop. Despite his remarkable reserves, the physical exertions alone should have been enough to bring him to his knees. The artificial boost to his metabolism at Hell Gate and the vicious effects of the Sklug's music had put him at the end of his rope's ravel.

The sun was coming up. The sky was clear. Rising light was starting to touch the WJUG broadcast tower with gleaming lines.

Johnson and the Detective surveyed the rooftop. Each had a gun in his hand.

Without a word, the two separated, checked out the entire rooftop.

Nothing.

The Detective peered over the edge of the building to the street. The dogs were gone.

He and Johnson converged at a small shack at the base of the tower.

A padlock secured a hasp on its door.

The Detective rapped the lock with the Rigelian Zapper. The lock dropped open.

<<Drastic security measures they got here.>>

He removed the lock, swung open the door.

The shack was empty except for some spiders and a big circuit box fed by two thick metal conduits and sporting a large lever. The lever was in the ON position.

The Detective looked at Johnson.

Johnson shrugged.

The Detective stepped into the shack, grabbed the lever and shifted it to the OFF position.

There was a sudden silence, which meant the investigators hadn't even been aware of a low-level hum that had been emitted from the shack.

"Holy Moses."

Johnson's exclamation was hardly more than an escape of breath, barely audible. But it carried the sense of awe he clearly felt at that moment.

The Detective stepped out of the shack, joined Johnson in peering up into the air above the shoulders of the surrounding buildings.

The sky was filled with dragons.

PART FIVE

Dragons

CHAPTER ONE

World War One was called The War To End All Wars.

That wasn't true.

By war's end, Germany was in ruins. It was relatively simple for the Vikings to take power. These were descendants of the pagan Vikings who had driven their Christian cousins into exile to Vinland centuries ago.

The Norse move into Germany was a natural step in consolidating power in Northern Europe. The Vikings had been insinuating their tentacles of influence into the shambles of the Austro-Hungarian Empire for generations. The Balkans suffered greatly during the War, and the Norsemen welcomed the opportunity to remove any remaining internal barriers to their rule.

The World War had been a bloodbath. After the treaties were signed, the other Western powers were focused on licking their wounds; in private, politicians probably remarked that having an external power take over Germany was a deserved punishment for the country's involvement in the recent hostilities. Perhaps some thought the Vikings would lend stability to the war-rocked Germans. If any forward-looking strategists considered the expansion of Norse influence with misgivings, no one expressed them at the time—or else their concerns went unnoted.

After the War, each nation turned its attention inward to repair and seek a return to normalcy.

So for those who awoke one day to bold, 72-point headlines announcing Germany's invasion of Poland, the blooming of fascism's flower may have seemed to happen overnight. But civil war had been harrowing Spain's countryside for years. Italy's trains had been running on time. And stability had come to Germany with a militaristic nationalism fired by its Viking leaders invoking the country's pagan past.

That dense packet of information filled the mind of every person in New Angoulême who saw the dragon ships suddenly revealed in the sky.

<<Whatever the tower was broadcasting—it must have prevented anyone from seeing the ships.>>

"Even Jupiter and me," the Detective said.

Johnson was too stunned by the fleet in the sky to notice his companion responding to someone who wasn't visible.

A silence like a sort of fog enveloped the rooftop. After all the racket—the howling dogs, the battle in the radio studio, the destruction of the tower—the sudden quiet was uncanny. The dogs were gone. They ran away after the transmissions ceased. No traffic was moving, and none had been moving since the citizens went loopy in the streets. Not even the noise from any of the roaming JD gangs was apparent.

The ships overhead varied in shape and size according to their purpose, but most were lean and long or were designed to give that impression. These craft were intended to instill fear from the time they first were glimpsed approaching. Their skins were black or bronze, highlighted by golden designs: traditional Viking knots, swirling dragons, runic symbols. On the bow of some were painted stylized dragon faces. On others were mounted dragon-head shapes that gave their ships an even more fierce appearance.

<<Now what?>>

"Johnson," the Detective ordered, "report to Uncas, if he hasn't already seen this. Call the Commissioner."

The cop raced away.

"Jupiter?"

<<We're in communication now. He's awake again.>>

"Get him up here."

Less than a minute later, Jupiter joined the Detective on the roof. He was naked again. Pale green, yellow hair flowing in a Mohawk like a stallion's mane. Violet eyes.

<<You're going to have a great run on Broadway.>>

"Quiet." The Detective was getting cranky. "What do you make of this?"

Jupiter snorted. “You’re letting these kinds of advances take place under your nose?”

<<You've got a nose?>>

Jupiter continued: “No one on this planet should have technology for stationary flight yet. There are no rotors on those ships, they’re just sitting in the air like clouds in formation.”

“That’s off-planet technology,” the Detective said. “Someone has partnered with the Vikings—they have a culture of invasion, battle, and conquest. Some extra-system power has taken advantage of that. Given the Norse the tools to exercise their natural tendencies.”

<<That's a quick recovery.>>

“Recovery?” Jupiter sounded confused.

<<From the war. World War Two. Have you been out of the system the past twenty years?>>

“Off and on. Were these Vikings defeated?”

“No,” the Detective said. “The Allies and the Vikings battled tooth and nail to exhaustion. No one could gain a step over the other. Both sides agreed to a truce. A treaty.”

<<Since then, a sort of malaise has set in everywhere. Economies have been in the doldrums; countries have barely cleared up the rubble.>>

“Apparently someone stepped in to help the Vikings get back on their feet, take advantage against their enemies while no one expected it.”

The violet in Jupiter’s eyes swirled with golden flecks. “We need to move fast, before something happens that carries us beyond a point we can assert control.”

“Look!”

The dragon ships didn’t move. But from the belly of those in the front rank, pods began to fall toward the ground, like seeds being sown from the sky.

<<Something's happened.>>

CHAPTER TWO

"Dragon's teeth."

That's what Jupiter called the pods. No one other than the Detective was with him on the roof at the time, but in one of those strange cultural or zeitgeist synchronicities created by mass anxiety or strife, it was a name given to the pods by nearly everyone who mentioned them.

A single pod was large enough to damage any structure it might hit, gravity and the pod's mass removing the need for missile fuel and explosives. Once the thing came to rest, its armored skin would detach in sections and fall away, then blasts of compressed gas would blow the pod into wedges like an exploding orange. Each wedge might fly as far as thirty feet, then open, disgorging a warrior.

From the rooftop, the rending crashes of the pods striking buildings, cars, and pavement could be heard. Earlier everyone's ears were filled with howling. Now the shattering of glass gave the air a brittle quality as windows gave way from the vibrations of the pods' impacts.

Smoke and dust rolled in billows from the strike sites.

The dragon ships remained stationary in the sky.

Jupiter stepped forward, put a foot on the roof parapet as if ready to pounce into the street and take a fight to the invaders. The Detective put a hand on the giant's arm.

"We need a plan first," he said.

Jupiter frowned. The violet and gold in his eyes swam.

"C'mon," the Detective said. "Plan first, then you can go bash somebody."

He turned, went down the steps to join Uncas and the Harlem cops. After a moment, Jupiter followed.

<<That's surprising.>>

"Everybody's had a long day," the Detective said. Even though Jupiter was a creature who continued to survive despite his impulsive nature, the Detective took in stride the giant's going against his usual pattern of behavior.

When the Detective and Jupiter reached Uncas, we learned the plan wasn't much. At least, not immediately. The Chief Inspector said, "Headquarters. We talk to the Commissioner before anything else."

Then everyone left in the patrol cars.

None of them gave the melted Sklug a last look.

CHAPTER THREE

Johnson and Jones rode in the front of the Plymouth. Jones drove. Uncas and the Detective rode in back. No one offered Jupiter a ride. The giant wouldn't fit. No engineer had designed a passenger car to carry anyone with a mass approaching that of the giant.

He leaned to the Chief Inspector's window. "What's the address?"

Uncas stared at Jupiter, then answered.

Jupiter nodded. He looked up at the dragons dropping their wicked seed, then galloped away.

Jones put his foot into it. He kept the sirens off, as Uncas directed. "No need to draw attention from the enemy. We will have plenty before we are through this, I am sure."

The Plymouth piled down the street. Jones slowed as the car ran into the clouds of dust that were rolling from the direction of the dragon's teeth landing sites. Johnson craned his neck, kept a lookout for anyone in the car's path.

Uncas attempted to stare a hole in the Detective's helmet.

"If your friend is a genuine performer," he said, "I am Charlie Chaplin. Every showman in New Angoulême has spent at least one night in jail, and not one of them must be told the address for police headquarters."

<<I know this is getting old, but it might be a good time to pull out a copy of Leo Malet.>>

The Detective was slumped into the contour of the car's worn upholstery. Even a mystery man who deserved a comic book named for him could feel beat down after all the action he'd seen recently.

"Well," he said, then he stopped. His voice sounded as if he didn't have an answer.

Uncas didn't prod, just kept the high-intensity Stoic Mohawk Stare focused on the helmet.

The Detective spoke again: "The world is a funny place, Chief Inspector. It's bigger than your city, here. Bigger than just this world." He pointed skyward, although the rushing dust clouds obscured any view beyond a few yards. "That stuff in the sky," he continued, "that's bigger than Berlin. There may be a lot of technical know-how in Germany and the other Norse lands, but they didn't come up with that stuff alone." He returned Uncas' stare. "If there are lots of people on this one planet, there are lots of other planets in lots of other star systems. That flying Viking stuff in the sky didn't come from Wotan, but from some other planet where maybe Wotan got his start."

Jones kept driving, but tried to watch his passengers in the rear-view mirror.

"Keep your eyes on the road, Jones," Uncas snapped.

"Yes, sir."

The Detective said, "There are cops and crooks here in your city, and all over the world. Same as out there," and his voice had a quality—not the Smile he usually employed, but a ring of authority, of calm matter-of-factness. "One mob on the south side of town wants to move in on some territory on the east side of town. Same as out there. One mob wants somebody else's moon. Or planet."

Uncas leaned forward, just a slight movement. But for a small shift in position, it carried a heavy suggestion of threat. "And you?" he asked.

"I'm no mob," the Detective said. "I'm a cop. Like you."

"Not like me."

"Not here," the Detective agreed, "not for your city. Not according to your rules. But out there," and he waved with a gloved hand out the window in a gesture that encompassed some place beyond the obscuring dust, beyond the reach of the atmosphere and the gravity well for the solar system, "I'm like you. Official."

<<That is certainly a boat load of whale bait you just tried to feed your distinguished colleague. In a cop car, no less. Do you think he'll bite?>>

Uncas neither spoke nor moved. He continued to stare.

The Detective continued: "You'll note I encouraged you from the beginning that something unusual was up. I'll admit I didn't think the Berlin crowd would be involved. I figured it was simply an invasion from another realm of influence. It was clever to leverage the pagan Vikings' existing tendencies to lead the way. Not at all what I expected."

The Chief Inspector finally broke in. "Did you pull this so-called explanation from the pages of those funny books you claim have poisoned the minds of those children running wild in the streets?"

<<I'd hardly call this matter *funny*.>>

"You saw the evidence," the Detective argued. "Certainly you *felt* the evidence when that robo-roach took a chunk out of your leg. You wouldn't have known about the imposters in your ranks without my investigation. Clearly something in the ink on those comic books made those kids and others go crazy. And you saw with your own eyes what we found at Hell Gate. AND the radio station."

<<Pinch his nose for good measure. That'll teach him. The big bully.>>

Uncas could create the impression of a volcano ready to erupt without changing his expression, without huffing and puffing, without the color darkening in his face. It was something about his eyes. As if, too, his presence somehow exerted a physical force.

"Are you impugning my skills as a detective?"

"No! I'm trying to push you through the membrane of your perceived reality to understand something about a larger reality that's been hiding behind that scrim you see every time you look out your eye holes at the world."

Uncas' eyes narrowed to slits. "What do you see through your particular and unusual eye holes, Space Detective?"

The Detective sighed. "A tired and frustrated cop. Just like the one I know is on the inside of my eye holes." He shrugged. "You wanted to know. You started this conversation. You asked about Jupiter."

<<I think it was less a question, more an accusation.>>

The Detective continued: "Do you have an explanation for those ships in the sky? They don't move, just stand in the air like they're parked on clouds?"

The Plymouth erupted suddenly out of a wall of dust into clear air. Jones stomped the brake pedal.

The street was filled with people. A man in a dented Civil Defense helmet was directing a huddle of women and screaming children to an apartment building. Another group, all men, trotted the other direction, toward the source of the dust clouds. Each carried some sort of weapon: a monkey wrench, a sledge hammer, a revolver, a rifle. Some of the guns looked like military issue brought home from the war. The crowd parted as a fire engine screamed and rolled past.

<<Looks like everyone has left Loopy World.>>

A man came toward the Plymouth from following the trotting men. He stopped at Jones' window. He wore a construction helmet. He looked about forty years old.

"I see the city seal," he said, "but I don't see any cops." He spotted the Detective in the back seat. "Hey, but I know you."

"Chief Inspector Jonathan Brewster Uncas," spoke up the official party in the back.

"Yes sir, I've seen your picture. Sorry to stop you. Taking precautions, you know."

"What is going on?" the Detective asked.

The man frowned. "I woke up, like. There was a pop, and . . ." a wave of confusion passed across his face, "and I woke up from something. A dream, I guess. Compared stories with the guys I found around me. Same sort of thing. We spotted the Vikings in the sky. Started getting organized. Lot of us saw the fight overseas. We know what to do."

"I am sure you do, sir," Uncas said. "Please carry on. We are on our way to Police Headquarters."

"Yes sir, thank you sir. Be careful out there."

"Thank you. What is your name?"

"Barlow, sir."

He saluted. Uncas returned the gesture. Jones put the car back into gear and roared along the now-open street.

The Plymouth pulled up before headquarters. One of Uncas' uniformed cops ran up to the driver's window as the Chief Inspector and the Detective climbed out of the car.

"Hey, you Harlem guys," the cop said, "report over to Precinct One-Two for orders."

Jones nodded; the cop rushed away.

Uncas leaned to Jones' window. "I would be grateful and would consider it a matter of professional courtesy if you gentlemen kept confidential any matters you may have inadvertently overheard from the back seat of this car."

Jones and Johnson both nodded. "Yes, sir."

"You both have been a great help to this city. I am sure you will continue to do so. Please be careful."

"Yes, sir."

Uncas patted the car hood, and the Plymouth rushed away.

The Detective waited at the bottom of the steps leading up to the entrance.

<<No sign of Mr. Planetary Party.>>

The Detective turned this way, then that.

Uncas scanned the street. It was crowded with official vehicles, cops, and mobilized squads of civilians who looked not so far from their military days fighting Vikings. Fire alarms and sirens sounded from multiple directions.

"Looking for your . . . colleague?" Uncas asked.

The Detective shrugged. "I'm sure we'll know when he shows up."

The Chief Inspector nodded. "I am sure that is true."

The Detective started up the steps. "Let's go see your boss," he said.

CHAPTER FOUR

"Whatever's happened doesn't matter." Commissioner Knifetongue glared at every person standing before his desk. "We're at war, and we appear to be on our own."

The room, large and ornate and filled with cops—some in uniform, some in plain clothes, some in very casual wear—breathed the atmosphere of a theater, with Knifetongue on stage. But there was no sense of entertainment. Every man there displayed a posture of tense and sober readiness for action.

The commissioner's eyes moved, his glances touching each face. If the bedraggled appearances of Uncas and the Detective registered, he showed no sign.

"The mayor can't be found," Knifetongue continued. "Federal authorities can't be reached. Ships in the harbor have been sunk by those things in the sky, and an aerial blockade of the port has gone into place. Somehow, we are essentially cut off from all outside help."

He glared around the room. "Our city is under attack. It looks like the Vikings are behind it. The city is depending on us to—"

The outside wall blew inward. Everyone in the room was thrown to the floor.

The Detective was blown through the door behind him and into the commissioner's waiting room.

<<Are you okay?>>

The Detective got to his knees. "Whew. Yes." He was shaky.

<<No sign of fire or explosives. It's like something rammed the building.>>

He staggered through the wrecked doorway into the office. Dust flew in clouds. Men groaned. Most were stirring, getting slowly to their feet. Some writhed on the floor.

<<Knifetongue's huge desk must have blunted some of the force and debris.>>

A ragged hole the width of the room where once had been a wall now gaped out upon the street below. The dust flew out in streams, improving visibility in the office. The Detective found Uncas at the foot of the wall by the blasted doorway. The chief inspector's beret was gone, his coat shredded. A bleeding gash along his left jawline and a rising goose egg over his right brow appeared to be his only external injuries. His eyelids fluttered. He gasped. "Get me up."

The Detective arranged him in a sitting position so he leaned against the wall. "I will be fine. Find the commissioner."

Screams and wails rose from the street outside and mixed with the sounds in the shattered office of the stirring cops. Chunks of splintered wood, broken stone and plaster, and buckets of dust dropped to the floor as men got to their feet and attended to their injured colleagues.

In the center of the floor, a large pile of debris heaved up and settled back. The Detective began tossing aside blocks of stone, broken lath and plaster, and lengths of splintered beams. He revealed a human form, a broad back covered in a shredded-to-slivers coat. Knifetongue.

The Detective heaved away the last of the debris. He took hold of one of the commissioner's flailing arms and helped the man to his feet. His formal uniform was tattered. Blood streamed down his face. His eyes rolled a few moments as he staggered. Then he shrugged, gathered his energies and composure, and shook loose from the Detective's grasp.

Oswald Knifetongue, Police Department Commissioner for the city of New Angoulême, turned and surveyed the room. The ragged points of his mustache bristled. His blood-spattered face grew fierce.

"This by God will not stand," he said. A barely restrained rage trembled in his voice.

He pointed to a patrolman who had appeared at the shambles of the doorway. "Get medical help for these men." The cop darted off.

Knifetongue looked around the room. He stepped to a corner and retrieved a battle ax that once had hung on a wall. Then he strode to the doorway. He turned to his men. "If you can stand," his voice rang out, "you're with me!"

He didn't wait for a response or reaction. He turned crisply and walked in his purposeful way toward the interior of the building.

Men in the room began to stagger out, following. Some appeared to be completely dazed, but with each step their gaits grew steadier.

Uncas had made it to his feet by now. He pushed off from the wall. Before he joined the crowd following Knifetongue, he clutched the

Detective's elbow. "Get to work," he said, then he was gone with the others.

CHAPTER FIVE

From the roof of Police Headquarters, the detective got a better view of the situation.

The dragon ships were launching large objects at the city. Not explosives—just squat battering rams, massive plugs that collided with buildings and caused enough damage to make most structures totter and collapse. Just such a juggernaut had caused the commissioner's office wall to blow to bits—and the building caught only a glancing blow. One roared overhead and the rush of wind in its wake staggered the Detective. The sound of the thing striking a building and the structure's subsequent tumble to street level filled the air with enough noise to block every other sound. Only after a few minutes could the sounds of keening, of shrieks be heard.

A pall of dust swam over New Angoulême, carried upward in swirling columns from the wrecked buildings. Fires were breaking out in many spots.

"Where's the military? The Air Force?"

<<Radio is spotty—apparently the dragons are jamming signals. But any military aircraft in the vicinity have been blasted into powder at their airfields. As for any other military help, I can't get a good answer from the existing frequencies.>>

"Cockroaches, comic books, bedeviled beer . . . now this."

<<Looks like you were right about the diversions.>>

"I hate being right."

He started down through the building. "Can you bring the Studie up?"

<<Could be tricky, could be slow. I'll work on it.>>

"Good." There was no Smile in his voice. I didn't expect to hear it for some time to come.

On the street, a cop pointed at Uncas and told the Detective the chief inspector had a word for him.

Uncas stood among a group of twenty cops, all armed with shotguns and holstered pistols. Uncas was similarly armed. His beret was back on his head. "Your magician friend, Mr. Jupiter, was spotted near Radio City. In the middle of a mob. We're going there now."

A few of the men, including Uncas, jumped into squad cars that remained operational. The rest—the Detective among them—started jogging through the mess in the streets to the music hall. Most were quickly winded, but they kept up a steady pace.

<<Could have offered you a ride.>>

"I'm just a citizen."

Knifetongue had already set up a perimeter with his and Uncas' men around a pile of fighting men—massive, muscled forms swarming over one figure at the center of the heap: Jupiter.

<<Looks like the brewery brawl all over again.>>

"But these bruisers don't appear to be slowed down by whatever the brewery group had been exposed to."

Uncas approached. "You see what we're dealing with?"

"Berlin Berserkers. Just like at Hell Gate."

"They appear to be the only troops on the ground so far. They arrived in that." The chief inspector pointed to a large object across the street. It had the general shape of the building busters the dragon ships were launching at the city, but was broken apart into symmetrical segments.

"When it hit," Uncas said, "it popped apart and these monsters jumped out and went straight toward your friend."

"Like they were seeking him out."

"Yes."

The Berserkers were in constant motion, clambering over each other to get at the purple-skinned giant at the middle of their mob. Jupiter would hit, swing, throw, and punch. If a Berserker was knocked loose from the swarm, he got to his feet and ran back to the attack.

During the war, about half-way through the third year, the Berserkers had appeared. Apparently they were the result of some genetic experiments the Vikings and Germans had undertaken to create a race of Ubermen. A squad of these super soldiers could wipe out an infantry company in an hour's time, with or without weapons. They were nearly unstoppable unless taken out by a direct hit from a bazooka or tank.

"Why are they using no weapons?" Uncas asked. "And why attack only Mr. Jupiter?"

"I don't know," the Detective said. "But let's be glad of it."

Knifetongue shouted and gestured. He and ten of his men advanced on the seething mound.

<<What's he doing? They'll be destroyed.>>

From twenty feet away, the cops started firing their shotguns. Chunks of flesh exploded from the Berserkers' bodies, but they continued fighting Jupiter. If one of the monsters received a shot to the head, it might go down or stagger away from the group. When that happened, a cop would advance and empty his pistol into the thing's skull until its head was a shattered mess and it stopped twitching.

Once the cops used all the loads in their shotguns' magazines, they unholstered their service revolvers, advanced again and began firing into the mass of Berserkers. The latter remained unfazed except in the case of a head shot.

The cops stopped firing. Knifetongue roared and raced forward. He swung the battle ax and hamstrung the closest Berserker. It went down, and the commissioner beheaded it. He turned, and lopped off an arm, then a head. He started chopping at all the writhing forms on the outside ring of the mob.

<<I think I hear Viking blood singing.>>

Finally a Berserker turned and swatted Knifetongue. The commissioner flew in an arc and skidded to a stop at Uncas' feet. The ax went spinning into a pile of rubble.

Uncas bent down. Knifetongue's nose was broken and streamed blood. Red also flowed from a gash below his left eye. His eyes were open, but he was dazed beyond speech. Uncas called over three cops, directed them to load the commissioner into a squad car and get him to the nearest functioning hospital.

He stood and turned to the Detective. Before he could speak, three blasts sounded overhead. Both men looked skyward. Fiery explosions bloomed in black billows alongside three of the dragon ships. Three more blasts peppered the same air within less than a minute.

<<What is it?>>

"The big guns at Battery Park," the Detective said.

Uncas nodded. "Some of the former soldiers from the war must have taken over for the military men usually posted there."

Another round of shells was fired at the ships. But when the smoke cleared, the dragons remained untouched, unharmed. They stood in the air, unmoved and unmoving, like the new gods of the city.

CHAPTER SIX

Jupiter and the Berserkers continued to slug away at one another.

The writhing mound did not move far from where the battle started. Endlessly, tirelessly, the warriors swung, pushed, yelled, kicked, pulled, thumped, and on and on. The sounds of their fighting could be heard a block away.

After Knifetongue had been hauled off, Uncas had stared at the teeming hill of flesh as though hypnotized. "Why are they using no weapons against him?" he asked aloud. He'd asked this before.

<<They *are* weapons.>>

The Detective said, "I want to take a look at the body of one of those Berserkers the commissioner brought down. Okay?"

Uncas simply made a vague gesture with his hand.

The Detective advanced slowly. He kept an eye on the flailing mob around Jupiter. "Make sure I don't get squashed by one of those bruisers."

<<Sure.>>

He examined one of the beheaded corpses. The Berserkers each wore a close-fitting battle suit of some sort of body armor.

<<Didn't help much against a Viking battle axe.>>

"Nope."

Around his torso, each Berserker wore a harness. Basically in the shape of a large X across the chest and another across the back, an octagonal plate was centered at the intersection of the X.

"Seen one of these before?"

<<Not at all.>>

Even without a head, the Berserker's body was hefty. The Detective unfastened the harness, but waved for a couple of cops to help him roll the body free of the contraption so he could carry it away.

Uncas asked, "What is that?"

"I don't know yet," the Detective said. "But I will. I have to go. I need to check on Hammer and Hack."

"Good luck."

The Detective paused and looked at the chief inspector. “Thanks. You, too.”

Then he trotted away.

CHAPTER SEVEN

The Detective found his loyal Louies at the same hospital he'd checked Rory Hack into after their Delta Printing investigation. He and Pete Hammer were helping move patients, directing new arrivals to triage areas, and lending assistance wherever they could do so.

"Boss, what's going on?" Hack asked after handing off a gurney to a nurse.

"Some sort of invasion," the Detective said.

<<Of some sort.>>

"This is all just . . . crazy."

Hammer joined the conversation. "You'd certainly be an expert witness about that."

Hack scowled. "You're lucky I'm injured, or you'd end up in one of these hospital beds, too. If I were at full capacity . . . "

"There's plenty of capacity left in your skull for filling," Hammer said. "But you're better than you were."

<Coming from Hammer, that's almost an expression of affection.>>

Hack ignored Hammer. "What do you need us to do, Boss?"

"Stay here for now. Looks like you're needed. But if things calm down here, find Uncas. He can probably find something for you easily."

Hack looked glum. "I don't think he likes me much."

"Doesn't matter. He'll take whatever help he can get."

He left them calming a mother with three kids, two of whom had been hurt during a building collapse.

<<Where now?>>

"The office."

<<Not much left of the tobacco shop.>>

"We'll try the back door."

<<If you can get to it.>>

The good thing about the office not actually existing in a building: if the building was inaccessible, as the first-floor tobacco shop now happened to be, the office still existed in the Nere, as the Detective put it.

As a precaution, he had placed a secret entrance to the office in the subway.

<<Some of the stations may have collapsed when buildings came down.>>

"We'll take a look."

Rubble was piled up before the entrance to the Forty-Seventh Street station. The Detective clambered over broken stone and concrete, twisted metal and shattered plywood. He moved slowly down the cracked steps. A beam of light from his helmet cut through the dark. Dust swirled in the ray of light.

The station was a shambles. The platform was a bigger mess, littered with shattered tiles from the walls and crumpled ventilation ducts, broken glass and dripping water. A single light bulb at the far end of the platform flickered into life occasionally. Debris covered the train tracks.

Midway down the platform was a door to a maintenance closet. The Detective used his Corbel key to unlock the steel door and entered into a brick-walled room. A dark niche was situated on the left side. The Detective stepped in, touched a particular brick. He took his next step away from the niche and his foot came down inside his office, just as if he'd walked through the door.

<<Home sweet home.>>

The Detective opened the file cabinet and dropped the Berserker harness into the Lab file folder.

"Look over that harness. I'm going to visit Ronnie."

<<Give him my best.>>

He had already slithered into the drawer.

When he faced Ronnie, the two were seated in upholstered chairs, leather-covered and comfortable. Or so it all seemed thanks to the cocoon in which Ronnie swam. A pitcher of lemonade and a pot of coffee sat on a low table between the two.

"What will you have, Ronnie," the Detective asked, "something cool and refreshing or something that's good to the last drop?"

Ronnie frowned with suspicion. "Nothing, thanks."

<<All of a sudden we're polite?>>

"Work on the harness."

The Detective poured a glass of lemonade and placed it before Ronnie.

"Been thinking about what I said, Ronnie?"

The kid looked down at his shoes.

"Okay, let me ask you this: Who are you working for?"

Ronnie's gaze came back to the helmet. "What do you mean?"

"Just what I said."

Ronnie tilted his head. "You told me I was working for pirates."

The Detective nodded. "That's right."

"Am I supposed to be working for someone else now?"

"You tell me."

"Hyrnavians."

"Yes."

Ronnie's frown didn't go away. "What do you mean?"

"You asked that already. Who did you report to? Who told you what to do?"

Ronnie's expression clearly showed he thought this line of questioning was some sort of trick. "You know. Gelinda."

"Yes, you're right, I know. Gelinda. Who else?"

Ronnie leaned back and shook his head. "That's it."

"Nobody else?"

"No, man."

"Always one-on-one? Always alone?"

"Yes, alone. Just her and—" Ronnie turned his head and stared at something over the Detective's shoulder. Something only he could see. "Wait. Once. One time there was another guy. He didn't say anything, just stood at the door, behind Gelinda."

"Hyrnavian?"

"Yeah."

"Have a name?"

"We didn't get introduced.'

The Detective nodded. "Did Gelinda ever mention anyone's name? Like, 'So-And-So wants you to do this'?"

Ronnie screwed up his mouth. His frown deepened as he thought. "I don't think so. What's this all about?"

"Just something I'm wondering." A television in a walnut cabinet appeared beside the Detective's chair. Its screen faced Ronnie, who remained unfazed by the addition to the furnishings. "Here's what's going on outside, Ronnie." Pictures appeared on the TV screen, transmitted from the closed-circuit cameras I had placed in the streets outside the tobacco shop below the Detective's office—rather, where people thought it existed. The scenes switched from street to street, but each showed the confusion, the mobilizing groups with guns, the rubble in the avenues, the broken buildings with smoke and dust drifting from their shattered debris piles. And the final shot focused on the dragon ships, waiting in the sky.

Ronnie stared. The Detective said nothing, just let Ronnie absorb the scenes on the TV.

Finally, Ronnie spoke up. "What is that?"

"It's the city, Ronnie. All of New Angoulême. Every borough, every block. Including your street, Ronnie. Your *home*."

Ronnie's face paled beneath the shifting light from the TV.

The Detective stood. "I have to go, Ronnie." He gestured toward the TV. "Good thing you're safe in here, huh?"

The Detective stepped out of the file cabinet.

<<Gonna let him stew awhile?>>

"Finished with that harness yet?"

<<Almost.>>

"Get to it, please."

Snippy. Snippy Space Detective won't be popular with the funny book crowd.

CHAPTER EIGHT

The rain of building busters slowed. Every few hours another would slam into a skyscraper and the roar of the structures' collapse followed the boom. After the rumbles subsided, the screams could be heard.

The first round of building busters had destroyed the bridges. All the islands of the city were cut off from one another. People rushed the docks to get away on any sort of available craft. There were riots. People were killed. Boats—all shapes and sizes—sank, overloaded by hysterical evacuees. Others caught fire or were wrecked. Perhaps through misadventure, perhaps because of sabotage.

An occasional round was fired off by one of the Battery guns, but with no better result than the first salvos had after the initial appearance of the ships in the sky.

The day after the dragon ships showed up, a small aircraft was spotted crossing the sky. Its trajectory across the smoky blue was aimed directly at one of the ships. Apparently some financial wizard directed the pilot of his company's private plane to crash into an enemy craft. People watched from the ground as the pilot parachuted from the airplane. His craft appeared to slam into an invisible wall before it struck the singled-out dragon ship. The crumpled plane tumbled from the sky and the ruptured fuel tanks burst into flame before the wreck smashed into a rubble pile in the streets shadowed by the very ship that had been its target.

Near Radio City, Uncas directed his men to circle the roiling mass of flesh that cocooned and pummeled Jupiter. He pointed out one Berserker. All his men targeted that figure and fired their weapons until the figure collapsed, dead or too filled with lead to continue fighting.

Uncas' expression remained unchanging. He picked out another Berserker. The cops reloaded and commenced firing.

Five Berserkers had hit the ground, lifeless, their bleeding corpses reduced to gory chunks by the relentless fusillades. Uncas' men were shooting at a sixth when another of the segmented building busters slammed into the broken pavement thirty yards away. The concussive force tumbled all the policemen off their feet. The buster's segments opened like seed pods from some devil's flower, spilling fresh Berserkers who swatted aside the staggering cops and joined the melee with Jupiter at its center.

Two of Uncas' men were dead. Two more were too badly injured to stand.

The chief inspector looked at the sweating mass of flesh that continually thrashed about.

"Put away your weapons," he said.

"Look!"

Uncas turned to where one of his men pointed. Toward the sky.

A fresh hail of busters hurtled from the dragons overhead.

Each bore segmented pods.

It was the beginning of the ground war.

CHAPTER NINE

I reported what I'd seen through my video networks.

"I want contact outside the city." Space Detective's mood hadn't improved.

<<I can't raise anyone.>>

"Reach out to The Reseau."

<<We're cut off from those lines, too.>>

"Shift the office to Paris."

<<It won't budge. Our only access and egress is for New Angoulême.>>

The Detective said a few words that probably had never been heard on Earth and shouldn't be said in polite company on several other planets.

<<I can't do that, either.>>

He sighed. He set his arms akimbo and remained silent for several moments.

"Are there any more transmissions going out like the Sklug was broadcasting?"

<<Not that I'm picking up.>>

He tapped his helmet. "I'm getting some kind of interference or something. Inputs just aren't clear."

<<Too much wear and tear the past several hours?>>

"Likely." He stepped to the file cabinet. "I think I'll switch it out, look it over." He *shlurrrped* into a folder.

He removed the offending helmet and placed it on a workbench. He picked up a fresh one from a shelf and donned it. He locked it into place.

The Detective disappeared.

<<Hey! Hey! Where'd you go? Hey!>>

No answer.

CHAPTER TEN

[*]
SPACE DETECTIVE LOG
[*] open [*]
ENTRY 3024
[*]

All this mess with the invasion has reminded me how smart Jupiter is.

Nearly everyone in The Reseau thinks of him as a brash and loud blunt instrument: throw him at a problem when brute force is necessary—or a gaudy diversion—and he'll knock down the obstacles like ten pins.

But you don't last so long as he has if you're just a big, dumb muscle with an easily ignited sex drive.

When I was first . . . recruited . . . into The Reseau, Jupiter was the one who told me to keep a log of my activities that was separate from my official documentation, which would be audited by different strands of The Reseau. Something I should keep private and secret.

Based on my recent suspicions, his call was a good one.

A few years back, through some contacts made on the sly through Jupiter, I outfitted this helmet with functionalities for blocking all sensors controlled by The Reseau. Even the connection with my Plutonian Pal In A Jar.

Now I could move about unseen and untraceable.

I really and truly was finally a *private* detective.

After trading helmets, I switched my suit for one tailored with similar trace-fouling features. The other one had experienced more than enough wear and tear the past days anyway.

I tucked a silk brocade handkerchief into my jacket's breast pocket before picking up a spool of fishing line and a few extra gadgets and pulling out a drawer in a cabinet I kept in this supply room. I could use the item stored there to move from place to place without returning to the public office. I opened a file folder and stepped in.

And stepped out into the warehouse containing Ronnie's blast buggy.

It was still there. So was the giant dreidel. I walked around the latter, scanning its surface closely without actually touching it.

I still couldn't make heads or tails of it.

I used the helmet's sensors to sniff for any smells that might be released by the thing.

Nothing.

I boarded Ronnie's impounded vehicle. Everything was as I'd left it. No flashing lights. Empty and dead.

After exiting the craft, I took a big step.

And came down inside my warehouse on the Mohegan River.

I called Federal Agent Van Eckk on the private connection we maintained to keep him out of trouble with his agency. He didn't answer with a hello.

"Where are you? What's going on?" he asked immediately.

"Just what I was going to ask you. We can't make contact with anyone outside the city. Apparently there's some kind of blockade keeping out air and sea support. And the sky is full of hovering dragon ships."

"What?"

"They're dropping ballistic wrecking balls, tearing apart the city. Oh, and Berserkers."

Van Eckk made a noise of deep disgust. "Damned Vikings." He cleared his throat. "Apparently something similar is going on in New Orleans and San Francisco, but reports are just as spotty there. And any military efforts sent by sea or air have been swatted from the water or air by some invisible force. We can't detect any source."

"Maybe something from high orbit?"

I could tell by the silence Van Eckk was pondering this idea. Finally he asked, "What about your pals? The Reseau?"

"They are . . . beyond contact as well." I let him chew on that. "Use your networks of influence as best you can. Encourage them to stay prepared to attack. If I learn something, I'll let you know."

"Roger. Good luck." He broke the connection.

Inside one of the Quonset huts I gathered several components for the frame I'd used to send the cockroach cartons to my NoWhere closet. From one of the coat's side pockets I took a container about the size of two stacked card decks. I flipped open the lid—like the top on a hard pack of cigarettes. Into this little box I fed the pieces of the frame, which were *shlurped* into a smaller, more compact construction by the gizmos in the box. Finished, I tucked the box back in its pocket.

Then I gathered another frame. I assembled it around me in the open space outside the hut. The thing looked tiny and fragile in the cavernous warehouse.

I ran through a few calculations in my head, then took out the remote control from a vest pocket. "Here's to luck."

I pressed the button.

I ended up NoWhere.

Here was the vast closet we used for storing Troublesome Stuff. Such things as the robotic cockroaches Uncas' patrols had confiscated.

It was a room—or a space—that had no discernable walls or ceiling. Everything was a velvety black, even the floor—if it could really be called a floor. There was a surface I could stand on and feel, even if I couldn't really see it. Crates and everything I'd stashed here sat on it. Only thanks to perspective—seeing a box resting several yards beyond a chair—was there any sense of depth when looking around NoWhere. No shadows, no visible light source, although every item I'd ever tucked away could be seen—otherwise, only a depthless black. But somehow I always had the sense of being enclosed when I was here. Weird.

I hadn't visited in a long time, so things were sort of higgledy-piggledy as if a kid had just tossed his toys into a box. I should have taken inventory up here every so often.

Up here. For some reason, I find myself thinking of this place as a sort of attic. It's dark, a little spooky and mysterious.

The chair remains right where it's always been. Nothing fancy about it. Just a straight-back oak chair like in libraries all over the place.

But this one was empty. No one was sitting in it.

I always get my man, I'd told Uncas. But there was one who got away.

He'd been tied in that chair.

I'd brought him here to stew in his juices while I figured out what to do with him. He played a part in a case I was working on a number of months ago. I know time doesn't work here the way it does elsewhere—maybe there is no time here at all, maybe NoWhere is just some type of stasis pocket—but back on Earth, about four hours passed before I returned to the closet for him.

He was gone.

No sign, no clue.

I think someone helped him escape.

Which meant there must be another way in and out of this place.

That realization was slow to come to me. But during the past year, I grew surer of it.

And it came to me one day when I was thinking about taking inventory here. In the closet.

And I was reminded of another closet. From my childhood.

We were visiting family. I was four or five years old. So was my cousin. She lived in this rambling house with my aunt and uncle, and while the adults ignored us, we played games.

On this particular occasion we played indoors for some reason. Maybe it was pouring rain or freezing outside. But one game we played was hide and seek. We took turns hiding and seeking. It was her home, so she knew all the good hiding places, but I managed to find her just the same.

Except once. I searched and searched. Nada. It was as if she had utterly disappeared.

Until she surprised me by popping out from under a bed I'd already checked.

She showed me her secret.

She opened the coat closet by the front door and crawled in, heading to the left. I followed her on my hands and knees, moving around shoes and shoe boxes and feeling the bottoms of coats brushing my back. And my cousin kept moving forward in the dark and I kept following. With the shoes below and the clothing above making for tight quarters, plus the surrounding darkness, I felt a bit like I was crawling through a cave.

And then she opened a door. We crawled out into the room where she'd appeared from under the bed.

I looked at the way we'd come. It was like magic to my young mind. Two separate closets were actually one big closet.

That memory rose up just a few months ago to explain why my prisoner had been gone when I'd come back for him. Somewhere in this big closet, this NoWhere, there was another door.

I just had to find it.

I took the fishing line and tied one end to the chair. Then I started walking away from the clutter I'd installed here and into the empty darkness. Eventually, when I turned around, the chair and other items were no longer visible. I experienced a moment of frightful vertigo—the sort a person feels when he's on a guided tour in a cave and the tour guide turns off the lights so everyone can experience total darkness. Everything is invisible in the blackness; the only sure thing is the sensation of the floor against the feet.

I shook off the sudden sense of falling before I turned and continued walking forward. I had a variety of sensors built into the helmet, but they picked up nothing. No infrared emissions, no temperature changes, no up or down fluctuations, no radio waves—nada. Really, NoWhere was a great name for this place.

I reached the end of the string. I'd walked at least a hundred yards. I wrapped the end of the line around a finger. I turned to the right and resumed walking. With the string's help, I would survey a clockwise circle through the closet until I came across something—or nothing.

I'd switched on the light mounted in the helmet's forehead during my stroll away from the chair. It didn't really help. The cone of brightness seemed to evaporate a few feet beyond me, as if the dark simply swallowed the light. I could raise my hands and see them, or look down and see the rest of my body, and I could see the length of fishing line disappear into the black behind me. That was all.

I had glanced at the string to make sure it wasn't too slack—that would mean I was drifting back toward the center of my clockwise circle and not examining as large a territory as possible with my rudimentary tether.

I turned away from the invisible center of my circle and I froze.

I'd seen something.

A *glint*.

Fleeting, just long enough so that a few seconds after it vanished I doubted whether I'd actually seen it at all.

I moved my head and the cone of light—slowly, trying to recreate the movement that originally revealed the flicker of what I thought was reflected light.

Nothing appeared.

I slowed my movements further, achingly slow, moving my head, then my body, this way and that, trying to see with my eyes and the helmet's sensors whatever might be out there.

Nothing. The blackness remained absolute.

Maybe, I thought, *I was seeing things*. Because I had wanted to find something.

I closed my eyes. Relaxed and focused on my breathing.

After a few minutes I opened my eyes. I looked into the dark. I moved the cone of light.

I saw something.

Again, just a flicker. But I held the light steady once the apparent reflection was caught.

Now what? I couldn't determine its size or distance in this volumeless void—the helmet's sensors were useless for that here. One thing was clear—whatever the thing was, it was beyond the length of the string. And without the string, I would be lost.

I slipped off one shoe and pointed its wingtip toe toward the unknown object.

Then I removed the other shoe. I untied the fishing line from my finger and tied it to one end of the lace of the second shoe. I used a sheet bend, which was good for joining two strings of different diameters.

I made sure the helmet's sensors were attuned to the chemicals and gadgets embedded in the Florsheim now anchoring the near end of my tether. Then I carefully began walking in the direction my other shoe pointed.

I didn't know how far away in the dark the object may be, so if my sensors' readings from the shoe flagged for even a moment, I would return to the end of the lifeline. I didn't want to be adrift in this blank blackness without a marker.

I counted forty steps—about one hundred and twenty feet—when I reached the thing.

It was small, apparently metal, and was suspended about four feet above the invisible surface of the floor.

It was a doorknob.

CHAPTER ELEVEN

[*]
SPACE DETECTIVE LOG
[*] continued [*]
ENTRY 3024
[*]

It was a no-frills knob, brass needed polishing, no keyhole, attached to the blank nothing that made up NoWhere.

I walked a circle around it. When I went around what would have been the knob's door—had there been one visible—the knob disappeared. Just as if something existed between it and me. Clearly something *did* exist between us: It simply wasn't visible or tangible.

Because I'd swiped my hand around the knob and felt nothing. My hand hadn't encountered anything and the helmet sensors hadn't picked up a single sign of any door, curtain, portal, route of egress, nada, nuttin', zero.

But the thing had to be attached to something.

I grabbed the knob as if to open whatever it belonged to. But I didn't twist it.

I tugged it, gently.

It came to me. There was a little resistance, but not much. When I let go, the knob stayed in place, right there in midair.

I looked at it. I grabbed it again and started pulling it back to the end of the fishing line by homing the helmet on my shoes. Once there, I donned the Florsheims and started back to the chair. I put the knob in my coat pocket—again, there was some resistance as I moved it around, similar to that felt when moving a toy gyroscope while it's spinning—and coiled the line around one of my gloved hands while keeping it taut so I wouldn't lose my way in the dark.

At the chair I retrieved the knob from my pocket and hung it on the air again. It stuck in place once I released it.

The knob's presence explained in part how my once-upon-a-time prisoner had escaped. Maybe. And only in part.

Where had he gone?

I unholstered the Hand Zapper, grabbed the knob and twisted.

I pulled the knob's Door open a crack.

I peered through.

Dark on the other side, too.

I clicked on the helmet's cone of light again. The Door's opposite surface was visible, as was a handle. The light revealed a floor and walls.

I opened the door further and stepped through, but kept my arm stretched through the portal and my grip on the knob on the Door's NoWhere side.

Now what?

The helmet light revealed an enclosed space: a small room, maybe five by six feet with a low ceiling. Closed lockers of varying sizes covered all the wall space. A closed door—no, a bulkhead—occupied a spot among the lockers opposite the door I held open.

Each locker door was labeled in a non-English—maybe a non-human?—script. I stared at one label for a few moments.

This was all starting to look familiar.

The helmet's sensors weren't picking up any sounds beyond the closed bulkhead. I stepped further into the room—a storeroom, I'd decided—and left one foot between the Door and its frame to keep it from shutting and possibly cutting off my access to NoWhere. Then I unlatched one of the lockers and raised the lid. Several jars and packages were stored inside. I checked labels on a couple, and I nearly laughed aloud.

I rummaged through some other lockers until I confirmed my suspicions.

I was in the equivalent of a broom closet filled with cleansers.

I needed to know what lay on the other side of that bulkhead. But if the Door closed behind me, would it still give me an escape route back to NoWhere if I needed it?

I took a deep breath, held it, and moved my foot out of the way of the Door.

The Door closed. It didn't make a sound, not even a little *click* or sigh.

I didn't notice the lack of sound. I was busy losing my feet.

Gravity was gone! Apparently NoWhere's influence on Up and

Down disappeared when I closed the Door. My surprise lasted a couple moments, then I activated the Florsheims' tool that kept me stuck to whatever surface I stood on.

My artificial gravity in place, I went back to my original experiment: I turned the knob and opened the Door.

There was NoWhere and the chair.

Relieved and breathing normally again, I closed the Door and turned my attention to the bulkhead.

I took another deep breath and opened the bulkhead.

Nobody in the passageway.

I noted the identifying label for the room on the door, then closed it behind me before advancing along the way, Zapper in hand. I could adjust the Florsheims' pull so I didn't have to struggle with walking but could maintain a normal stride.

The passage had a distinct curve to the right, so whatever may have been ahead of me was out of sight around the bend about ten yards ahead. After walking a few yards, the layout was starting to look familiar.

I thought I could possibly be inside a Dragon ship, but I doubted it.

Every ten feet on the left, a bulkhead interrupted the curving wall. Halfway between each of those bulkheads, one was set into the right-hand wall. I slowly opened the first three of these I came to—nothing behind them but large arrays of machinery and a low humming.

I walked more quickly, confident that I had recognized my surroundings and that hardly anyone would be around to catch me trespassing.

I came to a ladder and ascended.

Once I reached the next deck, I was sure of where the Door had brought me.

The left wall continued the series of bulkheads I'd seen below. Instead of a wall on the right, an open space filled with consoles was visible from where my helmet rose just above the deck level where I'd stopped on the ladder. I recognized this arrangement. It belonged to a particular type of spacecraft. I'd been aboard one like it once before.

It was a ship designed to be part of a network over a vast area—usually for communications, but it could probably have other uses. The entire craft was chock-full of devices meant to support that network, receiving and sending signals similar to the way a chain of semaphore stations moved information from one point to another before electric communication gadgets were invented and widely used.

Such a ship needed only three crew members—four at the most—trained as technicians to keep everything functioning.

Usually padded chairs—or whatever support device was appropriate for a given alien species—were arranged with the consoles in these control stations. But no chairs were visible in the area before me. The technicians deployed here didn't need chairs.

And that explained the lack of gravity: Why expend energy on maintaining something the crew didn't need?

Three Berrybots floated in the control station, flitting from one console to another. That wasn't their actual name, but it's the name I gave them because of their shapes and pebbled skins—they looked like giant raspberries. They were even the same color. They had no visible eyes or mouths or ears. They moved through the air by expelling gas from the tiny fissures between the drupelet shapes that made the pebbled surface of their bodies.

They weren't living creatures, although they had an artificial sentience of sorts that supported their functions as technicians. Berrybots were essentially complex machines engineered to maintain and repair other machines.

They didn't really need an atmosphere except as a medium for their flight, but the technology they maintained probably required a controlled environment for proper functioning.

I raised the Zapper and blasted the three Berrybots. Each one floated to the floor accompanied by the sound of hissing gas.

Up the rest of the ladder and into the control station. A couple minutes to reacquaint myself to the consoles' set up, then I touched two controls.

The console challenged me, requesting an identification.

I entered an overriding ID I'd learned in my training for The Reseau.

A bright flash illuminated the room. I blinked. I didn't know what had happened, and I wondered if my response had fired off some sort of security system lock out.

Surprisingly, a display opened up, floating above a console. The Berrybots didn't need a visible display—all system monitoring happened in their "heads" through a direct feed—but my head didn't work that way. The technologies used here and in other spacecraft were advanced far beyond the need for screens of the type used on Earth for displays, such as TVs, and the information I'd pulled up simulated a three-dimensional projection that hung in the air before me. I could easily move its focus, enlarge or diminish its coverage.

At the moment, the display showed the position for the craft in which I stood.

My ship was one of twenty that formed a loose sphere that enclosed the Earth and the Moon. Each ship was a node between the electronic threads forming an invisible net around those two globes to allow communications or data streams to remain continuous. The ships were relatively small—again, their primary purpose was to function as a purely mechanical component—but that only twenty were required to maintain the net demonstrated their power and efficiency.

I could shut down the ship's functions, but that would be only a temporary disruption: It would create a hole in the net that would last only until someone showed up to turn the machinery on again.

So I decided to disable the ship's functions entirely by destroying it. Again, this was only a temporary measure and a minor interruption, as eventually whoever ran the ship-net would put a replacement into the empty node space. But the disruption might distract the invasion leaders enough to cause them to make a mistake that could be exploited by the Earth-based defenders.

Fingers crossed.

I looked around once more to see if any clues to the meaning for the bright flash might be visible. Finding none, I hustled to the ladder, descended, ran around the curving passage to the ship's opposite side, where another ladder led down to the third and lowest deck.

At the bottom of that ladder, I stood in the ship's engine room.

My engineering expertise was at a pretty basic level, but I'd gone through some sabotage training when I'd joined the galaxy-spanning organization intended to prevent invasions of this sort. I started shutting off governors and reconfiguring power settings and overriding safety thresholds. Once things started to shake, rattle and roll, I'd have about ten minutes to get through the Door to NoWhere and safety before the power plant blew and took this node ship with it.

I completed every monkey wrench move I could come up with, then watched the displays start marching into the red.

Sirens and klaxons started sounding, accompanied by a series of syncopated beeps and boops. Satisfied, I hurried to the ladder and climbed.

I hadn't yet reached the top step when something slammed into the top of my helmet, throwing me off the ladder so I spun through the zero G and hit the wall. I kicked my legs until the Florsheims connected and stuck to the underdeck. I had hardly gotten anchored before something hit me again, this time in the back, knocking me loose from the underdeck.

I flailed through the air and hit the deck.

The Florsheims had just secured a grip and I was managing to stand when I was hit again. I didn't lose my footing, but my shoulders and helmet jarred against the wall behind me. I finally got a look at my attacker.

It was a Berrybot.

I'd zapped three in the control station. This fourth one must've been behind a bulkhead somewhere tinkering with the networking gadgets while I was otherwise engaged. Once the engine room alerts triggered, this technician came to check out the problem. Clearly it saw me as at least part of that problem.

That was a problem.

Because I had a limited number of minutes to skedaddle before this little ship was broken down into its component atoms.

The alarms were going crazy.

I was sure the Berrybot's programming compelled it to respond to those alarms. But so long as I was a perceived threat, it would deal with me first.

I slumped to the floor and played possum.

The Berrybot wavered overhead a moment, then flew to the source of the klaxons and beeps.

I gave it a second, then got to my feet.

"ARRH!"

It had slammed into me again.

I reached for the Zapper.

The Berrybot's drupelets—the little berries that make the big berry—are its tools. Each little berry can expand into a prehensile, shape-changing whatever-the-Bot-needs-at-the-moment to repair a broken module.

Or pummel an intruder with fist-sized thumping lumps.

Two of the thumping lumps hit my helmet while two more hit my gut and another whacked my hand, and the Zapper went spinning away, clanking against the wall and underdeck in freefall.

I reached for the Berrybot. It swerved and swam away.

Three more drupelets slung out and smacked me. I hit the floor.

I got back up, a couple of steps to the thing's left.

The Bot swung and connected, knocking me off my feet. I tumbled through the air. I clicked off the Florsheims, and when I got close to the wall, I turned and kicked off its surface: I was chasing the Zapper.

A glance back: The Bot was coming after me, tendrils extended, hooked barbs rising along their lengths.

I caught up to the Zapper.

Snatched it from its twirling flight.

Clicked on the Florsheims.

Hit heels-down on the deck.

Stood tall.

Aimed.

Fired.

The Berrybot flashed into raspberry jam.

I started running.

A roaring and thumping had joined the sirens and alarms. My ten minutes—about ten minutes—were nearly gone.

I reached the ladder, clicked off the Florsheims, and jumped off the deck, free of gravity.

Reached the next level, turned on the Florsheims again, and hustled back to the broom closet. A roaring had joined the noisy alarms, and I ran faster. I found the correct compartment label and tugged at the bulkhead. A vibration was running through the entire ship, and it took three tries to get the bulkhead open. If not for the Florsheims, I would've been whirling out of control along the passageway.

Inside the storage room, canisters and packets had jumped out of their lockers.

I grabbed the knob, opened the Door.

Stepped through into NoWhere, slammed shut the Door.

Then I blasted the knob to dust with the Zapper.

I let out a long sigh and sat on the chair while I caught my breath.

I was back home.

CHAPTER TWELVE

[*]
SPACE DETECTIVE LOG
[*] continued [*]
ENTRY 3024
[*]

The adrenaline was draining from my system and suddenly I felt exhausted. I slumped and a painful jolt in my side had me sitting up straight immediately. My fight with the Berrybot did more damage than I'd noticed.

I figured my escapade had put the node ship out of action. Even if it hadn't, I had plenty of questions.

Who put that Door to the node ship here in NoWhere?

Why had whoever it was taken my prisoner?

Were there any other secret passages into this place I didn't know about?

Those were just for starters. A really big worry was bothering me: The hidden Door opened into a standard Reseau node ship, which suggested to me that someone in The Reseau—the same policing organization I worked for—had installed it and stolen my prisoner. Among the people I worked for and with—including the Plutonian In A Jar—who could I trust now? And who could I not?

The NoWhere closet was a good place to hide and think and ponder these questions. But I needed to get back to New Angoulême to see what had happened while I was snooping aboard the node ship. From my coat's side pocket I took the flip-top container and released the pieces of the transport frame. I assembled it around me, then took out the remote control from a vest pocket and pressed the button.

I was back in my office's repair shop.

I switched my suit and helmet for a normal set. I hesitated a few moments before doing so, because as soon as I did, I'd be reconnected to my Plutonian Pal.

But I didn't see a way around it.

[*] close [*]
ENTRY 3024
[*]

<<Hey! Where'd you go? Where've you been? What happened?>>

"I was pondering our dilemmas and considering opportunities. I only just realized I hadn't heard from you for some time, so I checked my helmet. Turns out to be defective. So I replaced it, and here I am."

The Detective stepped out of the file cabinet into the main office and caught his breath.

<<You're hurt.>>

I ran a scan through his suit's tools.

<<You've got a cracked rib. Maybe two.>>

"Must've gotten hurt more than I knew during the fight at the brewery. Or the radio station. Or the commissioner's office. Or—"

<<There've been plenty of opportunities. Step into the medical lounge. We'll wrap your ribs.>>

The Detective pulled up the proper file folder and stepped in. He was quieter and shared less snappy patter than usual. Whatever he'd been pondering while he was incommunicado had put a damper on his personality.

Afterward, he sat in the captain's chair at his desk and brooded. I kept quiet and watched videos of the battles in the streets. He finally broke the silence: "This mess in the streets—this invasion with the Vikings getting help from, well, the Hyrnavians—this is unprecedented, isn't it?"

<<In my experience? Yes. But I've only been part of the organization just a little longer than you've been.>>

He was quiet a time before asking, "What would Barzello do in this situation?"

Barzello—there's a name that didn't come up often.

While Jupiter worked in this sector of the Milky Way and served as a sort of Dutch uncle to the Detective—although sometimes his advice could be boiled down to "Go ahead and do what you want, then ask forgiveness later," Barzello was the Detective's original mentor in The Reseau. It—Barzello belonged to a people who changed sex according to interesting biological cycles, so calling him *he* or her *she* wasn't always correct—worked out of the Tau Ceti station and was rarely in the Sol neighborhood, so had assigned Jupiter as the Detective's advisor in various matters.

<<What would Barzello do? Yes, that's a good question.>>

"Is it possible to reach him? Can you contact him?"

<<I'm still cut off from The Reseau communications network.>>

"You don't have some sort of back-door, secret way in? A separate hotline to your bosses?"

<<They're your bosses, too. And no, I don't.>>

"No cocoanut telegraph? Morse code? Smoke signals? Semaphore?"

<<No, no, no, and no.>>

"So you can send no messages. And you're not receiving anything?"

<<Correct.>>

"Okay." The Detective left the desk and stepped into a file folder. He soon had exchanged his clothing for a combat suit and battle harness with pouches carrying plenty of Zapper charges. The Florsheims were switched out with a pair of heavier boots. The Detective put a spare helmet and other supplies into a pack he slung across his back.

<<Never expected you to be wearing that gear.>>

"That makes two of us." He returned to the main office. Before he fuzzed over to the secret entrance installed along the subway rails, he said, "I'm off to work. Keep tinkering with that Berserker harness."

Then he was gone.

CHAPTER THIRTEEN

The Detective found functioning automobiles or hitched rides from militia vehicles—which not so long ago had been taxis and delivery vans and freight haulers—to the various hot spots in the city: places the locals were having slugfests or gun battles with the invading Berserkers. Booms and rattatats rattled through the city. Columns of smoke and dust rose and joined the aerial shroud that hung over everything happening in the streets. Fires roared while consuming entire blocks; sirens wailed and fire companies not engaged with fighting the Berserkers tried to control the flames.

The Detective managed to get to the warehouse holding Ronnie's rocket. Inside, he made a tour around the giant dreidel. It remained an inert mystery.

He climbed inside the blast buggy. He removed the back pack and sat it on the deck before dropping into the pilot's chair.

<<What are you expecting to find?>>

"I don't know yet. I keep looking, but I haven't found it yet."

He reached for some switches on the console. He hesitated a few moments, then he touched the buttons in a particular order.

<<Hey!>>

He'd disappeared again.

[*]
SPACE DETECTIVE LOG
[*] open [*]
ENTRY 3025
[*]

I hadn't expected to file another entry so soon, but that's how things happen sometimes.

I felt compelled—by something I couldn't identify—to return to Ronnie's blast buggy and enter a particular code on the control console.

When I did, I felt separated from the Plutonian connection—he'd been locked out of my helmet and network in some fashion—and I felt a mental release, like something was unlocked in my mind. As if I'd closed a circuit and something was flowing freely that had been restrained by—I didn't know what.

That isn't very clear, is it?

Once I punched in the code, a floating display appeared over the buggy's console.

It showed Barzello.

This was surprising. While seeing his face was unexpected, it was a relief to see him. At the same time, Barzello's appearance generated some anxiety, because he was part of The Reseau, and I had a strong feeling that the organization was complicit in the invasion happening outside the warehouse doors.

"Congratulations!" Barzello said. "You figured out how to reach me!"

The Plutonian says it's not correct to call Barzello he, because sometimes he's a she. But the alien in the display was currently in his male aspect. And most of the time he was mentoring me, Barzello had been in his male aspect. So I habitually called him *him* and considered him male. Well, except when he wasn't.

Barzello belongs to a people he calls the Mazzas. He's humanoid, with blue skin and green freckles around his ear flaps and top and back of his skull—essentially where humans would have a head of hair. His almond-shaped eyes are yellow.

"You're looking for answers," he said, "and I have some, but not all." His face showed a brief smile.

"Let me explain. This is a recording. If you are seeing this, you've succeeded in maneuvering through some of the difficulties I'm sure are now besetting your part of the world. In that case, my confidence in your skills is vindicated."

I wasn't sure where this was headed, but I couldn't ask a question. I just had to wait and hope the information I received would resolve at least some of my puzzles.

Barzello continued, "I put that Door in the static area you call your closet. I also took your prisoner from there. I have reasons for that, but you'll have to wait to hear them."

What else could I do?

"I made sure your prisoner was unconscious when I removed him from your closet, because I didn't want him to know how I released him. That's why I hid the Door in a storage room on a node ship. No one would look for a Door in a node ship. And that particular ship had only artificial—eh, I think you call them Berrybots. No true sentients were ever aboard. Except me, when I needed to use the Door. And I was an acceptable visitor, because I belong to The Reseau, which owns the node ship."

That explained one mystery—the Door and its location on a node ship.

"If you entered any kind of override code while you were aboard that node ship, the ship's systems were programmed to load a mission through your helmet into your brain. You may have seen a flash of light, but that was just the mental shock of receiving that burst of data. The mission: return to Ronnie's ship and enter a code to open this message."

Okay, boxes checked for a couple more mysteries.

"If you've been on Ronnie's ship previously—and I'm sure you have, because I know the kind of detective you are—the control console blinked some lights at you. That loaded an earlier code into your systems compelling you to visit the NoWhere closet and seek the Door I'd hidden there."

Check.

"If you're still listening to this, I appreciate your patience. Because you've got an invasion disrupting your home."

Disrupting isn't the word I would've used. But Barzello's an alien, so I cut him some slack.

"The secrets and subterfuge I've used to get you to this point are confusing, I know. But I've used them to protect myself and others in The Reseau. And I've used them to protect you as well."

He took a deep breath. "The Reseau has a noble purpose, and it's performed its duties well for more years than I've been alive, and long before my fore-broods were born. Yet some members within the organization see its mission through different eyes. They see balances and imbalances of power, and they see ways of redistributing and leveraging power by using The Reseau's resources. So they have allowed the Hyrnavians to collaborate with the Vikings on your world to shift the balance of power dramatically. And they have supported these efforts by supplying resources, such as the node ships, flaunting The Reseau's foundational orders.

"So I and some others are working to confound their work. We appear to be in league with their plans, but we are serving The Reseau's true mission covertly. While I apologize for the—what did you used to call it?—ah, I apologize for the 'smoke and mirrors,' but they are necessary for us to succeed in making our internal foes fail."

Barzello scowled. The blue skin around his broad nose paled as his flesh grew tight across his face.

"It is still probably difficult for you to trust my words. Perhaps this explanation appears to be just another means of twisting words and work." He shrugged. "I could load another compulsion into your systems—similar to what your Earth showmen call a post-hypnotic suggestion—but that would defeat the intention of this message. I need you to believe me, my friend. And if you can't believe me without artificial manipulation, my work has failed."

He held up a hand, a Mazzan gesture of respect and affection. "The coding of this message has circumvented your Plutonian partner's connection. You may rely on it to do your bidding, but know that its allegiance is to The Reseau—which facet of the organization that may be, I'm not sure.

"You may depend on Jupiter. He has been a member of The Reseau since its founding, I believe, but he is fiercely independent and his integrity is unshakeable. He will be true to what is just."

Barzello lowered his hand and smiled.

"Even though your connection to The Reseau's network has been cut during the playing of this message, I'm sure your training has led you to record it in some sort of private journal. That's fine. But for the next part of this message, that connection, too, will be severed."

[*]
SPACE DETECTIVE LOG
[*] interrupted [*]
[*] reset [*]
[*] interrupted [*]
[*] close [*]
ENTRY 3025
[*]

CHAPTER FOURTEEN

“Something must be interfering with our connection.”

The Detective was trying to explain why he kept disappearing from our links—both electronic and the mental one that I guess is most easily described as telepathic, although actually it’s all possible because of technology.

<<I've checked our connections. I can't find any problems there. So maybe you're right, the dragon ships are jamming us somehow.>>

“There you go. I guess. I’m not the Plutonian genius of this partnership.”

He’d made his way back to Central Market Place and stood looking up at the giant wooden gun over the door to Frank Lava’s gun shop. The street was littered with piles of smoking rubble splayed out from the remains of buildings. And paper—sheets and torn bits alike—was tossed by the wind and collected into tangled nests caught in nooks and niches. Paper may be more ubiquitous in the city than cockroaches.

The big black pistol hung crookedly by one chain, the barrel pointed precariously at the sidewalk—only one iron support remained bolted to Lava’s storefront.

Unpainted plywood was screwed over the display window and door to Lava’s shop, and the door was locked. The Detective hammered on the plywood with his open hand. “Frank! Open up!” he yelled. “It’s Space Detective!”

A window on the second floor pushed up and a woman stuck her head out. She was middle-aged, had black hair pulled back from her face, and worry lines creased her forehead. “He ain’t here!” Anger and fear rattled her voice.

The Detective waved. “Hi, hey, are you Frank’s wife?” The Smile was in his voice. The city was collapsing, but he could still generate the Smile.

“Yeah. Yes, I’m Mrs. Lava. I’m Anna.”

“That’s great. Nice to meet you, Anna. I’m Space Detective.”

<<Gosh, who could've figured that?>>

"You can call me Space, ha. Frank did some work for me. Do you know how I can find him?"

Some of the worry had left her face. The Smile was working. "Yeah, he carried a bunch of guns over to Sal's place."

"His cousin? Salvadore?"

"That's him." She yelled down the address.

"Thank you, Anna. I'm going there now."

She waved a finger at the Detective. "You tell him to be careful! He don't listen to me, but you tell him! I worry."

"I'll do that. Stay inside and cover the windows, Anna."

The Detective hustled to the next block and around the corner. On the way, he asked, "Got that Berserker harness figured out yet?"

<<Just about. I get into the middle of it and then get distracted when you simply disappear from the face of the Earth.>>

"So it's my fault you're not done?"

<<Did I say that? Yeah, I think I said that.>>

"Just figure it out."

Sal's shop was covered and locked just like Frank's had been. The Detective went around to the alley behind the building and found a heavy metal door labeled with a number that matched the one over the shop's front door. Beside this was a large overhead door that was also shut, but there were voices shouting on the other side of it. The Detective hammered on the overhead door.

The shouting stopped and the metal door opened. A head poked out, saw the Detective, then the rest of his body stepped outside. He was a short, dark man with a pencil-thin mustache. He was broad-chested, and had long arms. In fact, he was Frank Lava's twin, except he was bald.

"Whadda you want?"

"You must be Salvadore!" The Smile was working even more potently than it had for Anna, because Sal's posture and stance changed from being hunched forward and aggressive to relaxed and interested. "Frank did some work for me. I'm looking for Frank. Actually, I'm looking for both of you. Is he here?"

Sal nodded. "Yeah, he's here. C'mon in." He gestured and held the door.

Inside was a large workshop filled with tools, sawdust, and pieces of wood in various sizes, along with some partially finished pieces of furniture. Frank was standing beside a lathe, his arms akimbo, his face red. But his expression brightened when he saw the new arrival.

"Hey! The Space Detective! Sal, you gotta meet this guy."

"Yeah, we just met."

While Frank pumped the Detective's hand, the gunsmith said, "You shoulda seen the pistol he brought in, Sal. Nothing like it I ever saw. Prototype, he said. Smuggled outta Berlin. Amazing."

Once the Detective rescued his hand, he said, "I hope I'm not interrupting something."

Frank shook his head and Sal said, "Just a family conversation. Frank wants to go get *il suo sedere* shot off by the monsters from space." He glanced at the Detective. "No disrespect intended."

"No, not at all. We're from, ah, different parts of space."

<<So everyone just assumes you're from outer space now.>>

Frank interrupted: "We gotta defend ourselves! Our families! Our country! These—jerks have invaded, and they gotta be stopped."

"I understand exactly what you're saying, Frank," the Detective said. "And you can help do that, but I need you to do it my way. I need your help. It'll help fight the invaders, and it'll keep you safe. You and Sal both."

"Ah!" Frank waved his arms. "'Safe!'"

"Look, Anna is worried about you, Frank," the Detective continued. "You don't want Anna to worry, right?"

Frank's expression softened. "No, I don't want to upset Anna. But I have to do something."

"You can. You will. I need you guys to build something for me."

A puzzled look appeared on both men's faces. Sal said, "Build something. What?"

"That big wooden gun in front of Frank's store? I want you to bring it here—can you manage that?"

"Yeah, yeah," Sal said, "I got a truck."

"Good. And I want you to make a sabot that will fit inside the barrel."

Frank and Sal looked at their guest as if he'd started talking in a foreign language that wasn't Italian. "A sabot," Frank said. "Let's make sure we're talking about the same thing. A sabot, a support for some projectile you're going to shoot from a gun. Keeps it lined up in the barrel. Then it falls away after your projectile leaves the barrel. We're talking the same thing?"

"Absolutely."

"And we're making it for a wooden gun that has working parts, but doesn't really shoot anything. A *giant* wooden gun."

"That's right."

Frank and Sal shared a look, then turned back to the Detective. "Yeah, we can do that."

"Great! I knew you were the men I needed."

Sal asked, "Uh, the sabot goes in the barrel. What's going inside the sabot?"

"A giant dreidel. I'll write down the measurements."

CHAPTER FIFTEEN

<<Do you know what you're doing?>>

"Not entirely, but the farther along I go, the more I'll be sure."

He'd started an abandoned taxi and was heading to Sixth Avenue to check on Jupiter's melee.

<<What's going on?>>

"What do you mean?"

<<You're acting different today. Like you're working a plan.>>

"I know what's going on now. I didn't before. Too many mysteries. Now we know who to strike. Just a matter of making it happen."

<<That's what Frank and Sal are for? To fix up a giant toy gun?>>

"Yep. And I need you to come up with a way for that wooden gun to fire and make that dreidel fly."

<<Me?>>

"Frank and Sal have no way to make it work. But you can put cameras all over town and put heat sinks in cars and, heck, I don't know what else. And you sit in a jar all day. I'm pretty sure of it: You can make a toy wooden gun shoot a dreidel."

<<I'll have to think about this.>>

"And stop malingering on that Berserker harness."

The mob swarming Jupiter came into sight. A squad of Knifetongue's cops stood in a loose circle around the skull-thumping crowd. Pavement was broken all around, where the scrum had shifted position over the course of the battle that had had no breaks since its beginning.

The Detective blew the car's horn and put his foot to the floor, and the taxi accelerated the last fifty yards. A cop danced out of the way and the cab rammed into one of the Berserkers. The Detective was nearly thrown through the windshield, but he held tightly to the wheel. The Berserker went down. His two nearest companions spun and slammed their fists into the taxi's hood. Everyone could hear the mounts break and the engine drop to the street over the racket from Jupiter's fight.

The two giants bent, grabbed the front undercarriage, and heaved.

The vehicle was flung back so its tires pointed at the sky like a turtle stuck with its shell on the pavement. Then the brutes returned to slugging Jupiter. The one bashed by the taxi lay underfoot and didn't move.

Three cops ran and helped the Detective out of the mashed taxi. "You okay?"

The Detective dusted off his clothing. "Yes, thanks very much." He flinched as his ribs pulled a little spike of pain, then he looked over at the mob. "I didn't do much, but I got some satisfaction."

Everyone turned as a howling roar erupted from the midst of the swarm. The fighting didn't pause. The crowd looked like a twisting nest of giant snakes.

Another roar. And then everyone within two blocks heard Jupiter bellow:

"I have tunneled through the living ectoplasmic atmosphere of the Ghost Planet!

"I have sung chorales with the anaerobic Frrossnnerrll giants swimming in the cold wastes between star systems!

"I have coupled for thirty-seven delirious qaxnals with the thirty-eighth princess of the cephalopod molluscracy on Murkalor 12!

"I will not—*I will NOT*—be humbled by bacteria-infested anthropoids sired by muck and sulfur!"

A Berserker went flying through the air and landed with a tremendous thud two yards from the Detective. Every cop in the squad raised his gun and emptied it into the brute, who staggered to his knees, then collapsed to the street.

Another giant was flung from the mob, then a third. They scrambled to their feet and rushed back to rejoin the fray.

Another roar rattled the windows that had remained in their frames so far. Then the only sounds were those of flesh smacking flesh and grunts and panting.

The cops stared at the Berserker leaking blood on the street, then glanced at the fighters surrounding Jupiter and started back to their places encircling the battle. The Detective raised a hand. "Carry on, gentlemen."

Then he headed off to find the street fighting.

CHAPTER SIXTEEN

<<I've got your answer.>>

"Give me a few minutes here."

Three hours after the Detective rammed a Berserker with a taxi, he was hunkered behind an overturned public bus with ten citizens armed to the teeth. They were part of an ambush party. Another group of self-appointed militia members hid within a shattered storefront to the right of the bus, on a corner of the intersection in which the bus lay.

Fifteen men ran along the middle of the street toward the intersection. Chasing them were ten Berlin Berserkers. Every few yards, the defenders stopped, turned, and triggered several shots at their pursuers before fleeing again.

The quarry passed between the bus and the ruined storefront.

The Berserkers entered the intersection.

From a rooftop behind the bus, a citizen stood and aimed a bazooka.

<<A bazooka? Where'd that come from?>>

"People always tuck things away for a rainy day. And it's pouring."

The bazooka launched its rocket. It exploded in the middle of the running Berserkers with a blast that shook the bus.

A second after the boom, the pursued civilians stopped and turned back. The ambushers in the storefront and behind the bus all appeared and began shooting their rifles, pistols, and shotguns at the surviving Berserkers.

It took a little more than a minute, but then all the giants were down and none were going to get up again.

"Okay," the Detective said as he walked away from the celebrating defenders, "now I'm ready."

<<The harness you brought from the Berserker. I haven't got it entirely figured out yet, but there's this: It's constructed with panels that absorb kinetic energy. So every knuckle sandwich served during the fight is absorbed, if the expended energy isn't transferred to Jupiter's noggin or whatever is getting hit at the moment.>>

"Wow. There are a lot of knuckle sandwiches and kicks and squeezes and every dirty trick in the street-fighting book being exchanged in that battle." He paused and leaned against the last-standing ten feet of an apartment building's wall. "So what happens to the energy? Are these panels just batteries?"

<<If that were so, we could call them *battery batteries*.>>

"Ugh. That's bad."

<<I knew you'd appreciate it. But no, they aren't batteries. In a very simple analogy, the panels are like walkie talkies—they gather the energy and transmit it elsewhere.>>

"Those Berserkers have been fighting for hours—what's keeping them on their feet?"

<<I said I haven't figured it all out. Maybe they also act like batteries and are helping power the Berserkers? Or maybe the giant thugs' metabolisms have been modified by the Hyrnavians or whomever the Vikings are working with.>>

"Hm. So where is the energy going?"

<<Based on what I've tracked down, the panels are sending the energy up to the dragon ships.>>

"That's interesting."

<<That explains why the ships aren't just dropping bombs on the city. Those building busters also are collecting kinetic energy from their destructive paths.>>

"That's interesting, too. Maybe the ships' fuel expenditures are so great they need an extra power source—the kinetic energy is supplementing whatever power plants are onboard the ships."

<<Could be.>>

"Good work."

<<Hey, thanks!>>

"How's that wooden gun propulsion thing turning out?"

<<Working on it. Gotta go.>>

CHAPTER SEVENTEEN

Near dusk, the Detective had gotten cut off from a group of defenders in Greeley Square and been chased east by a gang of raving Berserkers. He ran into the shattered Broadway lobby of the Martinique Hotel. The structure's French-Renaissance style was dramatically marred now: a building buster had blasted to bits the mansard-roofed penthouse and the top five floors.

The lobby floor's broken mosaic tiles clattered and slid under the Detective's feet as he skidded into shelter. He was headed deeper into the building when he heard the rattling fire of a submachine gun. He whipped back to the entrance, using the collapsed awning bearing the hotel's name as cover. A citizen was at the corner of Thirty-Second and Broadway firing an Army-issue M3 submachine gun at three Berserkers. The fire was holding them at bay momentarily, but once the ammo clip was empty, they would charge.

"Over here!" the Detective shouted.

A quick glance at who was yelling, then the gunman dashed for the entrance, firing off several rounds on the way. He hopped over the corner of the awning that rested on the pavement and stumbled inside the lobby. The Detective grabbed his arm and tugged him along. "This way."

They hustled to the back of the lobby. "We'll hole up in the kitchen until they ramble on. There's enough steel in there to slow down a couple of buffalo."

"Better make sure the gas is off."

The Detective stopped and looked at the gunman. In a bulky jacket and rolled-cuff jeans, he looked like an average-sized man in clothes that were a little too big. But the gunman's voice was that of a gunwoman.

"C'mon," she said.

Once in the kitchen, they shoved every heavy table and bin they could find against the doors. The Detective made sure the gas was shut off.

Then the woman pulled off her Yankees baseball cap and revealed her wavy dark hair. Even with the dark smudges marring her features, she was now recognizable.

<<She's Hazel!>>

"Miss Byrne, you surprise me."

"I told you, my name's Hazel," she said and smiled like she'd just pulled a trick on him.

"I didn't know your skills extended from copy editing to combat shooting," the Detective said.

They heard the Berserkers crashing around in the lobby and registration area, so the pair kept quiet to see what would happen next.

Several strong blows bashed the other side of the kitchen door. The barricade shook, but it stayed in place. The attackers gave up on the door. Once the invaders passed and the subsequent quiet suggested they had left the building, Hazel went to the walk-in coolers. "Let's see if there's anything still fit to eat." She pulled open the door and a light clicked on. "Hey, there's still power here. Hungry? Thirsty?"

"Uh, no, I'm fine, thanks."

She cut some ham and made some sandwiches with lettuce and sliced cheese. She leaned against a wall and sat. "Come on over and keep me company. Do you know how to load a .45 caliber magazine?"

"I can manage."

"So do that while I eat." She tossed a purse-sized pouch to the Detective. It rattled with loose cartridges.

<<Armed and dangerous and hungry.>>

The Detective started pushing cartridges into the grease gun's long clip. "How'd you learn to use one of these?"

"My grandpas and all my uncles were Navy and Army men. My dad was in during the war. My mom spent some time in the military, too. I'd go into their bedroom, and a Colt .45 was holstered on both sides of the headboard." She shrugged. "Learning to shoot was just part of family life."

"Taking on Berserkers by yourself isn't the best way to face them."

Hazel rolled her eyes. "I know that. Our squad had to scatter, and those three followed me. I'll rejoin them after a little rest."

"What's happened to your boss? Mr. Grimsson?"

"Eirik? He disappeared. He started raving about—I don't know, some sort of conspiracy out to get him and to stop his publishing company. He ran out of the office. Shouting all the way. It was right before everyone else went loony and started wandering moon-eyed through the streets. Morrie—Morrie Cortland, the business manager? He and I went looking for Eirik, but we couldn't find him. And then everyone seemed to wake up once the dragon ships appeared in the sky, so I hope Eirik woke up and returned to normal, too."

<<That might wreck your chances for a Space Detective comic book.>>

The Detective punched the last cartridge into the last clip. "There you go."

Hazel patted the floor tiles beside her. "Come sit with me."

<<Be careful. You've loaded her weapon. That means different things in different cultures.>>

The Detective sat beside her and leaned against the wall. Hazel rested her head on his shoulder. "Running and shooting and hiding and shooting. It's nice to just catch my breath for a few minutes."

"It's full dark by now." The kitchen had no windows, so the Detective was basing this on the time that had passed since they ran into the hotel. "Getting some sleep is a good idea."

"I'm too wound up right now to sleep. Tell me, how did you turn to this Space Detective act?"

<<Act?>>

"Act?" The Detective sounded a little huffy. "I'm a genuine, licensed private investigator."

<<For proof, you've arrested people. And you've blown up a printing company and a brewery and shut down at least one radio station.>>

"Ha. You know what I mean," Hazel said. "Why did you choose this spaceman shtick?"

<<Shtick?>>

"Maybe the, uh, shtick chose me." He cleared his throat. "It's been a good marketing ploy. Captured something in the zeitgeist—the fascination with UFOs plus my distinctive garb have brought in clients I might've missed otherwise. There are plenty of competing private eyes in this town."

"Hm. Don't you take it too far? We're fighting invaders—an army in the sky." She yawned. "But you're still wearing that helmet. Isn't that silly?"

The Detective cleared his throat again. "The helmet is distinctive.

People recognize it from my advertising, so they know me when they see me. Know I can be trusted, I'm on their side, not one of the invaders. Gives me some authority among particular people when it can be handy. So yes, I wear it while we're all fighting an invading army."

Hazel was snoring.

<<Apparently you're not so fascinating as you thought.>>

The Detective adjusted his position so Hazel's neck wasn't twisted at such a sharp angle.

<<I had high hopes for Hazel. A gal with a gun—>>

"'Gal with a gun'? What sort of magazines have you been reading lately?"

<<Not Leo Malet.>>

"Consider something with more elevated language. Just what kind of high hopes for Hazel did you have?"

<<Why, I thought that Space Girl proposal was a great idea. But she's all tuckered out, and the fight's hardly started.>>

"Space Girl. I thought that discussion was behind us. And don't Plutonians ever need sleep?"

<<Sleep? When would we get all our work done on heat sinks and battery batteries?>>

"Never mind. I'm going to take a nap, too. Wake me up if something bad starts happening."

<<Something *bad*?>>

"Something worse."

CHAPTER EIGHTEEN

<<Time to rise and shine—or at least be less tarnished.>>

As the Detective stirred, he saw Hazel had already prepared and packed some food for her squad.

"Breakfast?" she asked.

"No, I'm okay. Thank you." He stretched the kinks out and flinched when his cracked ribs tweaked his memory. "Ready?"

"Ready. Our team has a pre-arranged spot to meet if we ever have to split up."

The pair broke down the barricade and made their way to the hotel entrance. Morning sunlight, reflected from the street, illuminated the lobby's interior. Outside, no immediate threats were in sight. Gunfire popped several blocks away.

All the vehicles on the block were wrecked, so the Detective escorted Hazel along Sixth Avenue until they encountered a flatbed truck hauling armed civilians as they passed the Herald Square Building. They hitched a ride to the corner of Seventh and West Thirty-Seventh, where Hazel rejoined her squad at the lofts adjoining the Mills Hotel. She waved before turning and entering through the shattered doorway.

The Detective decided to ride further on the truck.

<<You're getting a lot of long looks from your fellow passengers.>>

"I noticed. What's that about?"

<<Maybe it's the lipstick kiss on the front of your helmet.>>

"What?"

<<Yeah, if you have to use that headlight, it might be blocked a little bit. Really a nice, robust, fire engine red.>>

He muttered something and swiped his gloved hands over the spot.

<<That got most of it.>>

The truck dropped him off on West Thirty-Seventh under the Twelfth Avenue elevated before roaring off. Someone yelled out through the departing cloud of diesel smoke, "G'bye, Lover Boy!" No catastrophe was too dire to prevent a good-natured razz from a New

Angoulême citizen. I could almost make out the receding laughter over the clash of the changing gears.

The Detective went the rest of the way on foot to the Mohegan River warehouse. Once again he met Special Agent Van Eckk inside. Despite the federal operative's military-style buzz cut, his usually crisp-and-sharp appearance looked rather careworn. A sky filled with hovering Dragons will do that to anybody. He wore a .45 automatic in a shoulder holster under each armpit, and a Browning Automatic Rifle slung over a shoulder. A belt carrying extra clips for the rifle was wrapped around his waist.

<<He's armed for BAR, I mean bear. And lions and tigers, too.>>

"Agent."

"Detective."

"How'd you get here?"

"Collapsible raft—loaded it and paddled across the river in the dark." Van Eckk gestured at a box truck parked just inside the closed overhead doors that led out to the street. The cargo box's sides were dented and a big scorch mark stretched across half of the passenger-side wall. "It's all in there, like you ordered. It may be the strangest thing I've ever delivered to you, but I gotta trust you know what you're doing."

"Thanks. I know it's weird, but it should help. A great deal."

"I had a heck of a time pulling together guys to do the work, and finding equipment shops that hadn't been wrecked by the Vikings upstairs. But it's all there."

"I knew you could get it done. Thanks again."

"Good luck. I'll be seeing you." Van Eckk made a loose salute as he turned and headed out the door.

<<What's the big secret?>>

"No secret." The Detective pulled a little box out of a pocket. From the container he *shlurrped* out a collapsible frame that he expanded and sat on the floor, arranging it around the truck. It was waist high and looked a little like the baby barriers the newspapers advertised for placing inside door frames to keep toddlers out of hazardous rooms, but it was a lot longer. The Detective stepped inside the frame and snapped together its ends. He removed a small control box from another pocket and touched a button.

The truck, Detective, and frame all disappeared and reappeared in another warehouse—the one containing Ronnie's blast buggy and the giant dreidel.

And half an acre of stacked wooden crates.

<<It's a secret if you know what's going on and I don't.>>

"You heard me when I called Van Eckk and told him what I needed."

<<I did? No, I didn't.>>

"Maybe that's when the interference was blocking our connection." He left the expandable frame and walked over to the dreidel. He put his arms akimbo and just stared at the big toy.

<<So if it's not a secret, what is it?>>

"Don't worry, you'll find out."

<<What's that mean?>>

"Oh, just think of it as some of that mystery I'm adding to our relationship. Like you were reading about in the magazines." He walked around the dreidel. "Can I still get to the office?"

<<Wait a minute. What are all those crates for? They weren't here earlier. I didn't put 'em there.>>

"It's okay, you'll find out."

<<Okay, okay. The tobacco shop is still demolished. And the back door you used in the subway station is inaccessible—big collapse in the tunnel.>>

"All right. Let's try this." The Detective pulled another expanding frame out of a box. He stepped inside its ring and pressed the button.

He arrived inside the main office. Safe and undisturbed in the Nere.

<<Nifty. You don't even need a door now.>>

"Uncas will still need a way to visit. I like the way the fizzy door raises his hackles."

He stepped into the file cabinet.

Within a few minutes, he was sitting in an Automat across from Ronnie. It wasn't a real Automat, of course, but projected into Ronnie's mind by the cocoon.

"I like Automat coffee. How about you, Ronnie?"

The young hood was hunched over his side of the table. He stared at the Detective through the curtain of sand-colored bangs that had lost their pomaded styling. "I don't care about coffee at the moment. What do you want? Gonna show me more awful pictures from the world?"

The Detective leaned back. Relaxed. "No, no more scenes from outside. But they all look worse today compared to the last views you had."

"Then whatta you want?" Ronnie slammed the tabletop with a fist.

"It's not what I want, but it depends on what you want, Ronnie." He spread his gloved hands. "It's a chance to redeem yourself. Would you like that?"

Ronnie frowned. He looked like someone who suspected a trick was being pulled. "What do you mean?"

"Want out of here?"

"Sure. Yeah."

"That can happen. But you have to do something for me."

The suspicious glare was stronger. "Like what?"

"You can do something that makes up for what you did that helped cause all that mess you saw happening in the city."

"You haven't said what, yet."

"Something simple. For you, it's simple. Pilot that blast buggy you're so crazy about."

That got Ronnie's attention. He straightened up in his chair, but the suspicion hadn't left his eyes. "That sounds like a trick. You're trying to trap me into doing something that will get me in trouble." He scowled as he thought about it. "With somebody."

"No one has to know about the deliveries you brought down for Gelinda," the Detective said. He kept a relaxed posture. He didn't want to raise Ronnie's anxiety by trying to oversell his offer. "There is a fleet of dragon ships in the air over New Angoulême. They've dropped all that destruction you saw onto the city. You just need to fly up there, close, but not all the way."

"And do what?"

"Carry something for me. You just fly up there, then turn around and head back home."

Ronnie looked puzzled. "That's it?"

"That's it."

"I don't have to dock with a ship, or—or ram it, or—anything?"

"Nope. You wouldn't be able to dock anyway. What you'll be carrying, you won't have to put onboard a dragon ship. Just get close enough to do what it needs to do, then you bring everything back to ground."

Ronnie's eyes shifted, looking at different points within the Automat. A desperate hope was working its way inside him, but the hope was tangled with a fear that he was being set up.

The Detective nudged the hope: "You tired of living in the cocoon, Ronnie?"

"Yeah. Yeah, I am."

"This is the way out."

The kid chewed his lower lip.

The Detective waited. Finally, he asked, "What do you say?"

"Yeah. Yeah, okay. I'll do it."

CHAPTER NINETEEN

The Detective removed Ronnie from the cocoon and brought him out of the file cabinet into the main office. The young blast buggy pilot wasn't really conscious yet, and the Detective carried him like he was lugging a man-size bag of jelly.

"Is the load for Frank Lava's wooden gun ready?"

<<Yep.>>

"'Yep'? Really? Honestly?"

<<Yep. Impressed?>>

"On the verge. If it really works, I'll be impressed."

<<Be still my heart.>>

"You have a heart?"

<<I could go into my metabolic processes and the minutiae of Plutonian gross anatomy, but I fear you'd be so dazzled by my instruction you'd be distracted from your mission at hand.>>

"No doubt. Is the Studie still operating?"

<<Yep.>>

"Great. Load your new little toy in the car and send it over to Sal's workshop. Send me instructions over our connection so I'll know how to load it in Frank's pistol. I'll meet the Studie there."

<<You're not worried the car will be wrecked by Berserkers or the militia on the way?>>

"My new confidence in your abilities makes me believe you'll get it to Sal's place without a scratch."

He used his collapsible frame to disappear with Ronnie.

They reappeared in the warehouse next to Ronnie's rocket.

The Detective set up a cot and draped the pilot on it. "He'll still be out of it for some time. I have plenty to do, but he won't be awake until I'm done."

<<If you say so.>>

"Just be sure that propulsion load for Frank's gun will work. We only have one chance at this."

<<Yeah. Got it. It'll work.>>

He checked his watch, then took a deep breath and let it out slowly. “Okay. Things are going to start happening fast now. We can’t make a misstep. Ready?”

<<Well sure, I guess. Thanks to all this mystery in our relationship these days, I’m not really sure what the next steps are. But ready? Of course I am. Maybe.>>

“That’s the can-do spirit I count on from you.”

The Detective checked his pockets, made sure his Zapper charge was adequate, then built a frame around the spot he stood on, touched a button and fizzed away.

He arrived at Jupiter’s melee. Nothing had changed, except the shift of cops on duty, and more of the pavement was crushed into pebbles and grit. The Detective pulled another collapsible frame from a box in his pocket. With the cops’ help, he arranged the frame in a wide circle around the swarm of Berserkers assaulting Jupiter. Knifetongue’s men gave him puzzled looks as they did so. When the frame’s ends were connected, the Detective was inside the circle with the fighters. He watched the mountain of squirming flesh a moment while he held the control box. He shook his head and looked at the box, but before he could press the button, one of the Berserkers spun out of the mass and smacked the Detective a glancing blow as he tumbled past. The Detective cartwheeled backwards and broke through the transportation frame.

Two cops helped him to his feet.

<<You okay?>>

“Ye-ah.” The battle suit he wore had helped soften the blow, but it couldn’t have felt like just a love tap. He’d held onto the control box. But the frame was broken at the point he’d collided with it.

<<Now what?>>

The Detective turned to the cops. “Anybody got some chewing gum?”

“Yeah, I do.” One of the uniformed fellows—a Viking, not one of Uncas’ Mohawks—handed over a package.

“Share the sticks with your buddies,” the Detective said, “and bring me the foil wrappers.”

The cop blinked, then followed the directions he’d been given. When he came back with a handful of creased foil patches, the Detective had the cops hold the broken ends of the frame’s struts together. The

Detective smoothed out the rough edges at the breakpoints, then wound each repaired connection with a foil wrapper. When he was done, everyone released the frame gingerly and stepped back.

The repairs held.

<<It ain't baling wire. And it ain't pretty. Will it work?>>

"Let's find out. Thank you, gentlemen."

The Detective was back inside the area enclosed by the frame. He retrieved the control from a pocket and pressed its button.

The cops gaped when the mob disappeared.

The whole gang arrived at the Detective's big stasis closet in NoWhere. No one moved except the Detective.

From a pouch on his battle harness, he removed a small tool that quickly expanded into something that looked like—and was about the size of—a pogo stick. He held the handles and pushed the other end against the tangled Berserkers. Whenever the Detective thumbed the gadget's switch, a jolt would knock one of the big brutes loose from the swarm and he'd collapse to the invisible floor. Sometimes more than one jolt was needed to break a Berserker free from the mass.

He did this work for more than an hour. Finally, Jupiter was the last standing figure, frozen in place, his limbs twisted in a fighting posture, his face that of a screaming beast.

The Detective stood behind Jupiter and grabbed the agent's ears with his gloved hands. He ran a burst of electricity through the gloves and jumped back, because Jupiter completed the mob-flattening swing he'd begun before the frame fizzed him and the NoWhere closet froze him. His fist whipped around, but encountered no resistance, so Jupiter lost his balance and crashed to the floor.

He roared his indignation as he leapt to his feet, then he noticed the crowd of frozen Berserkers splayed around him, and he saw the Detective. Then he bellowed some word or phrase—probably something dramatically profane, but I'm just guessing, because it was a language I'd never heard—then grinned like an ape.

An indigo-skinned ape with pink eyes and a green mohawk haircut, true, but the simian resemblance was unmistakable.

"What a marvelous battle! I've not enjoyed its like for a few years. I almost regret your interruption, but perhaps I could enjoy a slight repast."

"Sorry to spoil your fun, but we have plenty of work to do, and you need a little rest. You'll have time for a snack."

<<Maybe he could eat one of those battery batteries. Like a cracker. Spread with a little pâte. What do you think?>>

I didn't get an answer. The Detective just fizzed the two of them back to the blast buggy warehouse, where he pointed to a coffin-sized locker. "There's a stash of field rations. Eat your fill. They aren't necessarily tasty, but they're full of essential vitamins and minerals."

Jupiter gestured at Ronnie, who was still stretched on a cot. "Who's this?"

"An ally. Just go eat."

Jupiter made a sound of joy before digging in.

"I'll be back." The Detective joined Van Eckk's box truck inside its expanded transit frame, pressed his button box, and fizzed away.

He landed in Battery Park.

<<The subway commuters will be wanting your magic if you keep using it so publicly.>>

"Hopefully the rigors of current events will make their memories fuzzy where this bit of magic is concerned."

Special Agent Van Eckk strode out of a crowd of national guardsmen gathered around the big guns still aimed skyward. "Welcome," he said. "I wasn't sure if you'd be able to keep our rendezvous, what with all the hubbub." He pointed at the truck. "That's quite a trick."

"Legerdemain. Smoke and mirrors," the Detective replied. "Are all the guns still operational?"

The agent nodded. "Apparently beneath the notice of the dragons. Since our shelling had no effect on the ships, couldn't even get close to touching them, they just ignored them."

<<Ah, the conqueror's hubris.>>

"Very good. Their arrogance plays in our favor. You know what's in the truck. While you're distributing that load, I'll collect the rest."

The Detective fizzy-fuzzed back to the warehouse. He set up another collapsible frame around the stack of mysterious wooden crates that had been in place before he'd brought Van Eckk's truck from the Mohegan River warehouse. Jupiter just watched while he continued wolfing down Army rations.

By the time the Detective had finished assembling the frame, Ronnie was stirring on the cot.

The Detective fizzed away. He returned to Battery Park with the crates. Van Eckk came forward again. "Y'know, the subway people are going to want to know about this."

<<What did I say?>>

The Detective put the Smile in his voice. "I think we'll keep this under wraps awhile longer." He gestured to the militia moving around the guns. "Any problems with the supplies?"

"Nope, everything's just right."

"Okay. You know what to do with these." He patted one of the crates.

"I know. Sounds crazy, but I know." A look of skepticism played across the agent's face as he scanned the just-arrived boxes. Then he grinned and offered his hand to the Detective. "We'll do our part."

The Detective shook hands. "You'll see the signal. I hope there'll be no way to miss it."

Van Eckk gave a loose salute and turned to the guardsmen. "Let's move these by each gun and break 'em open!"

The Detective returned to the warehouse in his fizzy manner.

Ronnie stood behind the cot. He stared at Jupiter.

"Ronnie, good to see you on your feet." The Detective strode over to the blast buggy pilot, who spun and faced him with a look of crazed fright.

"Where'd you come from?"

"Running errands." He pointed to Jupiter. "This is my colleague, Mr. Jupiter. You'll be working together during the next phase of our mission."

Jupiter waved and grunted while he chewed his food.

Ronnie wasn't reassured. His eyes still were wide and wild looking. "What is he?"

"He's part of our team. He knows Gelinda and the pirates, and many other things." He patted Ronnie's shoulder. "Go get something to eat." He called to Jupiter, "Did you leave anything for our pilot?"

Jupiter nodded and grunted.

The Detective gave Ronnie a gentle push toward the locker.

<<I'm sure this will begin a beautiful friendship.>>

"What you're sure of, and what I'm sure of, are sometimes very different things."

Once Jupiter stopped smacking his chops and had licked his fingers clean, the Detective had him pick up and carry the giant dreidel over to

Ronnie's blast buggy. He had already arranged a transit frame around the rocket. "Put on some clothes," he directed. "We don't want to shock our friends at their workshop."

While Jupiter complied, surprisingly docile, the Detective asked me, "Did the Studie get to Sal's okay?"

<<Still in one piece. Parked in the alley by the workshop door.>>

"Thank you."

The Detective had Ronnie and Jupiter, with the dreidel, stand alongside him inside the frame. "Here we go." He pressed the button.

They arrived in the alley alongside the Studebaker. Jupiter's belly laugh drowned out the sounds of Ronnie's hyperventilating.

While the Detective hammered on Sal's door, he directed Ronnie, "Get in your buggy. Check out that it's ready to fly. Catch your breath later."

"Yeah, yeah, okay."

Ronnie opened the buggy's gull wing and clambered in just as the workshop's overhead door rolled up and revealed Sal in a dusty apron. He caught sight of Jupiter and his mouth opened, but no words came out. Frank walked up from inside the shop and displayed the same silent reaction.

"Frank, Salvadore," the Detective said, "allow me to introduce Mr. Jupiter. He's going to help us clear out the dragon ships."

The indigo giant grinned and extended a hand in a dainty manner so he wouldn't crush the cousins' fingers while shaking. Jupiter's eyes twinkled. No, really, there was a little spark of light in each of them. Frank and Sal nodded their greetings, but still couldn't utter a syllable.

The Detective broke through their fascination with Jupiter: "Is everything ready?"

"Oh," Frank said, "oh, yeah."

Talking about work seemed to do the trick. Sal waved his visitors through the door. "Here we go, Mr. Detective and—and Mr. Jupiter. The pistol is in fine working order, and the sabot fits perfectly." He spread his arms to show off the results of his work on the giant pistol, which lay on a worktable along with the polished-to-a-shine sabot.

"That's wonderful!" The Detective turned to Jupiter. "Make sure the sabot fits the dreidel."

Frank elbowed Sal. "It really is a dreidel."

Sal nodded. “What a world we live in.”

“Anna will never believe this.”

“Talk to me tomorrow. I’m not sure I believe it.”

Satisfied that everything fit as planned, the Detective directed Jupiter to bring his giant toys to the Studie. “Tell Jupiter how to load that propulsion pack,” he directed. “I’m checking on Ronnie.”

<<Will do, General Space Detective, sir.>>

Jupiter retrieved my device from the car and loaded it according to my directions. He did so with no chit chat, which was unusual. He really was like a big kid with really big new toys. “This is quite something,” he admitted.

The Detective stuck his helmeted head out the gull wing hatch. “Don’t shoot it.” Then he disappeared back inside the buggy.

When he dropped back to the alley pavers, he said, “Ronnie says all systems are go. I’ve given him his flight plan. Jupiter, is the gun loaded?”

“Oh, it is, yes.”

“Okay. Carry it up on top of the rocket. Make sure you can’t fall off. Ronnie’s going to fly you up to the dragon ships.”

<<But nothing can get close to them.>>

“He’s not going all the way there. But close enough.”

Jupiter hopped onto the blast buggy’s hull. He carried Frank Lava’s gun. Loaded with the dreidel sticking out the end of the barrel, it looked like some crazy thing from a Tex Avery cartoon.

Jupiter’s feet changed. They widened and flattened, and then his toes began stretching out as long tentacles that wrapped around the hull. From the smacking sounds they made when they pulled away from the hull’s surface, it was clear Jupiter was extruding some sticky substance that would hold him in place while Ronnie was flying his little bucket.

Frank and Sal stood in the workshop doorway watching. They said in unison, “Oh my God.”

Jupiter showed his teeth. “Let’s go!”

Grit flew through the alley when Ronnie took off with a roar and a cloud of dust. As the buggy rose above the rooftops, Jupiter’s bellows of mirth were easy to hear.

<<He’s just not a sneak-up-on-’em kinda guy, is he?>>

“Hardly ever.”

The dragon ships hung at various heights over the city. They differed in size, but there wasn’t a single one that was marked or stood out as the command ship or flagship of the fleet. And the invaders hadn't sent out any communications to the city's leaders or general population—they'd just arrived and started a war—so there was no one to point to and say, "He's in charge." So knowing what Jupiter was going to do with his big gun and single piece of ammunition had me baffled.

<<Is he just going to shoot whichever one is closest?>>

"You'll see," the Detective said. "He knows which one to aim at."

<<How?>>

"A little bird told me."

<<A bird?>>

"Sure, they're up there flying around all those dragon ships. They know what's going on."

Obviously I wasn't going to get a straight answer.

I wondered how Ronnie felt, heading right up there in his little boat in plain sight of all those very large ships. Like a gnat that could be swatted out of the sky at any moment? I wondered if he was rethinking his deal with the Detective—maybe days and nights in the cocoon didn't seem so bad when he was flying into the teeth of ravenous Berserkers.

He must have had a specific target in mind, because the buggy curved to the right and gave plenty of airspace to a couple of lower-hanging ships. Ronnie piloted toward a ship near the middle layer and stopped.

I zoomed in my optics. Jupiter raised and aimed the pistol. I didn't see anything particularly distinctive about his target—it wasn't the largest ship, nor was it one of the smaller ones. Jupiter managed to pull the trigger as if it was something he'd done every day for years. The propulsion mechanism I'd devised made no sound, but even our team in the alley could see a burst of blue light as the payload left the gun barrel.

Ronnie's blast buggy swung in a fast arc away from the ships. The sabot dropped away from the dreidel, which seemed to travel slowly compared to a normal bullet. But Jupiter's weapon was hardly a normal pistol.

The dreidel got closer to the target ship—this was all easy to see with my close-up view. It passed the invisible boundary that had stymied all the earlier cannon fire. It closed in on the dragon ship, and punched through the hull of its belly.

And then—nothing seemed to happen.

Ronnie landed the buggy, and Jupiter peeled his feet from the hull. Ronnie stepped out of the hatch and stood beside the Detective.

Everyone in the alley turned to watch the punctured dragon ship.

It started to sink. Nothing dramatic: It kept an even keel, but it drifted downward at a slow, even pace. Finally it passed the lowest level that any of the other ships floated at.

Then the dragon ship's bow tilted downward, and it zoomed to the ground. Fire and clouds and a tremendous *boom* burst upward from the site.

Shouts went up from every throat in Sal's alley. And from people all across the city who had been watching that strange aircraft with its stranger passenger ascend to the invading fleet. But no one could hear them: thundering roars of heavy artillery fire erupted from Battery Park. The air over New Angoulême was filled with dreidels—*dreidels?*—flying toward the remaining dragon ships.

The fleet hadn't budged since Jupiter's initial shot punctured the first ship. All those dragon ships just hung there as if stunned or waiting for the Battery Park guns to target them.

The dreidels all punched through whatever invisible barrier had repelled all earlier fusillades. Every one of them hit its target.

The ships at the upper level began to stir as the lower ones, hit by flying dreidels, began to sink and then plummet to earth. But they were slow to get started, and Battery Park fired more rounds that hit more targets, until only about a dozen dragon ships finally ascended and headed east and over the bay and then out over the ocean.

When the Battery guns went silent, and the explosions from the crashed dragon ships finally muttered down to the sound of leaping flames, the shouts and cheers could be heard. They rattled the windows that remained in their frames.

Black columns of smoke rose from the wrecks and darkened the skies in ways the dust of the structures battered by the building busters hadn't done. But the thick pall was a new sign of hope to the city's people.

Jupiter carried the wooden pistol back into Sal's workshop. "Gentlemen," he said, "that is an excellent piece of gunsmithing. I am honored to have gotten to fire it."

<<That little bird was certainly a sharp one.>>

"What's that?" the Detective asked.

<<The bird that told you which ship to shoot.>>

"Ah. Yes, indeed. Our feathered friends love New Angoulême very much. Especially its park benches and statues."

<<You're not going to explain?>>

"No time right now. We need to get people into the streets to sweep up the stranded Berserkers."

Those battle-hungry brutes sure seemed to be a good excuse at that moment.

CHAPTER TWENTY

Maybe my comments about bringing mystery into our relationship was a bad idea.

Three weeks after the dragon ships crashed in New Angoulême, and I still didn't know anything: where the big dreidel came from, and how the Detective knew to shoot a particular ship with it; where the other dreidels came from that were shot from Battery Park; and that's just for starters.

It took ten days to take down the rest of the Berserkers running loose in the city. The few we could round up with one of the Detective's tricks, he put in the stasis closet. He asked if I could figure a way to send a reverse jolt through the others' harness batteries that would incapacitate them, but nothing worked. They wouldn't stop their rampages, and the cops and national guard worked street by street to hunt them down.

The Detective didn't hang around all that time. He found a way to get to New Orleans and then San Francisco to deal with the invasion in those cities.

Not long after the dragon ships came down, Jupiter disappeared. I guess once the tables had been turned in New Angoulême's favor, the sweetness of the challenge was gone. He didn't even say goodbye.

Ronnie Roquette cleared out, too. With his blast buggy. I guess he lit out for the Territory—somewhere.

I learned something about the dreidel after the Detective returned from San Francisco. He was sitting on a park bench with Uncas, who was taking a break from clean up and recovery efforts. The chief inspector was back in his usual uniform, wearing a black beret and a dark topcoat with the traditional black feather pin of the Algonquian nation.

"The dragon ships were repelling metal projectiles," the Detective explained. "The dreidel was made of densely packed cellulose, so it passed right through whatever magnetic or other barrier the ships were projecting."

"Wood chips?" Uncas frowned. "And it punched a hole in the hull of a ship?"

"Very densely packed, as I said." The Detective put the Smile into his voice. "And maybe there was something else that helped, but it worked."

The chief inspector's frown suggested he remained unconvinced. Instead of chewing on that topic further, he moved to something else: "When the immediate state of emergency is dissolved, you and I shall have a long conversation. About many things. Make sure I know where to find you."

After Uncas had departed, it was my turn to ask a question.

<<Cellulose?>>

"Just as you said back in the warehouse. Special cellulose," the Detective said. "Made to hold programming. It was a transport vehicle for its programming. Like tobacco is a vehicle for nicotine, or a kid picks up a toy that carries a virus and gets infected."

<<The dragon ship caught a cold?>>

"Something like that. The programming interacted with the hull material and the ship's machines. Once the programming in the cellulose hit the hull, it was like a bomb going off. Without gunpowder. Threw a monkey wrench into the works, and the ship spiraled out of control."

<<Why that first ship Jupiter shot? Any particular reason?>>

"It was the command ship. All the others were slaved to it for the kinetic energy the Berserkers' batteries were beaming up. And other controls as well." That explained why we found nearly no crew members aboard the wrecked dragon ships. Almost everything was controlled electronically by the flagship.

<<You know a lot about this stuff.>>

"I'm a detective. I work out puzzles. And clues."

<<Uh huh. What about the office? The tobacco shop building is gone.>>

"Yes, we'll need a new façade. Look around, see if you can find something that will do in the meantime. I'd like to stay in the vicinity. People know where to find us there."

<<We'll have to change the look of the real office. If Uncas visits in a new location and the office looks just like the old place, he'll have puzzles and clues.>>

"I'm sure you can manage that."

At podiums and across conference tables and through the broadcast frequencies, politicians and diplomats were feuding about the Vikings' breaking the treaty.

But other news was in the air as well: How did the Vikings get the technical know-how to float ships in the air? Were they behind all the disruptions that led up to the ships' appearing in the sky? What was that funny-looking little ship that flew up to the fleet and fired the first shot?

Questions everywhere.

The Detective was volunteering no answers.

And rumors and conspiracies were marching hand-in-hand.

UFO sightings and reports had been on the rise the past few years. Now more than one genius was interviewed on radio and TV, and in the newspapers and magazines, who stated the Viking invasion was really an attack from outer space.

Okay, maybe they really were geniuses.

But there was no evidence in the sky. The Detective told me about the network of node ships around Earth, but they had all skedaddled right after the dragon ships retreated. And I'd had no updated information from The Reseau. Nor from Jupiter.

In some ways, I was as much in the dark as the average citizen helping move rubble and clear the streets. Maybe the boss and I need a little less mystery between us.

The rumors and conspiracies led to an interesting encounter a few days after the park bench meeting with Uncas. The Detective was helping Hammer and Hack set up a new office, because the previous one had collapsed after the next-door building fell on it. The two private eyes were getting along better than they had before the dragon ships arrived. The Detective was carrying a box of papers—they'd once been part of organized case files—from a pickup truck nosed-in at the curb when a young woman called while approaching at a steady trot along the sidewalk.

"Mr. Detective! Mr. Detective!"

<<It's Hazel!>>

She wore a black V-neck sweater over a black-on-red plaid skirt that swirled as she strode closer. The wave in her dark hair bounced and her brown eyes flashed in a way that went with the determined-looking smile on her red lips. This all suggested to me that Something's Up.

The Detective placed the box at his feet so he could shake her hand. "Miss Byrne, good to see you. I'm so pleased you got through the recent unpleasantness unharmed. How'd you find me?"

"Were you hiding?" She looked cross.

"Uh, well, no—"

"Call me Hazel, like I told you. Someday you'll have to tell me your name. A dashing young man named Conrad at Moe's Magazines told me I might find you here."

<<Good ol' Connie. Selling the news everyday whether rain, sleet, snow, sandstorm, or alien invasion.>>

"Do you need help finding Mr. Grimsson?"

"Oh, no. We found Eirik downstairs huddled beside one of the printing presses. He was twitching and muttering, but he was safe and—mostly sound." She shook her head. A look of concern passed quickly across her features. "No, I have a business proposition."

"Business? While everyone's trying to clean up and rebuild?"

"That's just it! Eirik is in no shape to get back to work, but Morrie Cortland—the business manager, remember?—and I have employees who need money, and that means they need work. We want to put 'em back to work, but we're afraid no one will buy the books we were doing before because of all the kid crime and craziness that's happened recently."

"Okay. So how can I help?"

<<Here comes the windup.>>

Hazel's fingers rested on the Detective's near forearm. "I want to—we want to do a Space Detective book, monthly, like I said before."

<<Here comes the pitch.>>

"I'm not sure—"

"Word on the street," she barreled on, "is you had a hand—a really big hand—in knocking those Viking ships outta the sky."

"Rumors have very little to do with reality."

"What people believe is what helps 'em through each day. And they believe you did it, you stopped the invasion. You're a hero." Hazel gripped his arm with both hands and she looked intently into the face of his helmet.

That made the Detective lose his vocabulary for a minute.

He finally found some words to scrape together: "Miss Byrne—"

<<Hazel.>>

"Hazel," she said.

"Hazel," he started again, "that's very kind and generous, but I'm no hero. I'm just a citizen. A book like that, it would look like grandstanding, taking advantage of the situation."

"People think you're a hero," she insisted. "They need a hero. It's not grandstanding. And besides, I wrote the—I mean, the first issue is already written and drawn, and I need to put our people back to work." She put her fists on her hips. "The people of this city need you. Are you going to let them down?"

The Detective lost his words again. Only for a moment, this time.

He sighed, then said, "What do you need from me?"

Hazel pulled open the bottom of her sweater from her waist just enough to reach under and pull out a sheaf of stapled, typewritten pages.

<<Whatever happened to purses and pockets?>>

"Here's a contract," she said. "Read it over. Sign it. Or wait, because I'll be back here in an hour to pick it up. If you have questions when I return, ask 'em, and then sign it. I've got a business to get back on its feet, and I'll have that signed contract by nightfall."

Hazel grinned like an imp, shook the Detective's hand, then turned and headed away on the sidewalk.

<<Eirik Grimsson may be looking at the next phase of his publishing career. Whether he's *compos mentis* or not.>>

The Detective stared after Hazel before he picked up the box of papers at his feet. Rory Hack joined him from the doorway of his new building, where he'd watched the encounter with Hazel. "Who's that dame?" he asked.

<<That's no dame. She's a ball of fire.>>

The Detective started for the door. "She may be our new business partner."

"Hot dog! This operation's been needing some class."

<<No kidding. I wonder if there'll be a Space Girl?>>

The Detective shook his head. "I bet if Miss Byrne has the final word, Space Girl will be Space Woman."

Glossary

Cahokia – The largest pre-Columbian urban center in North America, this city was located in what is now Illinois across from St. Louis, Missouri. It was first inhabited around 700 AD and flourished until 1350 AD. It supposedly was larger than London in 1250 AD. It served as the center of Middle Mississippian culture. The site is now a state historic site. In Space Detective's world, it is a sovereign nation-within-a-nation governed by descendants of the Native Americans who originally established Cahokia.

Hell Gate Brewery – An actual brewery founded in the year 1866 by George Ehret, who had arrived in New York from Germany in 1857.

Huguenots – French Protestants of the 16th–17th centuries; many fled France to escape persecution from the country's Catholic population.

Mohegan River – The Mohegan people are an Algonquian Native American tribe, distinct from the Mohican people (made famous by James Fenimore Cooper's 1826 novel, *The Last of the Mohicans*) and from the Mohawk people. What we know as the Hudson River has had many names throughout North America's history, including Mahicantuck, Shatemuc (and probably others, depending on the history books you read), as well as the North River. In Space Detective's world, it's called the Mohegan River.

New Angoulême – New York has carried many names during its history. The Dutch called their colony there New Amsterdam. Before that, Giovanni da Verrazzano—an Italian exploring in a French ship, *La Dauphine*—arrived in 1524 and named the area Angoulême in honor of Francis I, the king of France, whose title had been Count of Angoulême before his coronation.

Satellite communications – In Part One, Chapter Six, Space Detective's Plutonian pal mentions satellite communications: "The concept had been published by the scientific community here, but had yet to be put into development." The concept was first proposed by Sir Arthur C. Clarke in a letter published in the February 1945 issue of *Wireless World*. The premise Clarke put forth wasn't possible to put into play until the 1965 launch of the first commercial geostationary communication satellite, *Intelsat I*.

Singstad Tunnel – We know it better as the Holland Tunnel, which runs under the Hudson River and connects Lower Manhattan to Jersey City in New Jersey. New Angoulême's tunnel owes its name to the Norwegian-American civil engineer, Ole Singstad, who designed its ventilation system and the method for building underwater tunnels using prefabricated modules.

Uncas – Chief Inspector Jonathan Brewster Uncas picks up his name from Sachem Uncas, who was a leader of the Mohegan tribe in southern Connecticut in the 1600s.

Vinland – *The Vinland Sagas*, written in the Thirteenth Century, include the story of Eirik the Red and his son, Leif Eirikson, who explored the eastern coast of North America 500 years before Columbus. According to modern archaeology, the Vikings were unable to establish a permanent colony there. In Space Detective's world, the Christian Vikings were chased away from their lands by the pagan Vikings, and the exiles settled in Vinland.

Walloon – The people of Wallonia, the southern region of Belgium, are historically Roman Catholic. The Walloons who emigrated to New Angoulême did so as the pagan Vikings began annexing parts of Europe following the end of hostilities at the end of World War I.

ABOUT THE AUTHOR

Coming from a long line of long-winded tall tale tellers, Duane Spurlock loves good storytelling. A professional writer since the last century, Duane writes adventure tales informed by a lifetime of omnivorous reading and studying great storytellers. Duane has contributed to various fiction and nonfiction anthologies. In addition to his own titles, he is the co-author, with Jim Beard, of *Airship Hunters*, an 1897 action-mystery based on actual newspaper reports about strange objects flying in the skies of western North America. You can learn more about Duane and his books and sign up for updates at www.duanespurlock.com.

ABOUT THE ARTIST

Mike Fyles: "As an illustrator I tend to concentrate on Cover Art primarily. It remains a challenging brief because of the balance that needs to be struck between form and content, design and narrative. Cover Art, like the short story, gets a limited shot at content and meaning. Much of what I have produced has been described as 'nostalgic sci fi and pulp' and sits alongside continued revivals of the adventure genre in film and fiction. Stylistically, I've always liked the commercial illustration of the mid-20th Century that was made to promote mass publications (especially children's annuals, pulp magazines, lifestyle magazines and comics). The creativity and artistic competence found on the covers and within the pages of these products was far-reaching and still has currency."

www.ingramcontent.com/pod-product-compliance
Lightning Source LLC
Chambersburg PA
CBHW030934260626
47169CB00002B/474

* 9 7 9 8 9 8 7 7 9 7 0 1 3 *